THE MUTUAL FRIEND

Books by Frederick Busch

FICTION

Long Way from Home (1993)
Closing Arguments (1991)
Harry and Catherine (1990)
War Babies (1989)
Absent Friends (1989)
Sometimes I Live in the Country (1986)
Too Late American Boyhood Blues (1984)
Invisible Mending (1984)
Take This Man (1981)
Rounds (1979)
Hardwater Country (1979)
The Mutual Friend (1978)
Domestic Particulars (1976)
Manual Labor (1974)
Breathing Trouble (1973)
I Wanted a Year Without Fall (1971)

NONFICTION

When People Publish (1986)
Hawkes (1973)

THE MUTUAL FRIEND
Frederick Busch

A NEW DIRECTIONS BOOK

A section of this novel, under the title "George Dolby. Or, The Cannibal Sheep," appeared in *The New Review* (London) and *New Directions in Prose and Poetry 33*. "A Maid Looks Back, and Laughs" appeared in *The Iowa Review*. "Mr. Dickens (As It Were)" appeared in *The New York Times*. A small section appeared in England in *PN Review*.

Manufactured in the United States of America
New Directions Books are printed on acid-free paper.
The Mutual Friend was published, clothbound, by Harper & Row in 1978; reissued as a paperbook by David A. Godine, Publisher, in 1983; and first published as New Directions Paperbook 774 in 1994.
Published simultaneously in Canada by Penguin Books Canada Limited

Library of Congress Cataloging-in-Publication Data
Busch, Frederick, 1941–
    The mutual friend : a novel / by Frederick Busch.
      p.   cm.
    ISBN 0–8112–1258–0 (pbk. : alk. paper)
    1. Dickens, Charles, 1812–1870—Fiction. 2. Dolby, George, d.
1900—Fiction. 3. Novelists, English—19th century—Fiction.
I. Title.
PS3552.U814M8 1994
813′.54—dc20   93–31458
                                                    CIP

New Directions Books are published for James Laughlin
by New Directions Publishing Corporation
80 Eighth Avenue, New York 10011

Judy

CONTENTS

THE MUTUAL FRIEND

It is the winter of 1899. I have been here a short while and shortly will be here no longer. The usual coughing of the usual pint of bright blood, I suppose, and then the usual death. But I am comfortable, within the limitations of disease and the cheer of the coughers' ward, and I've my notes. I've my comfortable heap of cheap paper which I cover with cheap ink—*aides-mémoire*, a visiting governor of the hospital called them. But my memory needs no aids, it's my flesh needs help; my memory's well, and I hear their voices. Some might say it's disease calls their voices up, names the facts of their lives and my own. Call it disease if you will. I hear them. And I set them down.

No, the memory needs no assistance. It's the long white limbs ropy with veins, the toes with their nails too long and yellow, the eyes in a pudding of black rings beneath and little maps of red just around them, the hands which shake sometimes so that the writing wanders. And once in a while, with the righteous tight lips of the downtrodden striking back, Moon—or so they *think* he's named: they don't really care, since he's shiny brown and short and comes in a cloud of Asiatic smells—Moon, with his humped back and little fingers, his one good eye bright black and outraged, his other eye a flowerfold of puffed lid above the vacant socket,

1

his delicate lisping servant's whispers, Moon brings in at night when the ward's a chorus of gagging and lament one of his little tributes to the slowly dying man. A vial of the cheapest gin betimes, or a pottery jar of navy rum. He expects no payment, but I offer a sort: I read to him from my papers in the usual breathless whisper punctuated by spitting and coughs. He is learning the language, he insists. A beneficial balance of trade, I call it. What the Empire was built upon.

And sometimes as I write, late, in the odours and sounds of the charity ward for grave-bound gaspers, I dream not only their voices and their shapes, but receipts of the sort I've come to cherish. The stalwart negus, for example, which I could easily render had I but a quantity of port to add to a double quantity of hot water. I could sweeten the mixture with lump sugar, some lemon and grated nutmeg, and the merest touch of the lemon's rind. Oh, and a drop of ambergris or, that lacking, some drops—no more than ten—of the essence of vanilla. Serve smoking. Drink every drop.

Or, still in the vein of what the body requires in such a cold season, your basic ale flip. Heat the stove up merry. Three or four pints of ale in a pan, a generous spoonful of butter, blade of mace, a clove. And then boil the jolly fellow, set aside. Use a spoonful of cold ale to mix with the beaten yolks of two eggs and the white of one. And then mix for all you're worth, with one of those French metal whisks if you can get it, and then mix more, adding the ale potation to that of the eggs. Pour between two jugs so as to froth. Might serve five persons. Drink it all yourself, I say.

Nothing wrong with *my* memory. I'm making more than *aides-mémoire* in my night-time vocalizings here. I've a purpose, and it isn't merely recollection, or the comfort of my flesh and blood. Attend.

A MAN OF PARTS

He said "Really, Dolby, I don't *want* to sleep in any more towns named Utica. Utica. *Utica*. Doesn't it sound like an herb you take for your health?" He rubbed the side of his face, which possibly didn't function—I doubted if he felt his fingers—and he sighed. Long moist sigh. "Perhaps it would help."

Because he needed some. Because he was the whore of self-pity, and also brave. He was the Chief. And what he saw—I calculate this, I'm guessing only a bit, I all but wiped his arse so many days and nights—was the right-hand side, just that, of any signs he claimed to read out whole. The feeling was dead, the vision crippled, his left leg dragged enough to make the carpets whisper. When he didn't know we looked, and maybe when he did, it seemed as though he heard his blood beat. But when he was on the stage he was a decorated panther, and he stalked, all giant eyes all-seeing, and hunger ready to spring. And he was tender, when he wished, as children asleep. The stage was his mind.

On the train sometimes he wore a gutta-percha overshoe on the left foot, claiming that a lingering touch of frostbite had swollen the toes. He never admitted to us he was ill. Sometimes he said he was exhausted, but never mortal, like men. When he wore the huge shoe, along with some pink silk waistcoat, his vanity kept him from the corridors of the railroad car; so I never sat, was always running his errands, opening windows, wiping the foul brown spit of some tobacco-chewing American traveler with a handkerchief he'd give me, then tell me to throw away.

Where does one deposit excremental cloths on a passenger train attempting to derail itself in New England or New York? No matter. Dolby will do it. Dolby will open the window so the Chief won't suffer from excessive heat—"My God, Dolby, they don't breathe *air!* They live in steam. They're orchids. Which rarely are watered. And spit tobacco juice"—and Dolby will fetch the trainman to move offensive passengers so the Chief will be surrounded by a wall of empty seats. And Dolby will listen when the Chief clears his throat, pressing the dead left side, rubs his pouter-pigeon chest, says "D-Dolby, it is the True American." Meaning—he loved his phrases better than the crowds who queued for days to hear him read from books they'd read before—that he had what he called the True American Catarrh. Meaning, too, that Dolby sometimes stammered when he spoke, that his affliction unnerved the big bald arranger of bookings, meals, even toilet-cleanings, and that the Chief found Dolby's difficulties amusing. Mouse in the paws of his language.

From Liverpool I came, on the loathsome boat. To meet with Bealpost and Fields, who treated Bealpost, his employee, like a son. To arrange first with Fields for the redistribution of books in cities where the Chief would read, and then to travel with Bealpost, rocketing back and forth in trains and often carriages, estimating audiences, booking the halls, drinking bourbon whiskey—my lord!—with ignorant journalists, sending wires home about America's love for the Chief, receiving wires about the birth of George, my only son, with whom I could not be. For I was on the Chief's business. Then back to Boston while Bealpost, mediocre assistant, returned to England to fetch the Chief.

Bealpost said that Boz, as he was called in his early writing days, often was gone from his quarters during the passage. Bealpost, because he is stupid, said the Chief paced the decks and thought of his absent wife. Never. His wife had been absent longer than the public knew. His wife had been dead to him for years. And it wasn't Ellen Ternan he thought of, either, though at night I wager he touched his body in her name. No, he was below decks. I saw this while I dined in Boston with fools and rich men's servants. I lay on the coverlet and smoked cigars and dreamed him, bilious with the motion and the rancid air, standing in the cargo hold he'd ordered opened to him, rocking in the *Cuba* and in his giant mind, staring in half-light at the stand and screen, the reading platform and the gas-lighting apparatus he'd insisted on loading himself. Staring at the gas pipes. Seeing flames.

"He is as tender as a woman and as watchful as a doctor" is what he wrote about me. He left his letters for me to seal and post. Scraps of his imagination. Everything changed by his pen to what he thought it should be. I didn't recognize the incidents he wrote of, often. Because America, the reading tour, Kate the soft wife he had thrown away, her sister Georgina Hogarth who stayed to care for his children in his home, the actress he sealed in apartments and paid for, the years of 1867–68 and Dolby, who stammered—"Whenever," he wrote, "the name Cambridge, that rock ahead in his speech, appeared in the itinerary"—all were in his mind. He was a pirate, he stole the living world.

That snowy moustache, and the visible pain, his monstrous strength when he whipped the weeping audiences—Little Nell's noisome dying, the wretched Paul Dombey in his mystical transports—and his letters to and about himself: "I cannot remember to whom I wrote last, but it will not much matter if I make a mistake, this being generally to report myself." And then, making me laugh and love him: "For now, farewell. My desk and I have just arisen from the floor."

In the Parker House, where he staggered in the hallway at the start of the tour, December 1867, bleating that the heat of hallways made him faint, we sat in the dining-room surrounded by white linen and threatened by an avalanche of crystal. He tapped a hard roll against his goblet—he was nibbling at partridge, too ill even then to taste his food—and he said "Dolby, the Negroes."

"Sir?"

"Where are the Negroes?"

"I see only Irishmen. Only Irishmen wait on table at the Parker, sir. This is Boston."

"Yes." He prodded the carcass of the bird with his bread. "All the servants are Irish—willing, but not able. You want a black man for the right service of a meal."

And that night the man who had taxed America for slavery wrote to Cartwright in London "The old, untidy, incapable, lounging, shambling black serves you as a free man. Free of course he ought to be; but the stupendous absurdity of making him a voter glares out of every roll of his eye, stretch of his mouth, and bump of his head. I have a strong impression that the race must fade out of the States very fast. It never can hold its own against a striving, restless, shifty people." He made up the entire earth!

Next morning, paler, and over the queasiness we'd both complained of, he called me into the sitting-room of his suite where he sat erect at the writing table, eyes bright with ink. I took a letter to post to Miss Hogarth. And wondered when he told the truth. "Dolby has been twice poisoned, and Bealpost once. When the snow is deep upon the ground, and the partridges cannot get their usual food, they eat something (I don't know what, if anybody does) which does not poison *them*, but which poisons the people who eat them. The symptoms, which last some twelve hours, are violent sickness, cold perspiration, and the formation of some detestable mucus in the stomach. You may infer that partridges have been banished from our bill of fare.

"Did I tell you that the severity of the weather, and the heat of the intolerable furnaces, dry the hair and break the nails of strangers. Dolby watches me brush my hair, which then falls out; then he gasps to see me coming apart; then rushes to my side. He is always going about with an immense bundle that looks like a sofa cushion but is in reality paper money; and always works like a Trojan."

Yes. And is often as full of spearheads and barbs. As in Providence, when the unstoppable ticket speculators had charged more than four times our price, and a crowd halted me at the hotel and I thought I'd be hanged on the spot. Inside, that evening, he said "Indispensable Dolby. Good Dolby!"

But he was the capable one. Arriving at the theater, interviewing the man who would control the gas—he always spent inordinate time with gas-men—and then, in a small room back of the stage, his face as white with pain as his moustache was with fifty-six years, sitting in the most arctic silence over a small meal, never eating it, never, then sending for an egg beaten up in sherry. Never speaking. Holding his prompt-copies, not looking at them ever, before he walked on stage. Sending me or Bealpost or one of the others to look at the size and quality of his audience. Then, suddenly, as if I had asked him: "Generally, Dolby, they are very good audiences indeed. Don't you think? Granted, they do not perceive touches of art to *be* art. But they're responsive to the broad results of the touches. I can't ask for more."

"No, sir. They love you."

"Love! I'm here for money, not love. The Inimitable does it for dollars, convertible to guineas. I've a houseful of children to see to, you know that."

"Yes, sir. Of course. The money."

"Yes."

Then a grimace as he moved his foot back and leaned his palms on his thighs. "My God, do you remember poor Longfellow?"

"I've never met anyone braver, sir. One couldn't tell, from speaking with him. That—"

"No. I knew, of course. I would have known. The horror, it was still in his eyes."

"I hadn't the opportunity to dine with him."

"Good Dolby. No, you were rushing about, carting all those crackling American dollars. Did you sleep last night?"

"A bit, sir. The journalists—"

"Why must they call me *Charley?* As if we chewed tobacco together in some frontier saloon. *Charley!*"

9

"They presume, sir. They slapped my back all night. It's quite sore."

"You do serve, Dolby." He drank his sherry and curled his fine nose. It was pale at the bridge. "And they asked about my wife? They questioned you about my—friends at home?"

"They're curious, sir. They would write about your gold studs—they do. They would write about anything."

"Write! They *pen*. None of them can write."

"True. They pen on, though. About anything."

"You told them—of course not. You were Dolby, weren't you?"

"Yes, sir. And still am."

The smile, and then its death, his dramatic faraway stare. "Yes, imagine Longfellow, still living there, in the same old house where that beautiful wife of his burned. I thought I still smelled the smoke when his cook brought in the roast. I couldn't get the scene out of my imagination. She was in a blaze in an instant, rushed into his arms with a wild cry, and never spoke afterward." Then: "I ought to be alone now, don't you think?"

And then, with no limp or frailty, the mounting of the stage as if it were a cliff he dared to look down from. And, starting softly with Bob Sawyer's party, and a gracious utterly insincere comment or two, and then David Copperfield, he squeezed them by the throat until they roared to be squeezed the harder. More sherry with egg between the parts. Silent sitting, perspiration and gauntness over him as if he were stone sprayed by a waterfall. And then back before them and—they were before *him*, performed for him at his command and never knew it—Nancy's murder by Sikes. When he cried "No!" in his grainy falsetto, a woman with a pearl collar shrieked back "No! No!" and young Kelly, always eager to be used by any of us, led her gently to the auditorium door. She wept on him. The Chief didn't pause, though he was grateful to her, I know.

So, on. Coughing from two or three in the morning until dawn—loudly enough for me to hear next door, and suffer on his behalf—and then less sleep, and tasting nothing, eating nearly not at all, taking laudanum for relief of the "frostbite," becoming more exhausted, more depressed. The incessant opening of windows, the complaints about lack of fresh air, the letters to everyone, as if their existence depended on what he said he saw, the America he invented.

When I brought him sherry in Albany, as he—what else?—wrote definitively of the city he'd visited twice ("a simulacrum of the western frontier" he decided to someone in London), he said "Do you remember when I visited the medical school in Boston, Dolby?"

"Yes, sir. You didn't speak much about it. Was it rewarding?"

"I saw where that extraordinary murder was done by that man Webster. You remember that I spoke of it."

"Yes, sir. The murder."

"Yes. There was the furnace, stinking horribly, as if all the dismembered pieces were still inside it." He was writing to *me*. "And there were all the grim spouts, and sinks, and chemical appliances. Ghastly. Fascinating. That was the night I dined with Longfellow. He is so dear."

"I believe he returns the favour with interest, sir."

"I flatter myself that he does. But what he told me—and after his own wife . . . He said he had dined with Webster less than a year before the murder, a party of ten or twelve. There they sat at their wine. Webster suddenly ordered the lights to be turned out, and a bowl of some burning mineral to be placed on the table. Longfellow telling stories with even a *spark* of fire in them! And in the weird light, all were horrified to see Webster with a rope around his neck! Holding it up, over the bowl, with his head jerked on one side, and his tongue lolled out, representing a man being hanged! Poking into his life and character, I find he was always a cruel man."

Yrs sincerely, etc.

"Dolby hardly ever dines" he writes to his daughter. "He is always tearing about at unreasonable hours. He works very hard."

Yes. And sometimes wonders if he will require a restraining jacket or a hospital ward for the Chief—which first? The night in New York City, when he smelled smoke and it turned out that a part of the roof was on fire: the dancing and jigging! the drool and little cries! rushing to gather everything into his pockets, including a face rag from his bathroom! He said to himself, as if it were a child's song, "Fire. Fire. We're on fire." I soothed him, at last. He cannot tolerate awfully much of the world.

"I took charge at once" he writes to Miss Hogarth. "I was not surprised, having smelled fire for two hours. I got Kelly up directly, told him to pack the books and clothes for the reading first, dressed and pocketed my jewels and papers, while Dolby stuffed himself out with money. After a little chopping and cutting with axes and handing about with water, the fire was confined to a dining-room in which it had originated, and then everybody talked to everybody else, the ladies being particularly loquacious and cheerful. And so we got to bed again at about two. The excitement of the readings continues unabated, the tickets for readings are sold as soon as they are ready. Dolby continues to be the most unpopular man in America (mainly because he can't get four thousand people into a room that holds two thousand) and is reviled in print. Yesterday morning a newspaper proclaims of him 'Surely it is time that the pudding-headed Dolby retired into the native gloom from which he has emerged.' He takes it very coolly."

Don't I? I carry the money in, then retire to the saloon-bar where I tell the journalists what he wants them to know. We discuss him as the greatest literary figure of the age, and they agree, and I do too. He is. He invented the age. It's his book.

"Our hotel was on fire *again* the other night. But fires in this country are quite matters of course. There was a large one there at four this morning, and I don't think a single night has passed since I have been under the protection of the Eagle, but I have heard the fire bells dolefully clanging all over the city. Dolby sends his kindest regard. His hair has become quite white, the effect, I suppose, of the climate. He is so universally hauled over the coals.

12

You may conceive what the low newspapers are here, when one of them yesterday morning had, as an item of news, the intelligence: 'The Readings. The chap calling himself Dolby got drunk last night, and was locked up in a police-station for fighting an Irishman.' I don't find that anybody is shocked by this liveliness."

Some of this, I know, is in his mind. He will use it sometime, so I may use it now. With a man like that, what's the difference between *as if* and *is?* Simply because he never gave me letters to Ellen Ternan, am I to imagine that he didn't write them? Part of his death-in-life was her absence, and his speculation—his constructing whole scenes and episodes—of her social activity in London. He never spoke of his wife. She and Thackeray had made trouble for him, despite his pained willingness to let her live in his house, sleeping alone in the room they had shared while he slept in his newly renovated dressing-room. She had borne ten children and she had bored the Chief.

I think—I have a right to: I carried his cash and curried his coat—that he was drawn to Ternan, as he was drawn to America, because she was a fresh start. He never forgave America for not being innocent. He despaired of Ternan not only because she didn't love him (I knew this, always), but because once she was his, she was sullied. He needed love, he needed more than any man I knew. But he needed more to live forever in his mind. Ternan didn't want to live there.

Most of us did, or had to: as in New Haven, after I had discovered that the wretched Bealpost, going on ahead, had been bribed by speculators to let them have great lots of tickets. "You know," the Chief said, "I'm a curious man. I conceived a terrible dislike to Bealpost on board the *Cuba,* coming out. He was ill all the voyage, and I only saw him two or three times, staggering about the deck. But I underwent a change of feeling toward him, as if I had taken it in at the pores of the skin."

"He's dismissed, sir. And the Steinway Hall people have threatened to beat him nearly to death when he returns to New York."

13

"No, Dolby, we'll let him stay. *Now* he'll serve: he doesn't want the dragging into court I could give him. His limits will be narrow, and he'll touch no money again. But now that he'll serve as he should (I can guarantee it), we'll let him stay. He needs my protection. He'll work hard."

"The man's a criminal, sir."

"Who isn't? In the larger meaning."

"Of course."

So Bealpost hated him then, and always, for canny salvation. He was owned. But, to quote the Inimitable, who isn't? In February, back in Boston for another long engagement of readings, we found that President Johnson's impeachment had kept the audiences away. There were empty seats, and the Chief cancelled the second week's readings: he hated empty seats. He thought to let his cough improve. How can mortality improve?

Restless in a lounge chair at the Parker—he was content only when he could complain of exhaustion—the Chief, then, announced to Bealpost and me "My merry men, I am pleased to proclaim The Great International Walking Match. You'll enjoy it, I think. We can't sit idle for a week."

Bealpost, smiling to his gums as always, asked him "Who's to run—er, walk, sir?"

"Good question, Bealpost. You are perspicacious, you will rise. But first you will walk. You both will, I think. Won't you? A select audience of enraptured spectators, ladies fainting, the booming applause as the English Champion first crosses the mark, swiveling his lithe b-body." I am not a small man. I do not parade myself, and I keep my overcoat buttoned. I looked at the carpeted floor and waited for Bealpost to fawn.

I *heard* his skin stretch into smiles before he said "A pleasure, sir. I hope, though, to show you some American mettle."

"Such as you tried to collect, eh? Now *we* collect the American metal. Don't we, Dolby?"

"Yes, sir."

"You're the Man of Ross, Dolby. I think it's rather good.

Bealpost, you shall be the Boston Bantam, eh? I've drawn up some articles of agreement for you to look at—all business, the Inimitable—and I, sporting my True American, shall be an umpire known as the Gad's Hill Gasper. Fields and I have laid out the course—a mere six miles or so to Newton Center and back. It was covered with ice and snow, needless to say, when we did it. A most murderous way to cure a cough."

I wrote a letter home, prattling about "the superb energy" of the Chief, telling my family how "delighted" villainous Bealpost and I were to provide him with this entertainment. Yes. Moving my thighs in public with ice about my ears because the Chief was bored. Our waiter smiled at me when he served the consommé that night, and I sneered into his red square Irish face "No potatoes, mind. And no familiarities." This pleased the Chief, though he whispered—his face burlesqued the cautious traveler—that we had to befriend the natives lest they eat us. Cannibal calling the cooking pot black.

But we all went laughing to the Mill Dam Road, and huddled over Bealpost's silver brandy flask, shivering. The Chief was a snowman, all frozen brows, his moustache hung with tiny icicles. But he kept laughing. So we began, the ladies cheering—most of them, then, returning to the fire-lighted parlour as we left—and the Chief crabbed behind us, bellowing encouragements to Dolby, the mount he'd entered in the race. When you walk as quickly as you can, your hips swivel lewdly, and your breath fails at once, especially if, as I had, you'd spent so much of your time with tobacco and drink. I was gasping before the turn, and at the turning itself I saw before me little red and yellow shapes, such as you might watch in the medical college microscope. They stayed no matter how many times I blinked. Behind them it was all white, soon enough, and I hardly heard my wheezes. Not a sound from little Bealpost, though, who smiled even then—he turned his head as he passed me—and slithered ahead. He wanted to win for the Chief, I had no doubt. And I was horrified to find that I did too, at least to shield myself from his generous humour, should I lose.

Mrs. Fields, the publisher's wife, was to await the winner at the finish-line, in the company of one or two other viciously pleased noncontestants, with a portion of bread soaked in brandy. Seeing that Bealpost was ahead, she directed her carriage driven toward us—at this time, I was trying not to fall down, and welcomed the thought of a ride—but had it stopped behind Bealpost's perky trail. Then she told the man to turn it, and drove alongside him; with silver serving tongs, she dropped a piece of brandy-soaked bread into his peeping birdlet's mouth. I stood where I was. I was overwhelmed by a need to urinate. The Chief in his carriage roared "On, Dolby!"

I replied "Sod, and go bugger!" But not with much volume. How often does food shout protests at the mouth it's lifted to? I walked to them, sauntered on my frozen feet, my hands in my pockets and my whiskers rimed so heavily my face felt dead—I thought I was becoming like him. So I smiled, to crack the layering ice. He thought I smiled for him. Good dog.

I smiled too, but inside my skull, as I watched him sneeze throughout the dinner he gave in our honour in the Crystal Room of the Parker that night. I had thought he was dying, that he'd suffered a seizure in England and hadn't received right treatment for it (if treatment there was), and the reading tour thus far had confirmed my feelings. It was suicide for a man in his poor health to make the journey to America and then exhaust himself with such ferocious work. He said he did it for his children. I told myself he did it for the adulation which the groundlings gave him. But seeing him pale beneath the pallor of the ice which hung on him, I thought that day, and later that night, of my original judgment: suicide. Why did he want so much to die? But he was a genius, I was not. He had written more of death, more movingly, than I would know in all my life.

Which didn't prevent me from smiling to my most appreciative self as he shivered and sneezed and coughed even harder in the grips of an oncoming illness he'd beseeched in order to see me jump on his strings. His spirits were high, though, and he drank a good deal, joking with Lowell and Holmes, Norton, Longfellow and his daughter, others of like reputation and dignified Bostonian bearing. I think he puzzled them. His running nose and yellow eyes were entertainment, though, for me—despite my concern that he'd pushed his health beyond its reserves.

At about ten, Bealpost and the Chief and I went up to bed. His bath had been drawn, and he insisted on our presence as he undressed for the tub. His left leg was swollen and the area around the toes was puffy. When he saw my attention to it, he limped exaggeratedly to the tub's edge, sat on it, and began to whistle and smile, saying "Grimaldi at the ocean's edge, eh, Dolby?"

Bealpost smiled his gums and nodded, though he'd never seen the clown—nor had I, though I knew his reputation—and I said "It's an ocean you could drink, sir."

"Ho!" he called, teetering. "Ha!" In his evening coat and boutonniere, trouserless and swelling, he rolled and whistled, clowning as I'd seen him do for whatever audience he could muster, usually his delighted children and his silent smiling wife. "A-*hey*!" he called, wobbling, thrusting his arms forward, losing his balance no matter, and falling into the tub—coat and golden chains and the carapace of brilliantined hair.

I said "On, sir!" as I went to help him out.

On the train, next day, he wrote a letter in shaking hand which I was to manage to get delivered to New York in time for a Cunard sailing. He complained of his quakings and cough, saying that "My True American has taken a fresh start, and I have terrified poor Dolby quite out of his wits by setting in for a paroxysm of sneezing." The letter was urgent, he said, because it contained a command to his eldest daughter that one Holman be asked for an estimate "1. To recover, with red leather, all the dining-room chairs. 2. To ditto, with green leather, all the library chairs and the couch."

I said "The postal connection will be difficult to make, sir."

Looking out the window, he said "The recovering, Dolby, is of the utmost importance to me. I have taken it into my head to have it done, and I will have it done. A house needs renewing."

Your humble servant.

So on, then, to Syracuse, Rochester, Buffalo and then Albany again, carrying the light of the world by train.

He grew worse. His True American seemed to hinder his breathing at times, and I often had to read out signs for him. At Syracuse, he had great difficulty in walking: he called it "an eruption of the leg." But he talked incessantly, of the recovering, and with lovely malice of the pirating of his books by American publishers, and of the food, which, though he ate so little, was of great importance to him: "Old buffalo for breakfast again, I see."

And he grew worse. Syracuse was a great success, of course, and some boys who had ridden miles from a small college called Hamilton wrote in their newspaper an article, reprinted in the local press, which was a hymn to his greatness. The Chief was enraged. "Read this, Dolby! They have no education at that place. They're training valets. *Grooms!*" It said "How did he look? Well, he *was* dressed a wee bit foppish, for so snowy a moustache, but after all with faultless taste. His great Shakespearean collar was very neat and white, so was his white tie, so was his white bosom. And the three little gold studs on his breast fairly laughed." He became silenter and more depressed, saying he would not be accused by tadpoles of being *nouveau riche*.

The newspapers in the area—a more backward place than the westernmost frontiers, he said—endlessly speculated about him: that he had recently sent $5,000 to his sister-in-law (with the implication that such a transaction meant a relationship barely moral, probably illegal); that he had asked the Secretary of the Treasury not to make assessment of the proceeds of his readings; that he would come to such-and-such a village to read its charter aloud, if they would pay him sufficiently. And the more said about his private life, the paler, more morose, he became. When we received a cable about the death of his friend Chauncey Townshend, he told me "Everyone is starting to die, now. When that happens, Dolby, there is an astringent stinking of mortality over everything, like a foul cloud."

Then something called "the freshet" happened. Between Rochester and Albany, we were caught by storms and the power of late March sunlight. A river named the Mohawk rose with water and ice, and the river became blocked. Driftwood and enormous chunks of dirty grey ice flooded onto the tracks sometimes to a depth of several feet, the tracks were impassable, rails were lifted off. We couldn't go on, we had to stay at Utica.

He fairly shook with fury in his lounge seat when the train stopped, hissing, at a darkened terminal. "I don't *want* to sleep in places named Utica" he said. "I want to go home."

He had learned from the motorman that Secretary of State Seward was stranded with him, though Seward was in a private car which was pulled at the end of the train. "You don't suppose he reads novels, do you? If their President interviewed with me— though he barely said a word that qualified him for low office, much less high—perhaps their Secretary of State, who is *not* being impeached, might consider—"

"Yes, sir?"

"An overnight guest?"

"No, sir."

"Why *no*, Dolby?" His eyes were narrowed, his nostrils wide. Although he wore a decent brown suit and his little round top hat and his gold waist chains, he looked like one of his murderers, bereft of hope, immersed in death, fearfully enjoying his victim's fear, and his own. "Pray, inform me why you wish to see me wrapped in a stale coverlet at some stale home for orphaned fleas in this stalest of grey-green cities."

"Politicians in America don't read words, sir. They only speak them. And read only numbers. You've written of it yourself."

"Twenty-five years ago, Dolby. Now, I'm not what you might call inconsequential, am I?"

"To politicians, sir, you are."

"Damn you."

"Yes, sir."

"Damn them *all!*"

So he limped to a wooden bench near a baggage camion, comforted by servile Bealpost, and sat in a pool of dim light, his legs stretched before him: an inconsolable boy. I walked near a street named Genesee, as I'd been directed, and in the city's other hotel, called Baggs', I requested rooms. The clerk was very thin and breathed through his mouth as he bent, his nose almost touching the page of the register, to examine our names. "Him" he said. "I heard of him. I'n't he English?"

A little cannon gave its cough near the train, and I said "That's he they're saluting now, I suspect."

"Nope." His breath should have been the colour of Stilton. "Seward." I knew who else would make the same mistake, and be similarly corrected, and I smiled.

At the station again, Bealpost stood when I approached and nodded his head at the large boy on the bench. The Chief looked up from the railroad guide and said "I'm really most entertained, Dolby. I know now that one can travel from here to famous Deansville in twenty minutes. And that the Franklin run is eight minutes less. Indeed. And that Mister John Butterfield is the Superintendent of these runs, and it's he we've to thank for ordering the trains shut down. How can I properly give voice to my appreciation of this diversion?"

Then he said nothing more as I and Bealpost—he was silent, and always, now, enraged—carried the bags (porters, it seems, had been swept away by the freshet) up four dark streets past wooden buildings and one or two monuments to the last century, and entered Baggs' four-story brick hotel, with its papered walls and imitation English hunting prints, and two huge clocks, each of which kept its own time. We shared a suite, the Chief in the bedroom, Bealpost and I on sofa and cot in the sitting-room. In about half an hour, Moses Baggs came calling with sandwiches and wine, and his ample hates.

The Chief greeted him with the usual charm he reserved for close friends and important businessmen and politicians: head erect, left hand in trousers pocket, chest swelled to set off his waistcoat chains, which draped him, a primrose and black dressing gown opened all the way; his mouth was curved down, his nostrils were wide, his eyes were hooded. He didn't smile, but made gentle motions in the air with his hands, as if to say how much at peace he was, now that Baggs had come. Some of the tranquility was the deadness of his left cheek and jaw: linen stretched taut.

They sat across an oval carved table from one another, drinking to each other, neither eating, probably so as not to lose the sense of utter sufficiency each one tried to radiate. Baggs was stockier than the Chief, dressed more quietly in broadcloth and a bow-tie, bat-wing collar. His lips curved downward too, but they were more compressed, suggesting resistance and disapproval at once. His nose was broad and hooked, quite gracefully, and his eyes, in large sockets, looked small. He was as vain about his straight silky hair as the Chief was vain about his much-pomaded curls, and he combed it across his forehead as a youngster in school might do.

They spoke without humour and, although Bealpost and I were near the sitting-room fireplace, across the room from the adjoining door, and could hear only murmurs and sometimes the fragments of words, we watched while sitting opposite one another's wing chairs to see how the rural landlord received the man who'd made a nation weep.

Bealpost leaned over, as if to prod a burning log with the brass poker, and whispered "He looks like a country parson."

"He's talking to the high priest."

Bealpost nodded his small head, his fine tight features. "The grand vizier. High poop and God-almighty godling."

"Don't be bitter, Bealpost. He's given you a chance."

"Sure. At a smaller salary. And the loss of my job when he squeals to Fields. I run his errands like a cabin-boy and never get thanked."

"Bealpost! You *cheated*."

"I used my imagination to better myself. Just like him. He came from nothing too, though he'd never admit it."

"He admits it all the time. The trouble, I'm afraid, is that you aren't bright enough to perceive it. That's why you cheated so clumsily, and got caught. And after what your machinations put me through, you won't get sympathy from me, my friend. Or any conversational betrayals. That one is a great man."

Bealpost crossed his little legs without wrinkling his trousers, rubbed his small fingers across his still clean-shaven jaws, sighed loudly and shook his head. "No, sir, Dolby. No. It doesn't work. I'm not convinced. No doubt I'm stupider than you. You're fooling him in ways that don't get caught, sure. But you're cheating nevertheless, and you can't say no. I've seen you read his mail, for instance, haven't I?"

"Witling! He gives me his letters to post. I have to address and seal them. *That's* what you've seen."

"Oh."

"Don't oh me. Don't be smug with your betters, friend."

"Ah, *friend*. And you watch him all the time. Look at him like he's chicken on your plate. You're doing something crooked, Dolby. Our little lamb shouldn't trust you very far."

"Bealpost. I'm tired, and my p-patience is thin as my hair."

"Very g-good, Mister Dolby."

"B-buggering imp!"

"Your servant, M-mister Dolby."

I was considering how best to bash him with the fire iron when the Chief raised his voice—that splendid baritone he used for summoning ghosts from the back of his mind to the stage—and called "Dolby! Can you join us a moment?"

I went in, half-bowing, to say "Mister Baggs? Sir?"

"We've had a curious conversation, Dolby. I thought I'd put you in the way of it, since we share so much." Which meant that I was now a foil. Costumed character. A theatrical event. "I cautiously inquired of Mr. Baggs, our host, as to the disposition of fire steps. America's the land of hotel fires, I said, and I am, as you know, disinclined to be roasted in foreign flames."

"Yes, sir. We've seen our share of smoke the past months."

"Yes, we have. So I tendered my inquiry"—he nodded to Baggs

and smiled his unfelt smile—"only to learn that our host is unsympathetic to suggestions that flammability, a universal law, extends to his historical pile."

In a hard voice Baggs said, to the table, "My hotel, which is built where my father's inn stood safely for more years than you can count, is the safest hotel in the Mohawk Valley."

"In the entire Mohawk Valley, Dolby!"

Baggs said "Brick throughout, and the most seasoned wood."

The Chief pounced like a rat-catcher: "Definition of an oven, I should say, eh, Dolby? No matter, though. We're safe in your hands. Taken as read. *You,* then, to return to the narrative, said—correct me, please, if I misrepresent you—'I understand that you work in the way of prostitutes.' Am I correct, sir?"

"You surely understand," Baggs said, "that I spoke of reformed prostitutes. Women of the streets now turned to women of virtue by virtue of yourself and some rich woman over there who shares your, ah, interest."

"Dedication, sir, not interest. I have no *interest* in whores. I work toward the cleansing of society by helping to remove them from the hovels and thoroughfares. Once the pollution's contained, and they're lodged in a well-regulated home under watchful eyes, I contribute a small amount of money, and a large amount of my time, and address them once a year to remind them of the holiness in which they must again learn to hold themselves."

"Very generous" Baggs said.

"And that 'rich woman' of whom you speak derisively is Miss Coutts, whose generosity and dedication are unsurpassed."

"Except by your own" Baggs said. "You are known for your generosity to women, may I say."

"No." The Chief's nose was whiter than his pale face, and his eyes were Jonas Chuzzlewit's, squatting over a warm corpse. "No. Do not. There's an inference in what you say."

"Inferences are as taken" Baggs said, folding his arms across his chest, almost smiling. "I'm enjoying our talk."

"You must have enjoyed your Civil War as well."

"No, killing's not *my* line of work."

"Dolby! My God! Am I hearing this? *Mister* Baggs: I have worked long hours to the ends of my strength and ingenuity in order to make our lives more happy. Hundreds of thousands of people, each month—every *day*—have—"

"Made you rich. I'm pleased for you."

The Chief stood, then sat as if his leg had given out. His face pulsed red and hot, then paler. He stood again, gold chains clanking, to stare down into Baggs' arrogant eyes, and whispered "You may not know who I am, although you know my name. You may not know *what* I am, although your most tobacco-sodden countrymen have acquainted themselves with that intelligence. I am here to read from my works, and you may pay to hear me do so if the revenue derived from this Mohawk Valley pleasure-dome permits such an outlay. But you may no longer hear my words for nothing."

"All right" Baggs said, standing. "I don't believe it's worth the price, and will have to deny myself any more noise like this. *You* may pay in the morning, at the downstairs desk. Thank you for your custom. And be damned." He left at an even easy pace, clicking the door gently closed.

The Chief sent me away, and through the closed door, whenever I wakened on the horsehair sofa, I saw the light beneath his door. I had no doubt he was writing it, transmogrifying it, for someone. But there was no letter in the morning, and the letter he gave me two days later said "The train gave in altogether at Utica, and the passengers were let loose there for the night. As I was due at Albany, a very active superintendent of works did all he could to get us along, and in the morning we resumed our journey through the water, with a hundred men in seven-league boots pushing the ice from before us with long poles." Eaten for supper in Utica!

Our train was moist and hot, Bealpost was sullen, the Chief in much pain. He sat panting near a window open to the long fields and flooded railroad bed, he said nothing. Four men walked before the train, pushing the ice aside, and children at the rails called to us not to hurry, and to get a horse. Our train took on the passengers of two other trains on which the fires had been put out by high water twenty-four hours before; so the seats were all filled, the air too muggy for comfortable breathing, and what there was of it was rank with the body sweat of farmers and the less excusably unwashed. The Chief held a newspaper in front of his head and leaned his face at the window so as to be unnoticed. Everyone stared at the man whose shoulders ended in paper and ink.

At the second transfer of passengers, we watched as cattle and sheep were unloaded from the train alongside. A dozen of the sheep were dead—our motorman explained they get maggots by the dozen as soon as they're cut, so septic is their wool—because they'd been stranded so long without feed that in their hunger they had begun to eat one another. The Chief's eyes widened and their fire jumped. He couldn't look away from the corpses of sheep, and the ones that staggered with bleeding wounds. "Horrible, Dolby. Ghastly to look at. Look!" He stared through the window and wrinkled his nose in disgust. He stared, said "Wond'rous sights in the New World. Most horrible, my God. Never, never—"

Bealpost said "Sure."

So we reached Albany, cutting through ice, with spring in the air outside, foulness within, and then a sudden change, more snow. I wondered if he would live through the reading, and then the trips to Boston and New York, then home. I think he wondered too. And I'm sure that Bealpost prayed for a timely seizure, a week of mourning, his freedom. I prayed for myself.

The Chief drank iced brandy and water in a weak solution, then dragged his foot to the front of the stage in a swarm of applause. By the time he was half a dozen feet from the lectern, his walk was balanced and steady as that of a great man's butler. At a side door, below the boxes, I watched his hatred for his body, and his love for the people's love—he thought that he loved *them*—transformed to a combination of scorn, for both himself and them, and a sly greengrocer's gratitude: Mrs. Gamp, in the most slum-dusted cockney, said, from the hairy hurt mouth of a man for whom little laughter was left, "'A thing,' she said, 'as hardly ever, Mrs. Mould, occurs with me unless it is when I am indispoged, and find my pint of porter settling heavy on the chest. Mrs. Harris often and often says to me, "Sairey Gamp," she says, "You raly do amaze me!"'"

Then—I had seen his specially printed prompt-copies, with their crossings-out, revisions, and their stage directions in the margin, *Breathe deeply here,* or *Horror! Disbelief!* in red ink—he was soon to Mrs. Prig's perfidy, as Gamp's best friend Mrs. Harris, so often quoted, is revealed as only her febrile imagination, a ghost in her waking dreams. "Mrs. Gamp resumed: 'Mrs. Harris, Betsey—'

"'Bother Mrs. Harris!' said Mrs. Prig.

"Mrs. Gamp looked at her with amazement, incredulity, and indignation; when Mrs. Prig, shutting her eye still closer, and folding her arms still tighter, uttered these memorable and tremendous words: 'I don't believe there's no sich a person!'

"The shock of this blow was so violent and sudden, that Mrs. Gamp sat staring at nothing with uplifted eyes, and her mouth open as if she were gasping for breath."

Etc. Yrs Sincerely, etc.

Dressed in what they assumed the English, whom they said they scorned, might wear to an evening's theater, they pointed and laughed—to hear the London diction, and to ridicule it; to share with the Chief his derision of the lower classes (whom he said he shielded from upper-class snobbery) and to thus be aligned with the landed and rich, whom their native comics daily wreaked their parodies on; to punish the audacities of imagination, though it was not just their evening's meal, but the chef who roasted *them*.

I saw, in the gas-light hissing above him, that his right jaw clenched and unclenched like the beating breast of a bird. He stood with his weight on his right leg, and his hands shook. The spectators doubtless laid it to his emotional raptures, perhaps even the subject matter which followed—Little Dombey's nauseous dying—but I knew that his final energies were giving out. Bealpost, at his post across the hall from me, stood with his hands in his pockets and probably thought of how to convince old Fields that he was pure. I wondered how to convince old Dolby that *I* was.

"The golden ripple on the wall came back again, and nothing else stirred in the room." He was whispering, and the weeping from the orchestra seats seemed to feed his clever grief. "The old, old fashion! The fashion that came in with our first garments, and will last unchanged until our race has run its course, and the wide firmament is rolled up like a scroll. The old, old fashion,— Death!

"O, thank God, all who see it, for that older fashion yet, of Immortality! And look upon us, Angels of young children, with regards not quite estranged, when the swift river bears us to the ocean!"

Pause at Estranged. Lingering sigh.

And then backstage: a greater exhaustion than usual. I was certain America would see the Chief give in to apoplexy and an attack of paralysis. His muscles jumped under his clothes, and his voice was husky, harsh. The Murder was next, and he held the prompt-copy on his old man's lap. I said nothing of his first-part's success, or of his fading strength. Instead, I squatted before him (wagging my tail) and said "Sir, the schedule you have given me for our next readings has something in common with this. Can you guess it?"

"No games now, Dolby. I'm spent."

"Out of four readings, sir, you have put down three Murders."

"And?"

"And since the success of the tour is so thoroughly assured, and since it no longer makes a jot of difference what you read, perhaps you will refrain from savaging your constitution every evening. You suffer most horribly after a Murder. . . ."

"Have you finished?"

"As you want it."

"I've said all I will say on the matter!" He threw a knife and fork to the backstage floor; his plate—the food untouched—fell too, and was smashed. "Dolby! Your infernal caution will be your ruin one of these days!"

"Perhaps, sir. But in this case, I hope you will recall that it was exercised in your interest."

Yrs etc., G. Dolby.

Then back to the applause, the darkness of the hall, the fearful women in the audience who had read in their papers of the fainting women in other halls, the men who prepared—their handkerchiefs were folded on their knees—to weep as their countrymen had done in other cities for many months.

When I returned to my post, Bealpost was there, wearing his bulky cloak and shod for snow. I said "Are you chilly?"

"I'm going" he whispered. "I won't be used like this."

"Won't you? And like what?"

"Handmaiden to the great girl up there in front of his violet screen and his hand-tuned gas lamp. Not any more. He can have me sacked, and roast in hell's own fire for his troubles. I don't care. *I'll* be my own man, Dolby."

"Meaning what, you vat of shit?"

"Meaning he owns these geese sitting here so dutifully. He owns you to your shoes. And he'd like to own me. The whole *world*. This is a free country, no one'll have me that way. No, sir. And he'll burn. He'll burn."

I yawned as hard as I could and whispered "Goodnight, Bealpost. Do write us for references, won't you?"

"Not where he'll be writing 'em from, Mister D-Dolby."

I felt him leave. My tongue was locked on my teeth. I closed my eyes and listened as Nancy, in the Chief's near-falsetto—true enough to be a frightened woman's tremulous croon—said to the monster she wholly loved " 'Why do you look like that at me!' "

"The robber sat regarding her for a few seconds with dilated nostrils and heaving breast, and then, grasping her by the head and throat, dragged her into the middle of the room, and looking once towards the door, placed his heavy hand upon her mouth.''

Now: despair.

'' 'Bill, Bill!' gasped the girl, wrestling with the strength of mortal fear—'I—I won't scream or cry—not once—hear me—speak to me—tell me what I have done!' ''

A woman in the rear, knowing she was supposed to, wept.

'' 'You know, you she-devil!' returned the robber, suppressing his breath. 'You were watched tonight; every word you said was heard.' ''

It still held me in its fist and shook me—not so much the fear but the lust to kill, the terrible passion for death he summoned into the dark air. And, I admit it, the destruction it worked on his feeble body by the end. I opened my eyes; more people were quaking with tears. His eyes were bright as fresh coals, and he loved his hatred, his face against the background screen was that of a corpse. And then I saw that above his head, protruding from the stalls, the gas-light reflector on its copper wire was threatened by a carelessly placed gas-jet. Its flame was high, it was heating the wires. Once burned through, they would release the reflector, which would fall into the stalls and set the theater afire.

Which of us had failed to oversee the gas-man place his lamp? Or: which of us—the thought came smoothly into place—had overseen him most zealously. Had moved the lamp ourselves, perhaps, with the tremble of a hand snaked down from the stalls when the theater was empty. Which of us had settled on a damp hall in Albany, state of New York, for suicide bier? And which of us had sought not suicide, but murder?

The wires glowed red, and I watched them. They grew larger, he diminished, and his voice sank away from my ears. The wires pulsed, and I studied them. He would burn first if the reflector fell, and his vision of flame would be true. His visions so often were. I stayed at my place. '' 'You *shall* have time to think, and save yourself this crime; I will not loose my hold, you cannot throw me off. For dear God's sake, for your own, for mine, stop before you spill my blood!' "

I pushed at the door, which led to the carpeted corridor, out to a cobbled alley, away to safety. But then I let it press back against my hand. Something made me—makes me—shake my head. I walked on my toes to the backstage steps and on my hands and knees (how right had Bealpost been?) I crept behind the folded stage curtain, watched from my squat. He bounced on his toes, his hands moved in health through the air. He was pawing his prey.

I hissed. His eyes struck down and sideways, and I stared up into them, and stared. Then I looked up at the cooking wires, pointed, opened my mouth as if to cry aloud, whispered "How long?"

The murderer's eyes lay on me like shovelfuls of wet earth. He didn't look up, but straight ahead, at his audience—at Nancy, begging for life—and then he let them fall on me again, studying.

One murderer's eye slowly closed into a rogue's long wink. He showed two fingers behind the podium, then closed his hand in a fist. He had seen it all, perhaps before I had. He was relishing his courage, timing himself to finish before the flaming fall. I crawled back and sat on the floor, my head against the cold brick wall. I closed my eyes and rolled my head from side to side, thinking of Bealpost. I knew he was thinking of us.

The Chief skipped parts, improvising elision and connection with invisible seams. I improvised too, for I was certain he would ask why I'd waited so long before warning him. And I was only Dolby, the clever character who did his bidding. I had no powers of my own for invention. I had no powers then even for simple thought. I was as limp as a dropped doll. Wood and paste don't answer.

Nancy was saying " 'Bill, Bill, for dear God's sake, for your own, for mine, stop before you spill my blood! I have been true to you, upon my guilty soul I have!' "

I heard his teeth click, and the spit popped from his mouth into the hot bright air around him. I knew that his eyes were bulging, his head shaking as if he froze, that the audience was stiff with expectation and emotion, that the wires were burning and the fire he feared, was always expecting, nodded above him as if in answer to what he constantly asked. The doxy and plunderer wailed to one another, pulling at each other, by his language bound.

"'Bill' cried the girl, striving to lay her head upon his breast, 'the gentleman and that dear lady told me tonight of a home in some foreign country where I could end my days in solitude and peace. Let me see them again, and beg them, on my knees, to show the same mercy and goodness to you; and let us both leave this dreadful place, and far apart lead better lives, and forget how we have lived, except in prayers, and never see each other more. It is never too late to repent. They told me so—I feel it now—but we must have time—a little, little time!'"

There was a rustle, and I knew that someone led a fainting woman from her seat. *Faster here. Profundo.*

"The housebreaker freed one arm and grasped his pistol. The certainty of immediate detection if he fired, flashed across his mind even in the midst of his fury; and he beat it twice with all the force he could summon, upon the upturned face that almost touched his own."

Screams and whimpers from the seats.

Remorseless, unrelenting.

"She staggered and fell, nearly blinded with the blood that rained down from a deep gash in her forehead, but raising herself, with difficulty, on her knees, drew from her bosom a white handkerchief—pure Rose Maylie's own"—*innocence! vaguest hope!*—"and sighed 'No, Bill! NO!' Then, weaker, holding the handkerchief up, in her folded hands, as high toward Heaven as her feeble strength would allow, she breathed one prayer for mercy to her Maker.

"It was a ghastly figure to look upon." *Slow down here.* "The murderer, staggering backward to the wall and shutting out the sight with his hand, seized a heavy club and struck her down."

31

First the shell of silence, then the bellows and cries of *Bravo!* which cracked the shell. The clapping of hands: a ceremony of drums. And in its midst, his growling "Gas down, there! Turn it off! Turn off the *gas*, you imbecile!"

And finally, then, the fire-lit bedroom of his suite, where he lay in the bed, a coverlet on his still-shod feet, breathing wheezily, slowly, untouched food and champagne on the bedside table. His eyes were closed, his left hand curled in a child's sleeping clench. As I watched, tears ran slowly onto his white-yellow cheeks. He still lived the killing. He might have wept for being killed, for doing the murder, for both.

In a very small voice he said "We gave them more than their money's worth, Dolby."

"You were magnificent, sir. I still, after all these Murders, am shaken by it."

"Yes. Bealpost is gone?"

"Thieves in the night, and so on."

"He arranged the gas-jet?"

"No, I don't think so. No: I mean I'm not sure. He never seemed to have the imagination or nerve."

"I've driven lesser men to do more, Dolby. It *might* have been he. I'll write to Fields in the morning, anyway. See you post it before we leave."

"Yes, sir." I looked into the fire, then saw that he looked there too, the tears still on his face. "We are booked on the *Russia*, sir, a Cunarder of course. From New York, as you directed, to Liverpool. To arrive the twenty-second of April, and I, for one, will be delighted."

"We cannot help but be transported, Dolby. Yes, I'll kiss the docks when we disembark, I promise it. Home is where you go to die. Not hothouse hotels in cities with pretentious names."

"Not you, sir. Some rest, perhaps a start on a new—"

"Dolby, please don't interfere in my schedule of writing. That is my concern, and bookings and arrangements are yours. Oh,

Dolby, damn-all, I apologize. And for snapping—before, about the Murder. I'm too tired, aren't I?"

He looked into the fire—partly because he was embarrassed, I think. He rarely apologized, except to the likes of Forster, say, or maybe Collins, and hardly even to them.

I said "A late squall of snow is expected tomorrow, I'm told. I wonder if you would consider staying in at the fireside and resting?"

He lay as if he had no muscles, said "Was there an afternoon post?"

"No letters from England, sir."

"No. I wonder how the children are, and everyone, that's all."

"I'm sure you're in mind at home as strongly as if you were there."

Pause here.

"Are you sorry, Dolby, for all the woe and work I've put you to?"

The scoundrel. "No, sir. I've—"

"Served. Miraculously."

"I was going to say I've learned."

His head turned toward the fire, his arms and legs lay loose. He sighed, as if half into sleep, "Learned what, my good, good Dolby?"

"You cannot imagine, sir."

Breathless silence.

I backed toward the door.

Deeper silence, still.

I saw the red pen moving in the margins, smoke of his language poured up. I booked his halls and blacked his boots. I was his page. He made me what I am.

New strength. A wicked low laugh.

"Can't I, Dolby?" *Dolby leans against door. Perspiration. In the darkness, pain.* "Haven't I?"

Moon here, and amply provided me with the old
blue ruin. He frequents a gin shop of the highest
standards of cleanliness, the Cap Raised High. I
knew it, once, first-hand. The publican never spat
directly upon the bar counter, but always into the
sawdust behind it or in front if it. If behind, where
he stood, he always stirred the phlegm into the sawdust and shavings so as to integrate the deposit into
the texture of his work. If he spat before, it was his
wont to require of a fat man named Smoky, whose
pipe was part of his jaw, I think, that Smoky do the
stirring. This was always an occasion of admiration
from those of us who nodded and drank. For it was
Smoky's custom to remove his battered boots upon
entering the shop in order, he claimed, that he feel
the more at home, as when his Meg was alive. His
Meg was crushed and ground by the wheels of a
camion bearing sides of beef from the Smithfield
slaughter. So Smoky would unflinchingly stir the
great slimy pool and, unnoticing, go back to his jar.
The rest of us would move our heads in celebration
of his stockings and his calluses and courage, and
would drink to Meg. We felt friendly, then, and
were grateful to Smoky and the publican for such
ease.

My notes proceed, I have an hundred sheets or
more inscribed, and am hardly beginning. Some-

times there is a high-pitched whistle in my brain, as of the chestnut vendor's waggon, which circled a neighbourhood I lived at for a while. I do not confuse it with the voices I hear, and herewith write down. Oh: in the west-country, there was a most glamourous customary harvest drink reserved for the early autumn. It had no name but the Nectar, and we treated it as such. We got a large cask, the eight- or nine-gallon size, and placed in it six pounds of moist sugar, five—you may prefer twelve or fifteen, why not?—ounces of bruised ginger, a few ounces of cream of tartar, four lemons, eight ounces of yeast, seven gallons of boiling water. We worked it several days, then strained and added a pint or so—you may prefer three or four or five, why not?—of manly brandy. It then was bunged in tight and, two weeks later, bottled. The caps, by the by, must be wired down, since the lovely fellow gets his spunk up in a very short time and wants to discharge.

There is discharge—I speak of blood and bits of throat coughed up into basins and onto sheets—and there is, again, *discharge*. And here I speak of the girl I dream of during these nights, when I can sleep, who discharged not merely her duties in the house. No, there was more. It begins with the usual story and then becomes much more. In my spinning head and heated brain—ah, Moon, you are so to be thanked—I hear it all.

36

A MAID LOOKS BACK, AND LAUGHS

When I am dead this Book will be found. I've faith, I've always had faith. Not in the God of my father. I take this opportunity to curse him again. Nor faith in much more than the tides. But I do believe in them. I can see them. Under the Embankment everything washes up. The Thames runs on. The earth itself is like a river. Even the tainted ground under Euston Station one day will turn itself up. The bodies of starved children and children dead of disease and whores with their throats squeezed shut by madmen will wash up from the foul ground after the Station itself has crumbled. So will my little Book. You who read this read my life.

Of my early days in the parish house at Canterton Glen in the New Forest there is little to tell. I was taught to read and write. I know the lives of my betters. They began not unlike my own. It was a typical English girlhood and that is that. The days I may have called my own no longer are mine. They have been cancelled. I put this down in my Book, that I died when I was aged thirteen years. Father appreciated Mr. Caldecott, and Mother, being dead, had no voice in the matter. My brothers and my sister of whom I intend to never speak again thought of him as I did. That his whiskers were too long for fashion and for comfort. That we were apprised of this quality by virtue of his kissing us with over-much frequency and too great a pressure of the lips. That he

often smelled of his own inner workings due to insufficient bathing. That we thought he carried the cholera and were relieved
each summer not to have been given it by him. That he studied us
overlong and me in particular. That he drank brandy with Father
when Father might have read to us aloud at night. That I understand today precisely what he meant by saying with a snicker
sliding off his large upper lip to Father "Oh, Jarrod, I do love you
as my own." Father's buggery was his own business. I assume that
still it is. The Church will not appreciate a bugger but that is the
Church's concern and mine no longer. Mr. Caldecott's hands were
furry as a beast's. In winter he perspired as much as in summer. I
have concluded that he knew no seasons but his own.

He held my hand in the last August I was alive as we rode a trap
to the station and then the train up to London. He told me how
Father and he had planned my trip. My day in the capital of
civilization. He cleaned the smuts from my face with a yellowed
handkerchief which smelled like his pocket. His pocket smelled
like him, a kind of meat or milk no longer fresh. He bought me
ices at the railroad hotel. We took tea at an inn where a hosteler
smiled to him and nodded his head. Somewhere on the Embankment we watched the River Police carry from their boat a woman
who had drowned herself clutching her baby. The baby's eyes were
open. They looked surprised. When I wept he comforted me by
squeezing under my arm with his long pelted fingers. He spoke
little and I spoke less. He seemed expectant and of course he was.
He showed me the clock at Parliament and examined some pendulum clocks in a window at Oxford Street. He showed me the
time he carried on his chain. Waiting.

So that at half-five he was able to say with a snap of his fingers
and shake of his head that we had missed the train. The last train
west and south. I was watching a night-man's wagon with its cargo
of excrement and trying to breathe through my mouth. He comforted me again with his hand beneath my armpit touching near
the breast. He told me of a pleasant night in a pleasant hotel, the
Telegraphing home of the news to my concerned Father, and then

the morning's first train back. I wept and he kissed me. His hand again. And I henceforth was to call him Uncle, he said. I said nothing more.

We rode a cabriolet to Curzon Street. In the gas lamps there the buildings looked yellow. Like the rotten undersides of logs in the Forest at home. No one attended us at the hotel but he seemed to know his way about and soon he had shown me the room. I asked why there was the single bed only and he snapped his fingers and shook his head. He smiled. His amusement seemed to be with himself. I remember his words: "One thinks one thinks of everything and then one doesn't. Ha!" One, one, one. I was to wait while he went down to attend to sending the news home. I sat on the edge of the unkempt bed and waited. The curtains were drawn and little noise came up through the window.

I was thinking about my brother and wishing I had the knife he carried. I had thoughts of killing myself rather than sleep there. For I still thought that life was like a book and in certain books that was what young ladies thought at times of extremity. The book had not yet begun. Then the door opened in and it started.

He was old and kindly-looking, his cheeks very smooth and a pleasant scent of clove hung on his quite nice clothes. I stood. He stood beside me, little more than my own height. He said "It will seem difficult and then awfully nice. It's always that sort of thing."

That sort of thing. For a small man he was strong. His little fingers exerted surprising force. I lay on my back beneath his hands and then his forearms and then all of him. It was like the dream of shrieking and being able to make no sound. I did make a little high-pitched bird's kind of noise but then he pushed the pillow into my face and leaned upon it and I stopped. He was forced to tear my clothes because I still struggled. He later apologized for the damage and offered me a sort of *pourboire*. I am surprised that at thirteen I knew enough to take the coin. But I was a practical country girl.

Of the pain I do not intend to speak. It was the usual pain. And from what I have since learned from others at Urania Cottage and elsewhere, it all was little different from a wedding-night, even the suffocation. There was blood and there were bruises. I had bit my tongue and cheek. My stomach hurt. Always that sort of thing. Later, I wondered what his organ had looked like. Later still I knew.

Of the weeping in the room on Curzon Street I do not intend to speak. Nor of the woman who later knocked, then entered bearing a basin and some balm. Nor of what she called "our arrangements for the future." Nor the knowledge we all of us shared, and none of us spoke, that I could not return to my home forever.

I wept much and spoke little and several days later the woman put me to work. In such circumstances I was lucky. I did not have to go blind in a factory or catch a disease in one. I never walked the street. Two of the women were intelligent and traveled, and they delighted in reading to me aloud and in refining my own skills. It is they who taught me to speak to you like this. One of them was a Jewess of considerable refinement. Her father owned three coal barges and a yard near Greenwich. She had enjoyed many advantages. Including a party at Piccadilly ending in rape and the accidental murder of a well-placed older man, her chaperon. The accident being his failing to lunge when a broken bottle was deposited in his throat and face. The rape being her introduction to Christian hardihood and communal love (there being three of them). It spoke well for them, I thought, that they raped her before the murder. At least she didn't have to use a cadaver for pillow.

No one at Curzon Street went home. I learned then that a woman's body, once it is opened to the world, is somehow allied to the door which closes on a hearth's bright fire. This lesson has held up well. Ask the Master's wife.

Susan read to me and I read to her and she insisted that I perform writing exercises to improve both my hand and my expression. She told me of her father's rituals and her mother's silences and of how her father was hated for a Jew. I asked her about the Jews' murder of Christ and Susan said, one night, sitting on my bed, her hand on my naked thighs and her finger making small delicate motions on the mound and hair, "Everyone murders Christ, Barbara. Jews and Gentiles alike. He was made to be murdered."

I pulled her wrist harder and rose to meet it, but I bit my lip and rode down again, saying "Do *you* believe in Him too?"

Her fingers followed me down and her lips, then. She whispered into me "No, love, we are alike in that we detest Him, you and I and the Gentiles and Jews. And of course He hates us in return."

I went out little. Sometimes I stayed in for fear of meeting someone from home. Sometimes because I could not imagine what I ought to do in the streets save look at men as customers, women as sisters in the house. Or each as opposites to us and our mistress's clients. And then I would hate them. I grew fat and Susan forced a regimen upon me. I grew lazy and she made me write. One day after shopping she returned to my room and, kissing me on the lips, bathing my lips with her tongue, she offered me a package. In it were three small volumes, *Oliver Twist: or, the Parish Boy's Progress*. At *Parish* I laughed, at *Progress* I howled. Susan said "So you've decided already that you like it?"

I said "No." I stood close to her and spoke onto her mouth, nearly kissing her. "No, I have decided that I am also a Jew." Then I did kiss her. Then the men came and we worked. Then that night I started to read my darling's gift.

It was early in the third year of my employment and the second week of my reading that in *Oliver Twist* Rose Maylie offered Nancy the whore a new life, safe from Sikes and the streets and all of London. Nancy refused. Not loving anyone but Susan, I wondered if I would stay a whore to be with her, or escape from the Life. It wasn't fair, for Susan was no murderer, but my lover and only friend. I felt nothing with the men of course. With Susan

I felt everything. Still, I wondered. And although it was only a book it was most powerful and I wept when Sikes dashed her brains out.

I told Susan of the passage. "He knows nothing about women" she said. She looked at me as if to determine what I had learned from the novel by Boz, for that was what they called him when he wrote it.

"If a woman could leave this" she said. And then I knew why she had given me the book. She was weeping. "If a woman could marry a man who knows what she is and leave for America. A farmer's wife——"

I cried too. I left her room and in my own I put the books into the fire. It smelled as if an animal were burning. When she came that night, after the men had left and the house was silent and the street silent too, I lay on the bed completely naked. My legs were wide apart. I rubbed myself. She stared. Removed her gown. Knelt between my feet, then went to all fours. I said "Come kill Christ."

She said "He was only a man."

As she lowered herself and started to tongue I seized her hair and squeezed my thighs and, holding her hair still, turned myself over upon her so that she was face-down on the sheets and squealing. I took the candle from the table. I held it like a dagger. Its flame sputtered when I drove, behind me, behind her, in, to put it out. She screamed and bucked and threw me off. I lay not laughing. She ran whimpering from the room, crouched over.

I held the candle and bit at it. I lay on the bed and moved the candle in myself. I even fell asleep. And next morning I left as if to shop. I hired a cab and was driven to Shepards Bush, where Susan had told me the author and Miss Coutts maintained the establishment for women like me.

And it was there, after the endless lectures and the bland wholesome food, the drudgery, the stares of the matron, the smirks of the gentlemen who came to inspect as often as they could, the baby's system of merits for resisting temptation and the long parade of bodies I often was hungering for, that the man who had written of whoring came to inquire if there was a girl there who could work in a kitchen and never let on about her past. I heard him say "I'd like a Jewess if there's one." And next morning, when the matter was broached after prayers and before breakfast, close on dawn, I raised my hand and told them I was a Jew.

He had been upbraided for making Fagin a Jew and such an awful one. One of his readers had complained and he could not bear the dissatisfaction of a single reader. And he hired a secret whore, a secret Jew. I lived below stairs at Gad's Hill and was his buried conscience. He was one of those who claimed not to have murdered the Christ. The hair in his nostrils was sometimes unclean. He was old.

Rising early was still difficult but not without its humour, for I rose to clean. Sprinkling dried leaves on the floors before dusting and scrubbing, sweeping up the leaves and laying the carpets again. Dusting the soot from the coal stoves, turning mattresses, changing sheets, emptying slop basins. I was told that the Master used to inspect the drawers of his children's bureaus to see that everything was in its place and lined up straight each to each. He was like that about the house and soon noticed disorder, and so the mistress Miss Hogarth was adamant on tidiness. It all was funny. Who was I to make things clean? But I did, his resident Jewess, and so did the others. We sometimes saw him, often heard him. Telling everyone the news of the world and the truth about living. Complaining about black beetles in the pantry or a hint of mice outside the meat larder. Declaiming on the luncheon menu even though, I was told, he rarely was able since his return from America to eat a healthy meal.

Once when I was pouring hot water to carry upstairs, I heard through an open window a woman cry in terror. It reminded me of me. Slowly with the basin in my hands I followed the noise. I saw the Master at the back meadow, his hands curved in the air and his neck shaking. A man's deep noise came and then the high cry. I dropped the basin on the lawn and ran to him. To see as much as to help. He cried again, shrill and high, in my weakest voice, "No, Bill! No!" He struck his fist down and staggered. Then he stood up taller and nodded his head.

In gnat clouds and over a tit's fearful cry from the elder beneath which he stood I said "Pardon, sir, are you well?"

He turned slowly and looked at me. He slapped his small hands against his waistcoat and limped toward me, his foot all wrapped in a black silk bandage. There was red in his eyes and perspiration on his forehead. He looked down to me, for I am a small person, and he said in his softest voice "It's Barbara?"

"Barbara, sir."

"And you wish to know if I'm well?"

"No, sir."

A great smile went over his face and the whole face changed. "And there I thought you worried for me. Ah, well." And then the face changed again, the lines around the eyes disappeared only to reappear around the mouth and he looked bloated with malice as his face widened and his nostrils flared. "Then *why* are you not in my house, where you work? Where it is *said* that you work. Where you are *hired* to work. Where I *require* you to work."

I curtsied like a good girl and laughed like a whore. "I came, sir, because I heard a cry as if in extremity. I had thought that rescue lived neither above nor below stairs. I desist because I recognize the nature of the cry. It's that girl. The whore with the heart of gold. Except she's too much gold and not enough whore, sir. Am I dismissed?" I curtsied again.

"From me or from my service?" he asked, and the lines returned to his eyes.

"From either, sir."

"Yes" he said, and laughed like a boy who'd found a fine joke. "No, I mean. No, you're still in my employ and I do not dismiss you from my meadow." He bowed to me, a mockery of bowing. I inclined my head in parody, but he was looking over the fields toward the school in the distance. "Well-spoken and brazen as a cathedral bell and a reviewer to boot. So you read your master's little books?"

"I read that one before Urania. It was why I begged them to let me in."

"All the better" he said. He smiled on me without meaning it and limped a few paces toward the house. Then he stopped. He said "Do you know, Barbara, that thousands of people have paid thousands of pounds to hear me read the Sikes-and-Nancy?"

"The mistress and others have told me so, sir."

"Are you impressed?"

"By the money, sir?"

He pointed a finger in the air, then dropped his hand. He nodded his head and his face was solemn. "Why are you so skilled in repartee?" he asked. "Why are you so well-spoken?"

"For a retired whore, sir?"

"You must be careful," he said, "that your wit not overshadow your gratitude. Mustn't you?"

"As you say, sir." I curtsied.

"As I mean, Miss Barbara."

"I'm sorry, sir."

"No you aren't" he said.

"No, sir."

He banged his fist against his thigh and winced. "*Learn* sorrow, then! Learn station! Learn *place!*" He limped toward the garden and I waited near the elder. I thought that he soon must die, he looked so feeble as he hobbled home. His strength was in his murders.

I said to myself "Learn sorrow." As I watched him scuttle slowly back the gnats settled at my eyes and nose. I followed him.

I have little interest in recounting my odious duties. It was harder than being a whore. Nothing's easier than that, of course. At least on Curzon Street. It wasn't one of those places where they work you until your flesh sags and you're dead of disease. They had us inspected by a doctor whose name you would know if,

45

when you read this, too many hundreds of years haven't passed. Of course there's the necessary rape or theft or drugging to start some of us off. Some volunteered and perhaps I would have been one, though I doubt it. Probably in my case what happened was what should have happened. But in a shorter time than you might like to think, the Life's the only life. We never worked mornings and we had our freedom. They knew, the Mrs. and her man, there was no place to run to. No place except a workhouse and the lashings and gruel. Or the factories. Or Urania Cottage. And he was the only reason I went there.

Not for his famous goodness or mild mercy. I'll talk of that. No. I went there because Susan sent me. If she was telling me goodbye she also was telling me that I must seek a life without her. We loved. She was my teacher. I'm not sad for my manner of saying farewell. For she deserved it. Punishment is what you deserve. It defines itself. You seek it. My punishment was to lose her and hers was to have me as a man since it was a man she sought and found and fled with. Her voyage was to America. Mine was to Gad's Hill Place and the carrying of slops. Once I was in the Life, the rest of my life was in her hands and she placed it in his. There I was.

Of the other staff and members of the household I shall have something to say. But essentially it was he and I. Trust him to have the cheap edition of his books below stairs. For our enlightenment I suppose. And because he assumed that no one could live without his language. Even the famous false door in the parlour which opened into his study was named, in a manner of speaking. There were leather backs of books which weren't books, all ranged in rows. Until you tried to move them for the dusting. Then you saw that there was nothing behind them except shelving. At a touch, the door swung to. Shelves and leather backs and all. And there was the room he worked in. I wonder why he had to skulk like that. But the artificial books had names. He and his guests used to laugh over them. I could hear him holding forth, saying "I call this one *Drowsy's Recollections of Nothing* and the other

Heaviside's Conversations with Nobody. Ha. Yes, and this little beauty, in only six volumes, mind you, is *Kant's Eminent Humbugs,* eh? And tell me, Forster, what do you think of *Socrates on Wedlock?* In twenty-one volumes, here, we've *History of a Short Chancery Suit.* This little pamphlet, on which I shall have to have the title printed sideways, is of course *The Virtues of Our Ancestors.* Understand? Virtues. Yes. Awfully good, isn't it?"

They all laughed for him. Mr. Collins and Mr. Forster were much with us in 1869, and Mr. Dolby of course. He was away from home with Dolby often in those days. Giving his Farewell Readings. I don't think anyone has ever taken longer to say goodbye. It was before and after his journeys to Scotland and Wales, Dublin and Belfast, that the talk filtered down below stairs and under the sliding hallway doors. Always talk of trains. This interested me much. But what was important and instrumental was *his* interest. Whatever he thought about seeped down under great pressure like thick Italian coffee. It pooled and then spread to the rest of us. So that whatever was on his mind, be it his son Plorn's departure for Australia or Henry's study at Cambridge, became a weight on the collective mind of the household. In mind as well as act he was a dictator.

Soon I heard of Staplehurst. This was before his journey up to Scotland for Readings. Some of the staff called it his "Holiday." It was four years before I came to his service, and they all spoke of it innocently enough. A trip to Paris. Only late at night, when the mistress was asleep, did they speak of his companion. Ternan the actress. She was the same as me. A whore. I say this with no blame. You who read this by now must understand me. She had her work, which was easy enough. To live in the flat he rented for her and to meet him in Paris on his holidays. They were returning on the tidal train in June, going fast through Headcorn toward Staplehurst. Cuddling in his compartment no doubt. The driver saw torn-up rails, some say. Others say the newspaper reports spoke of a flagman's red banner. Whatever happened to alert him, it happened too late. The train jumped a 40-foot separation on a dip in the tracks and ran off toward the bank of the river bed. Much screaming of brakes and people I'm sure.

First the engine, then the guards' van, and then the coach with Ternan and the Master. There it was, its rear end on the field, part of it hanging off the bridge. Miss Hogarth has said that the Master said " 'Suddenly we were off the rail, and beating the ground as the car of a half-emptied balloon might do.' " Not that he has ever been in a balloon. But he must use his words, mustn't he?

Well, he was a hero to hear it told by those who heard him tell it. Demanding the key of a guard and opening the compartment door. Helping Ternan and some old lady out of the car. Watching as guards ran up and down the train while the injured screamed and those who were trapped screamed louder. Miss Hogarth said he said " 'With my brandy flask in hand, I fought my way through shattered carriages and the bodies of the dead and dying. One poor fellow, staggering past, had such a frightful cut across the skull that I could see the grin of bone.' " Twice I've heard her tell it and twice she's said that. Grin of bone. Oh they love his mind. His ceaseless prosing. " 'I couldn't bear to look at him,' " she said he said, " 'but I did. It was my duty. I poured some water over his face, gave him some brandy and laid him on the grass. A lady had blood streaming over her face which was lead-color.' " Lead-color. He never forgets his language. It was only then, Miss Hogarth said he said, after surveying the crushed and dead and bloody, that he remembered that the manuscript of *Our Mutual Friend*'s next number was in the carriage. Cool as a cucumber, he climbed back in to rescue it.

I wonder. If he was cool as a cucumber, he probably shunted his mistress off beneath a tree where no one would notice her. Then with the manuscript under his arm from the start he probably strode about. Examining the corpses. Encouraging the employees. However. Everyone agrees that he was shaken when he returned to Gad's Hill. That his hand shook so, he had to dictate replies to queries about his health. That he told Forster, there on a visit soon after, "I am curiously weak, as if I were recovering from a long illness. I begin to feel it in my head, you know. I sleep well and eat well, but then I write half a dozen notes, and turn faint and sick. Drove into Rochester yesterday and bless me if I didn't feel more shaken than I have since the accident. A curious turn for a veteran traveler, don't you think? Is the Inimitable aging, old friend? Do say he isn't, I pray you. Ha! *Warn* you. Ha!"

They say he sent a pair of pigeons and some clotted cream to Ternan on the next morning. And I heard him speaking with Dolby, whining about his fears. "I cannot bear railway travel, I fear, Dolby. No, that is not true. I bore it through America and I *can* bear it now. But I am not always certain that I want to bear it. You know, I have, always, a perfect conviction, against the senses, that the carriage is down on the left side. Curious, isn't it? For at Staplehurst, it was the right side which sank. And anything like speed, as ever, is inexpressibly distressing. I must confess that now it is less tolerable than in the years intervening. Could you say your Chief is doddering off into his senility?"

Good Dolby said no. The Master knew he would. Good Dolby worried about the railroad rides as he worried about his Chief's poor health and good crowds for the Readings. Sometimes he looked as if he wished to lay his head on the Master's breast. Sometimes he looked as if he wished to bite him.

I do not read his travel books. They are as pompous as the response of any bully Englishman to a world he cannot own or hasn't invented. But I have read his books. They were there in the downstairs kitchen. I knew they were there for me to read. Not all of them, but most. For in his life and ceaseless language were the clues to where my own road led. I knew that. A precocious sixteen-year-old, and schooled by a teacher he couldn't hold a candle to, I read him. I liked his *Dombey and Son* because a father gets his due in that. Although he isn't punished nearly enough. That's because the Master deserved his daughters' punishment and knew it. He tried to forestall it with his books. And he saw his death coming and knew how it would travel to him. Listen: "The very speed at which the train was whirled along mocked the swift course of the young life that had been borne away so steadily and inexorably to his foredoomed end. The power that forced itself upon its iron way—its own—defiant of all paths and roads, piercing through the heart of every obstacle, and dragging living creatures of all classes, ages, and degrees behind it, was a type of the triumphant monster, Death." He wrote that book eight or nine years before Staplehurst. He knew.

Once, after the early trip to Scotland, he had Miss Hogarth send for me. Collins was in the sitting room with him, all tiny arms and hands and legs and feet and a giant round head. His spectacles glittered. He looked like a monstrous bee. He studied my body as I studied his. I was good to survey. He was not. He knew it. His ugliness and need excited me. The Master said "Mr. Wilkie Collins, this is Barbara, the girl I have spoken of."

I curtsied and Collins moved his enormous head. "You show no signs of your former life" Collins said. His voice was soft, like a tongue.

I said "I have but the one life, sir, and am still in the midst of living it."

Collins smiled like an animal, all tongue and teeth. The Master first smiled, then his nostrils widened and he looked grim. He tried to. "You see, Collins, what I refer to? A wit far in excess of what you would expect."

Collins replied "No, not necessarily, sir. Women, even girls— few of them live to be women in fact. Girls who follow the Life must sharpen their wits to survive. That is why I maintain they are a proper study and subject fit for art of the highest order. Barbara, I am told your persuasion is Jewish."

I nodded. The Master said "Ma'am!" I curtsied and said "Yes, sir, you are correct."

"Was your father a money-lender?"

I smiled, for I had been waiting. "No, sir," I said, "he is a minister in the South."

"You are a *convert?*" the Master said.

Collins said "You choose hardship and separation from the mass of your fellow beings. But why?"

"I was chosen first by a Life which is as far separated as any religion, sir. Once there, other choices are secondary."

"You call being a Jewess secondary?" Collins said.

The Master said "Is not salvation by your Lord of high concern?"

I said "Sir, I have been told that all men daily kill Christ. And women too, I suppose. What difference, then, under what name we do the murder?"

The Master's eyes were wide, Collins' narrow. Collins finally said, rubbing a carved lion's head on the arm of his chair, "Why, none. Given your supposition. We must speak at some length, my dear. With your master's permission."

The Master nodded wearily, as if he had predicted the invitation. What it might lead to. I of course was certain where it could lead. I curtsied. My nipples stung as they rubbed my clothes. And then the Master shouted "By damme, Collins, it *does* make a difference. Why change if we all do it. It isn't logical, by God. What is your *honest* reason, ma'am?"

I curtsied and said "I do not know which of my reasons is honest, sir. How do we recognize the honesty of our reasons?"

I was dismissed. Collins grinned wide. The Master frowned. His son Plorn had told me he would.

The more his life pressed in upon him the more the pressure seemed to reside in his foot. The more he limped upon it the paler he grew. The paler he grew the less he ate. As he ate the less he spoke of his Nelly more. No one else spoke of Ternan unless he did. And then it was with the disinterest you feign as you look into the noseless face of a syphilitic and pretend it is only another face. When a certain Bealpost was mentioned his face became a mask.

Charley his son at thirty-one with four daughters and a son to support was nursing a paper mill going bankrupt. Wills at *All the Year Round* was ill and the Master had to do his work too. Later he let Charley do it. Alfred was in Australia. Mary was as old as his mistress and neither she nor her father was comfortable with the fact. And Plorn was shortly to leave for Australia. He was almost seventeen. He learned.

Plorn was in bed one morning in October. The Master was in his study practicing his Murder. We heard the shrieks. I came in with linen to change the bed and saw him, but closed the door behind me anyway. I could see how under the comforter his feet were pressed together at the heels, his knees spread wide and flat against the sheets. His hand was at his groin. The other with white knuckles held the bars at the head of the bed.

"Oh Christ" he said. His little face was white and thin. His legs were thin. He was smaller than his father. He turned red and looked at the ceiling. His eyes were brilliant. His father's eyes.

I said "Am I disturbing you, sir?"

"I'll be up in a minute, Barbara."

I held the linen against me and said "You seem already to be up, sir. Shall I leave?"

He closed his eyes. He said "No."

"What shall I do, sir?"

He looked at me as if he were praying. His hand beneath the covers moved and then he stopped it. He looked away toward the ceiling again.

I said "Perhaps I can help, sir." I set the linen on a corner-chair and walked to the side of the bed. "It doesn't make you weak for long, you know. It may *be* as it's the life's precious fluid of a man. But it seems to regenerate, if you know what I mean."

With his eyes closed he nodded. His face was crimson and hot-looking. I touched the covers. He hissed as if I'd stung him. But his hips moved up. He was a sweet young boy. I moved the covers away and saw him. Innocent and small for all his excitement. Defenseless. It looked like a baby animal.

"Let me do it for you" I said.

"Whore" he whispered.

"That's right" I said. "Whore and Jewess from under the stairs."

"You shit-smeared kitchen-maid whore" he said.

"That makes it better, doesn't it?"

He called me all the names they like to use. Telling me how low I was. At the final instant I lowered my head like a bird of prey and sucked him. He whimpered like a child and tried to move away. I held him by his little thin buttocks and pulled him in. Like a bird again I fell upon his torso and pulled myself up him and seized either side of his face and plunged my tongue between his lips. He gagged.

He had nothing to say. I stood beside the bed again and licked my lips until he had to look away. I said "I'll come back later, sir, to change the bed."

I came in early the next morning again. He wanted me to do it the same way. I told him he must learn to be a man. He locked the door and I showed him. Like all young men he was quite unoriginal. Not very good. I told him I hoped in Australia he would learn a bit of enterprise. He bit my throat and cursed me for a serving-wench whore. I told him he sounded like his father's books. I tutored him for a week. It was good to have some pleasure again though soon I saw myself as if from a point on the ceiling. I was cold and clever. Businesslike, in all. One morning he said "Where are you? When we—"

"You must read more of your father's writings" I said. And next day I read him what I'd copied: "Oh for a good spirit who would take the house-tops off, with a more potent and benignant hand than the lame demon in the tale, and show a Christian people what dark shapes issue from amidst their homes, to swell the retinue of the Destroying Angel when he moves forth among them!"

"You think you are *above* . . . it?" he said.

"Like your father, sir."

"Don't call me sir like that, you bitch whore."

"Very well."

"No. *Do* say sir."

"Ah. You mean: Sir, my lord, may I rub your organ on my cheeks and lips. Like this. Or sir, may I kiss it. So. Sir—"

"Get off me! Get out! Whore! *Whore!* And never dare to think of yourself and my father in the same thought. Out! Away from me!"

They said his father's voice broke often as he spoke to Plorn of the coming voyage out. Miss Hogarth said that the Master had quite broken down when he said the final farewell. He gave his son a box of cigars. Cigars! And standing at the top of the stairs one afternoon two of us heard the Master declaiming to Dolby from the hall "Oh if you ever do come, Dolby, to send your youngest child thousands of miles away for an indefinite time, and have a rush into your soul of all the many fascinations of the last little child you can ever dearly love, you will have a hard experience of this wrenching life."

Dolby replied that he understood. His Chief hastened to say "No, you do not, dear Dolby. You cannot."

Dolby replied that he supposed, after all, he could not.

I whispered "He cannot let it go at that."

With surprise and pain in his voice, his Chief said "But you must, Dolby. You must *try*."

Dolby, lost in either the coming at or going from the issue, finally said just "Yes."

So he was alone.

Miss Hogarth was a solid slow woman. She had no wit. From what they said she was like the wife he'd driven out. A stolid steady performer of necessary chores. Her teeth were stained, her throat sagged. She loved him and his needs. She didn't respond to his needs: she worshipped them. I waited to hear they'd been lovers but everyone swore not. He was a moving statue of something sacred which she adored. She loved him as only a virgin can. Purely because from a distance. She spoke only when she had to.

She always was clean because he demanded a world without pollution. I think he demanded too that she instruct me so as to save me from a false god or my own false self. For every time she spoke with me she made a lesson out of something as simple as putting up pears or sweeping carpets. I didn't mind. I assumed that having a mother was like being preached at by Miss Hogarth. A little wordy, but not too uncomfortable. She always saw that our meals were good though she didn't permit us much ale except on holidays. She spoke of the many famous people who adored him. She spoke of the masses of the poor who felt the same. She spoke of how hard he worked at his Readings so as to earn an estate he could leave to his children. When I asked her if he might not also perform for the pleasure, she said "Pleasure?"

I said "The thrill of all those people gasping?"

"Your master does not threaten his health for the sake of a gasping crowd" she answered. Her thick lips tightened.

I said "Oh."

But he went on. His leg dragged, he panted when he walked. Sometimes he fluttered his eyes like a fainting girl. And always there was someone to hold to his arm and whimper on his behalf. St. James Hall, and the spectators, the friends at home who told him what he wished to hear. One, a critic, although I do not know of what, told the Master that when Bill struck Nancy he had an irresistible desire to scream. The Master said "You need not stifle the impulse on my account, you know." Another, a physician, said "If only one woman cries out when you murder the girl, there will be a contagion of hysteria all over the place." The Master did not correct the surgeon to the effect that it was Sikes who did the Murder and the Master who read it aloud.

And then Dolby was returned from his home at Ross again and they were to set off for Edinburgh. I brought in tea and heard Dolby say "Your mind is on Staplehurst again, sir."

"You do know me, Dolby" the Master said.

"And it is worse than in America?"

"Dolby, when I am on board of a train, I see the car leaning to the left. Always to the left!" His face was white and he pointed in the air.

Dolby, eager and awkward and large, said "And yet the car went down to the right at Staplehurst, did it not?"

The Master closed his eyes and nodded slowly, as if Dolby had disclosed a great sorrow. "Dolby," he said, "you know. You always know."

Dolby bit his lip. His teeth were close together. "I do my best, sir."

The Master said "Yes you do." He asked me to pour out tea and leave them. I curtsied. "Do you know, Dolby, how many shocks the nerves receive on a long excursion by train?" I stopped pouring. He motioned me to go on, then closed his eyes again.

Dolby said "No, sir. It hadn't occurred to me."

"No," the Master said, "you were not at Staplehurst."

Dolby said "Ah."

"Thirty thousand" the Master said. "I have calculated it. Thirty thousand nerve jolts."

I began to giggle but stopped. "You will suffer, sir" Dolby said. "But I will go on."

They left, with enough portmanteaux and apparatus to equip a traveling troupe. When they were gone, the house, as always, became silent and the work less arduous. But not for long. Some days later Miss Hogarth received a letter in which Dolby told her of the Edinburgh Reading. We were assembled below stairs in a smell of earth and leeks to hear of the Murder. "'The horrible perfection,'" Dolby wrote, "'to which he brought it, and its novelty, acted as a charm to him and made him the more determined to go on with it elsewhere, come what might. He ignores his health so bravely! The terrible force with which the actual perpetration of this most foul murder was described was of such a kind as to render him utterly prostrate for some moments after its delivery, and it was not until he had vanished from the platform, my dear Miss Hogarth, that the public had sufficiently recovered their sense of composure to appreciate the circumstance that all the horrors to which they had been listening were but a story and not a reality. And I must report that it was painfully apparent to his most intimate friends, and those who know his state of health the best, that a too-frequent repetition of the Murder will seriously and permanently affect his constitution."

She shook the letter at us and then let her hands drop to her ample sides. She sighed and nodded her head. "Why does he go on?" she asked us.

I opened my mouth to reply but she looked at me with such strength that I said nothing. To myself I said I have done much for the sake of a caress. Why should he do less?

And then, a week more into January of 1869, we received another letter describing the events which followed the Belfast Reading. They were on a mail train to Kingstown, where they were to catch the mail boat. There were but two carriages for passengers, the rest being guards' vans and post-office carriages. Dolby and the Master rode in a *coupé* composed almost entirely of plate glass. He had, Dolby wrote (and Miss Hogarth loudly read), arranged for the *coupé* in order to assure privacy for his Chief. As if she were reading of Arthur going to battle, she declaimed "'Whilst running along at a rapid speed, about forty miles from Belfast, we received a severe jolt which threw us all forward in the carriage. Looking out we observed an enormous piece of iron flying along a side line, tearing up the ground and carrying some telegraph posts along with it. Possibly having the recollection of the dreadful Staplehurst accident in his mind, my Chief threw himself to the bottom of the carriage, and we all followed his example. Later, taking stock, once the brakes had been applied and the train safely halted, we found that the great tire of the driving-wheel had broken, and that the piece of iron we had seen traveling with such destructive force was a portion of the tire, and that the noise we had heard on the roof of the carriage as we stopped was caused by another enormous piece of iron falling on it. Had this piece of iron struck the glass instead of the framework of the carriage, it would have been impossible for us to escape, and in all probability there would have been a repetition of the Staplehurst catastrophe.

"'Need I tell you, dear Miss Hogarth, that my Chief is an iron man? Two minutes later, he bounced onto his feet and was telling the driver that he was a good man.'"

Miss Hogarth held the letter to her starched bosom. We all sighed, as that was what she wished us to do. I would have given much could I but once have found her flesh-to-flesh with the Master. His buttocks jiggling. Cries belching from her wonderful girth. Our iron man. Steel seed.

We heard more. As if the saga of England's hero were published in parts, like the Master's books. Miss Hogarth would call us from the corners of the house and grounds and in the kitchen we would assemble. Standing at the metal-topped service table. Listening through Dolby and then Miss Hogarth to the Master's voice whose timbre and histrionics somehow animated Dolby's words and Miss Hogarth's tongue and rounded mouth. We learned of "'his own good nature'" and "'affectionate disposition, sense of justice,'" and we were told of "'his determination to go on which I cannot and dare not shake.'" We learned of pain. "'The awful swelling of his foot, and inclination when under duress to sometimes stagger as if wounded.'" He was at the same time "'graceful as a dancer despite his malaise.'"

When a letter in the Master's own hand first arrived, Miss Hogarth would compose herself on the sitting-room settee and read the letter aloud to herself, washing it down with green and yellow herbal tea. I remember her saying, as I poured for her, "Listen, Miss Barbara. *This* is what courage speaks. He writes: 'After the Reading some friends came to me in the dressing-room, but kept a good distance away. Not so much from respect or decorum, I fear, as from a subterranean, almost animal, intimation of the murderous instincts I had displayed at the lectern. My Murder, you understand, had gone off rather well. I did my best not to display my teeth in a frightening fashion, as I suspected that any sudden motion on my part might set them to fainting and chattering like goslings before the wolf. I was most mild, dear spirit of my household—'" She nodded to me as if to remind me of the esteem in which he held her. Then she said "And so forth, yes, yes, and so forth and—ah! Now attend! 'Having some vacant days before the Lancashire Readings, I concurred with good Dolby—he is as watchful as ever, my brother and my son—that a change of air would prove beneficial to what I fear is a further weakening of the Inimitable's constitution. We went, then, to Chester with its old walls and small crawling streets, and Dolby expressed satisfaction at the good Saturday night I passed. How he dotes! But on the Sunday, there was a reoccurrence of the symptons and I was, I must confess, most disturbed. More disturbed, if that is possible, than my friend and all-round Arranger. We went up to Mold, then, thinking that the softnesses of tone in the old Welsh market-town would prove restorative. My night there, alas, was a most miserable one.

"'Dolby understood that I would have willingly bitten at his throat, poor fellow, had he remonstrated again as to my health. So we drove, the following day, in silence. I had a sense, then, at one point, when a small boy waved to us from the side of the inferior carriage-road, that my traveling days were drawing to a close. Insupportable! And finally, when we were to walk about, and when my walking was most unsatisfactory to both my body and my Dolby, we broached the subject again as if by agreement that now I would not bite.

"'Primary concern, of course, was not for myself. I feared for the disappointment of my Lancashire audiences, and for the losses that would be incurred by Messrs. Chappell who had invested so heavily in the Readings. One has one's obligations. Dolby assuring me that my audiences would understand, and the Messrs. Chappell would do all in their power to adapt their arrangements to the altered condition of my health, I agreed that we should go to London and consult with Mr. Beard. But we were unable to return to Chester in time to catch the only train to London on that day and so I wrote at once to Mr. Beard, asking his advice, and we set out for Chester, and a rest.

"'I owed two Readings, and I gave them. The one at Blackburn

I found most difficult, and Dolby was almost in tears. I did not complain. Thereafter, I owed readings at Preston and Warrington. Dolby arranged apartments in the Imperial Hotel, and I found the sea breeze most invigorating. I told Dolby that I guessed, with luck, that I would get through the week's obligations. I wrote again to Beard, expressing the revivifying effect of the cool wet breeze, but also confessing to a certain deadness on the left side— do not *worry*, my dear!—and the difficulty of taking hold of any object with the most reprehensible left hand.

" 'The result was a Telegram from Beard announcing his arrival, and, before dinner, the presence of our friend the good medico. I showed Beard the Guildhall for the Reading, and then we returned to the hotel for the consultation. He was most thorough and, as ever, respectful. Afterward, Dolby came in and asked if he should ring for dinner. I told him "Listen first to what Mr. Beard has to say and then do as you think best." And Beard, as curt as ever in responding to medical matters, said this: "All I have to say is that if you insist upon his taking the platform tonight, I will not guarantee but that he goes through life dragging a foot after him." I confess to an unmanly seizure, for I did weep and hang on Dolby's neck, saying "My poor boy! I am so sorry for all the trouble I am giving you!" I then recovered my composure somewhat, after explaining to Dolby that I feared for the reactions of the crowd who had purchased tickets, and I said to Beard "Let me try it tonight. It will save so much trouble." "As you like" Beard said. "I have told Dolby what I think."

" 'My only thought, then, was for Dolby, and all the arrangements he must make. Dolby assured me that he would manage. At which point I decided that we must escape Preston at all costs, lest some ill-disposed person, seeing me there, report that, despite reports of my ill-health which Dolby would circulate, I was up and about.

" 'Dolby notified the newspapers and sent messengers to stops some fifteen or twenty miles away, to save the incoming audience the remainder of the trip. Arrangements were made with the local authorities, and with Messrs. Chappell, and I am sent home like a failing child.'"

With which she slowly tried to jump to her feet and, panting then, gave a series of orders for the house to be made ready for his imminent arrival. She quite forgot to discuss with me his bravery and the nobility of his steadfastness. I was much relieved at the omission. He came home. Bearing his paralysis like the shield upon which he refused to be carried.

Much to-ing and fro-ing, the Master sequestered, great hush at Gad's Hill, the silence of visitors, and the sense below stairs that soon he would die.

He did not. He refused to. In five or six weeks he was practicing again, and the Murder echoed down to us. There was talk of his going to Australia for a Farewell Tour of that most distant of places, and a visit to his sons. I smiled to think of Plorn. Polluted Plorn. But the journey was abandoned, out of fear for another failure of his health. I thought of Plorn and licked my lips.

With no Readings yet for a while, the Master resumed his literary life. He worked again at his paper, *All the Year Round,* turning the subeditorship over to his son Charles, who had miserably failed at business. He went to the theater and dined in town with Dolby and other friends. Mr. Collins returned frequently and studied my body when he could. His head looked too large for thighs to surround. Mr. Forster came. As if from the grave. He disapproved of everything but the Master, and approved of him only in his own company. The Master secured apartments at the St. James Hotel in Piccadilly, that he might the more easily entertain his London friends. His daughter and Miss Hogarth went with him and, though we heard of their tepid adventures when they returned to Gad's Hill for country entertainments, the house grew silent once again.

In the leisure thus offered, I read his books and thought on Mr. Collins. He was interested in whores. I thought, then, of myself and the day my life ended, of the time at Curzon Street. Of Susan in America, shooting Indians and preaching virtue to her farmer's children. I thought at night of the lit candle's quick extinction. It is true. I swear it. That for the first time I asked myself why I had come into the Master's service. I had left Curzon Street not because I was bored with whoredom but because I had stayed there for Susan. She had given me a family and a feeling of necessity. With her departure, my only occupation fled as well. Urania Cottage had been the only way away. But had I gone to it or to him? And why had I volunteered as a Jewess to be in his home?

One night I told myself that it was his smug assurance that a whore must die. That in heaven and on the earth there *was* no forgiveness for me and my ilk. What he said in his books was plain. If you err you cannot be forgiven. If you fail, no matter the reason, you are fallen forever, and lost. But had I not known so before his language and pomp came into my life? Perhaps. But he was the spirit of household and hearthside by whom such hypocrites as Father and Mr. Caldecott swore. His was the tone of assurance which rigidified the membrane between me, as then I was, and a possible life. His son would have nightmares and deeper night-time lusts because of me. I had fouled his home and witnessed his humanness. I was not an unhappy woman.

And then he returned to Gad's Hill, leaving his daughter and Miss Hogarth at the apartments, bearing with him the bulbous Collins and visitors from abroad, Mr. and Mrs. Fields of Boston, Mr. and Mrs. Childs of Philadelphia. He brought them out to see the country and his manor house. And one afternoon, as his guests were driven to the station to greet Miss Hogarth, who was arriving by train, he called me into the sitting-room.

I looked for Mr. Collins, but he was not present. The Master slouched in an easy chair with his foot propped on a large ottoman. A kerchief was laid upon the foot so as to hide its nakedness, which it did not do. He could not, that day, bear the pressure of a shoe. One arm clove to his side and the shoulder slumped somehow into the body. His head was tilted, his features drawn, his face white with strain. He told me to sit.

He said "My son has been gone more than a month."

"Somewhat more, sir, yes. I believe so."

He stared at me as Collins might. But differently as well. "This has been an expansive period for you, has it not? A time, shall we say, of growth? Have you not *grown*, Miss Barbara? Hey?"

I knew of course what he was saying. I replied "Not so much as to *groan*."

He did not smile, but nodded as if well challenged. "But you will" he said. "In—what?—eight months? Seven, shall we say?"

I nodded and folded my hands at my waist.

"Did you come here for that?" he asked. "I would not be surprised. My friend Mr. Collins has wagered that your purpose is somehow united to your . . . anatomy. You do not object to my discussing one of my staff with a gentleman and colleague?"

"Mr. Collins writes about whores and the physical instincts" I said. "I should be glad to have his opinion."

"You yourself are unsure?"

"We all are unsure, sir, are we not?"

He pushed against the gryphon's heads and bulbous carvings of the arms of his chair. As if he would rise. As if he could not, he slid lower. His eyes were somehow happy in their jellies of pain. Or pleased, at least. He sighed deeply and shook his head. "You are alone and yet show a fibre and resiliency. Of the streets, you read your betters' works and penetrate them. Brought low, you talk high. A vulnerable woman, you eschew protection. I do not understand you, Barbara."

"Are you trying to write me, sir, or comprehend me?"

He slammed his hands upon the chair and whitened. He opened and closed his small fists, then closed and opened his large bright eyes. "Be still! Do not be more impertinent—is it *possible?* I have contributed to your welfare in the general and then the particular. You have repaid me with upstart banter and a mind full of Billingsgate. And the corruption of my son. It is a vile and filthy matter."

"Pardon me, sir," I said, "but I did not know that your beneficence required payment. If I may say so—"

"*Yes*, by God! I predicted you would say so—that *your* profession is the one requiring payment. Eh? *Eh?*"

"It had occurred to me."

"Had it not" he said low. Despite himself (or because of himself) he was amused. There was a long silence in the cluttered room. The dark chairs and chaise-rests, the brown velvet cloth and dull-red rugs. The sense of heaviness despite the sunlight pressing at the windows. Then he said "Do you expect that I will pay for the midwife and confinement? The expenses of nursing? The . . . *costs?*"

"I do not require it, sir. But, yes. I do expect that you will become involved. I confess it."

Now he hissed. "Can you confess to me why?"

"Yes, sir."

A silence. "Then *do* so!" he shouted.

"Because you will think of the flesh alive within me as somehow your own. You are a man of immeasurable acquisitiveness. You sense profoundly what you own. Or feel you ought to own. I think that you will not permit an *item of mortality*—"

"I wrote those words" he cried.

I nodded, said "Your interjection is a type of what I try to describe. You claim much as only yours."

He sighed again and rubbed at his face as if to bathe it. "You suggest that I am no Christian" he said.

"No, sir, I do not. I suggest that there are no Christians. Everyone kills Christ, I have been taught."

"Surely not—"

"Sir: everyone. I fear I do believe that."

"Yes," he said, staring at me, "yes you do. Tell me about my son. No!"

And another silence.

And then he said "He is only a boy. And soon I will be dead."

"Perhaps his child will live" I said.

"And therefore? Miss, in light of the circumstances, therefore *what?*"

"There are no therefores, sir. Perhaps his child will live."

"Do you want it to live? Do you know what its life can be like? I have been showing my guests the Horrible London they crave to see. You have been of it, Miss Barbara. But you have never been confined to a workhouse. Aged people in every variety. Mumbling, blear-eyed, spectacled, stupid, deaf, lame, all vacantly winking at the sun which managed to creep in through the open doors. Weird old women, all skeleton within, all bonnet and cloak without, continually wiping their eyes with dirty dusters of pocket handkerchiefs. The ghastly kind of contentment upon them which, as you may think, was not at all comforting to see.

"Miss, I saw a young woman in deep grief, sobbing most bitterly and wringing her hands, letting fall abundance of great tears that choked her utterance. She spoke over and again of 'the dropped child.' The child that was found in the street, and she had brought up ever since, and which had died an hour ago, and see where the little creature lay, beneath this cloth! The dear, the pretty dear!

"The dropped child seemed too small and poor a thing for death to be in earnest with, but death had taken it, Miss Barbara. And ugly old women crouching, witch-like, round a hearth and chattering and nodding, after the manner of monkeys. All ignoring the diminutive form, neatly washed, composed, and stretched as if in sleep upon a box. Is that what you would wish?"

I breathed in deeply and then out again. Deeply again. I forced myself to laugh, my eyes to remain opened. I nodded as he sat forward to better witness my horror. Or my impudence. "Sir," I said, "I know for a fact that you have taken your guests in the company of a police-sergeant for some awful strolls. And that you have spent a goodly amount of time at the opium dens in the neighbourhood of the Ratcliffe Highway. And I should expect that those wasted victims of the dreamy obsession should have been dreadful to see." I drew another breath. "But I am a whore of some small learning, sir. I hope that my child might be intelligent on that account. You see, I have read what you have written. And what you have just told me was penned by you some many months ago. Your horror is accurate but perhaps no longer quite so keenly felt? Oh, I do admire you even more for that. You are one of our greatest dramatists. And clearly our greatest author. But I am an informed audience, sir. I shall not drop my child."

He closed his eyes as if in sleep.

My child is named Edward after his father, though I do not call him Plorn. I was provided for at the time of his birth, and after. Mr. Collins came to see me occasionally at Falmouth where I went to live, and where I keep this Book. Of him I could say much and intend to. He was gentler than my Master and more of a man than my Edward's father. He has written of me, using another name. He insists upon thinking of me as tragic. The Master wrote of me too—in his will. I am taken care of. The family do not speak of me.

Though Miss Hogarth came to visit after the Master's death on the fifth anniversary of Staplehurst. She sighed and heaved and was embarrassed. She knew him best, perhaps, of all of them. She devoted herself to his service as if at an altar. After his death her sense of service clearly continued. She leaned her elbows on the American cloth of my small dining-room table and bowed her head into her arms. My child played outside in the air that washed from the sea. The sea went over the world to Australia and America and then it came back. I often sat and listened to the tide of my history washing on the bright rocks. I did so as she wept. The terns cried with her. And then she lifted her head and looked beyond me as if to the altar of the man who was dead. She said "Barbara, did you love him too?"

"I liked some of his writings" I said. I made my voice coarse.

"But *him*, what of him?"

"He was kind to me. He used me well."

"Surely you think more of him than that?" She wore black. It did not diminish her size. Her face was that of an old woman. She had given him every young year. Her grief now seemed as old as she was.

"I knew him as little as he knew me" I said. "But I have written of him. I have constituted him according to my mind and body. You know," I leaned in closer to her sweet and unintelligent face, "I am not certain that he's dead."

Her eyes widened, first in surprise and then in horror. She composed herself a little, and very slowly, and then she said "You mean—his books?"

"No" I said, thinking of insipid Oliver and Nancy the spiceless whore. Thinking of even this Book. "No, a book is no more than a voice. There are many voices. All of them in time are lost, I suppose."

"Barbara, I have not always been your friend. I was your mistress for a time. But I have always tried to treat you kindly and instruct you. I beg of you to understand my bereavement. It is great. Will you tell me what you know?"

I heard my son's feet on the gravel at the cottage door. The latch rose and fell and rose and the door began to swing. I said "Here he is." Miss Hogarth rose from her chair and whimpered. The door swung in. She shielded her eyes. The sun burned bright as if the door-frame were afire. I licked my lips and laughed. The Master's eyes rode wide in the sun. I said "Mind you wipe your feet, love."

His poor wife wrote a book of receipts. She could cook, that woman; so it was said. She should, I sometimes think, have roasted *him*. She worked long and hard for their entertainments, and especially late into the night as Christmas Day approached. She herself made the christening cake, and the mince pies—no fewer than eighteen at a go—and an egg-nog which, I am told, was unsurpassed. Poor creature. Her secret was this: with six ounces of sugar she would beat eight egg yolks and add one and one-half pints of brandy or whisky, one-half pint of cream and one and one-half pints of milk. She whisked the egg whites stiff and stirred them into the mixture, sprinkling with grated nutmeg. The drink was to serve twelve persons. I would, if I could, double all portions. And then I would find an empty room with a crackling-good fire in the grate and, speaking in twenty-four voices— "Splendid party, isn't it?" "Oh, jolly true, jolly true!" "And the pies so chocked with sultanas!"— and I would drink for twenty-four mouths.

The little chap named Terry died today. No one came to see him, and those of us who are locked here by our bodies as much as we're locked within them pretended to notice nothing. For it was another passing, no more. A lantern in the darkness signaling that the locomotive, Death, was coming down the tracks toward each of us. He whimpered in his delirium and called for his mother. Of course. So many of us do. She was not present, having deposited him, carefully wrapped in a handkerchief she doubtless had stolen, on the steps of the Lord Mayor's house. He had kindly sent a servant to the Foundlings' in the morning, and they had kept him until he was six. Yes, it was mercy all round, and Christian goodness, and the customary vomitings of blood upon the coarse white sheets.

Terry's passing put me in mind of another child's death. They die all the time, you know. It is 1900, and we ought to be learning why the children die. No. No, we know that, don't we? We do know why. We ought, as he often said in his writings, to be seeing that they do not. I think it is sometimes mentioned in Commons that their deaths are occasions for public concern.

Moon is married! He instructs me that she resents his drinking, especially since spirits are forbidden by their faith. She additionally hates his service to his favorite member of the gaspers' ward. Yet she wishes him to perfect his English, that he may advance himself. I do not tell him that for dusky skins there may be no advancement. I encourage him to bring me my requirements, and I read him what I write. He must have his dreams, after all. As I must have mine.

AN ENGLISH MOTHER

Dora, you were among us the shortest of times, and when you died I was absent. That haunts me yet, as here, in this heart's long letter, I invoke you, and my absent self.

You were my ninth child, and we were in confinement together in the old Devonshire Terrace house in London. Georgina, as usual in charge, had the children with her at Fort House, Broadstairs, for their August by the sea. Your Father, occupied by the managing of his new magazine, *Household Words*, and by the difficulties of writing the numbers for his new book, *David Copperfield*, traveled between the two homes. It was 1850, the first of two years I shall always remember as the dreadfulest in all my life.

It is said by Mr. Forster that *Copperfield*, in many ways your Father's favorite work—"my favorite child" he has called it!—portrayed Maria Beadnell, his first infatuation, as Dora, the fumbling, foolish first wife who must finally be got out of the way so that David may marry Agnes. Without appearing to stress my own importance—I wish this were not true—I must reluctantly protest that the Dora of the novel seems more like myself. Did my Husband think I would fail to recognize myself in the portrait of a woman, gentle enough, who could not manage her husband's house? He has said as much to my face, and before Georgina, to whom, more and more, he has assigned the duties of the household and the rearing of our children.

So I—we—were in London, the family at Broadstairs, the summer passing, the moment of your birth approaching, and my Husband, your Father, nearing a crucial moment of his book. Dora, good of heart but feeble of body, and an obstacle to David's marriage to the enchanting and ethereal Agnes, had to pass from the pages and away. When he was home, in London, I could hear him speaking downstairs with Mr. Forster. He referred, once, to "her anti-Malthusian state." I took that to mean that I was swelling the population. I was not bitter. Although, darling, you were not "planned," you were welcome, you were loved as soon as we knew you would arrive. Although your Father at first complained bitterly of the burden of one more child in a large family, the complaint was merely petulant, and I know he adored you as I did. Although, I must add, my Husband did not refer directly, in conversation with me, to the dangers of another childbirth, I am certain it was in his mind. Georgina was at Broadstairs with the children. My Husband traveled to and fro, he wrote at his book and published his paper.

On August 16th, you were born, in a difficult delivery. Oh, it was not your fault! I expect that certain aspects of my woman's anatomy had got compressed and twisted by the other births—all of which I welcomed, though certainly none more warmly than your own. My mother was present, and soon enough, when he was sure of my satisfactory recovery, my Husband was able to leave for Broadstairs, to see your brothers and sisters, and of course to continue working on his book. We called you Dora Annie. He wrote from Broadstairs "I have still Dora to kill—I mean the Copperfield's Dora—."

It is curious, is it not, how what is written may later come to pass? Perhaps it is testimony to his miraculous powers over the word, how what is written may later come to pass. For he often wrote to me and your grandmother of little Sydney, then three, whom he called the Ocean Spectre. Sydney would sit at the ocean's edge and gaze strangely out into the sea. And that was what, some years before, young Paul Dombey did! The little

Dombey died, but Sydney lived, as a sailor, to squander his money in dissipations, and to be banished from his Father's home at Gad's Hill. Still, it is curious how what is written may later come to pass.

In September, we came, you and I, to Broadstairs, and the early autumn passed amid much ocean bathing and literary activities. The year passed along, with busy-ness and theatrical fervor. My Husband became involved, with Mr. Bulwer-Lytton, in a dramatic festival at Knebworth. Plans were made for productions of *Animal Magnetism* and *Used Up*, and my Husband was at high pitch, for he dearly loved every aspect of the theater, though none so much, it is true, as standing before a worshipful audience and declaiming, their hearts in his strong hands.

My Husband, admiring powerful actresses as he did, was overjoyed to learn that Miss Boyle could join the company as Lisette in *Animal Magnetism*. His admiration for Miss Boyle was profound. I was pleased to be in the production with her as Tib, which was a small part, but which placed me in the presence of my Husband nonetheless. However—and again, it is the clumsiness he painted into his Dora, my inability to even keep my bracelets from sliding into the soup while my Husband roared laughter until he wept—I tripped and fell through a trap-door onstage and so sprained my ankle that it was impossible for me to join Miss Boyle in the glow of my Husband's professional admiration. It was, I am afraid, that sort of autumn. But that, of course, is not the point, Dora dear.

What is, is that you became terribly ill, in early February. They told me it was congestion of the brain, and that we ought to have you baptized, and we did. I am afraid that I did not bear up well under the strain, although your Father was sufficiently strong for all of us. Mr. Smith advised a regimen of exercise and cold water at Malvern, and I took his advice at my Husband's fond insistence. And of course he was correct, for indeed I displayed a dimness of vision and an inclination to dizziness which left me quite unable to function as I should.

I reconstruct the rest from what I personally witnessed, and from what your Father, and Mr. Forster, and Georgina—she was there when he needed her—were able to tell me, months after the eventuality.

My Husband discussed with Mr. Southwood Smith his observations on certain instabilities of the mind he thought I had displayed for some three or four years, and so I was treated most gently. And, while I was away, his father died. Before he did, my Husband wrote, a surgeon was called "who instantly performed (without chloroform) the most terrible operation known in surgery, which was the only chance for saving his life. He bore it with astonishing fortitude, and I saw him directly afterwards—his room, a slaughter house of blood."

So he was in the greatest duress. He had his family to care for, although he had Georgina's immeasurable aid, and then the shock of his father's agonies and death, and perhaps considerations of how during his later years he had rebuffed the old man and rebuked him for his profligacy. He had my illness, which kept him traveling from London to Malvern. He had his literary work, and his long walks with Forster, and the business of the magazine. *David Copperfield*—"I have still Dora to kill"—was, thank goodness, done, and marvelously well done, at that.

Returning in April from Malvern, where he had comforted me, he passed an afternoon at Devonshire Terrace in frolicking with you, Dora Annie. He then went to speak at a dinner for the General Theatrical Fund, saying as he watched Forster summoned from the room, that part of an actor's magnificence was his ability to appear on the stage even fresh from a deathbed, were it necessary. Forster told him the news directly he was finished speaking. And then your Father hurried home to sit with your fresh corpse, Dora Annie, as you had died in convulsions an hour before.

He gave Mr. Forster a letter to bear to me at Malvern. Afraid for my health, he wrote me that I must read the letter very slowly and carefully. "Little Dora," he said, "without being in the least pain, is suddenly stricken ill. She woke out of a sleep, and was seen, in one moment, to be very ill. Mind! I will not deceive you. I think her *very* ill.

"There is nothing in her appearance but perfect rest. You would suppose her quietly asleep. I do not—why should I say I do, to you my dear!—I do not think her recovery at all likely.

"Remember, my dearest, and this is most important. If—*if*—when you are come, I should even have to say to you 'our little baby is dead,' you are to do your duty to the rest, and show yourself worthy of the great trust you hold in them."

While I was filled with terror, Dora Annie, and with disgust that I was not with you, I must confess to feeling, even then, an admiration for how well-constructed your Father's ingenious letter was. Even from afar, he was able to control great and shattering events with his pen. And is it not curious how what is written may later come to pass? I mentioned it to your Father and he did agree.

I will not speak of your appearance or the burying.

I cannot.

I will speak of your arrival. I was conscious throughout of an odor of thyme in the air, or perhaps of grape leaves. I tried to speak of it to our surgical friend (who was at the farthest end of the room, for the midwife, with my mother's assistance, was draping me with warm sheets), but he said it was merely part of the holy mystery of birth and perhaps a quickening of the eruptibility of my woman's fruitfulness. The pain became severe and I cried aloud, although my Husband had expressed to me the wish that I forbear from such utterances because they disturbed both him and the medical senses of our friend. The doctor, at my cries, came closer. I was not ashamed. A mother eight times before, I knew well that his elaborate modesty during my more conscious moments was intended for my sake alone. I admit to blushing when I felt his hands upon me, but I had felt them before. In the midst of the painful surges I recalled how once he had examined me, after Sydney's birth, to seek an explanation for my weakness and constant fumbling. This being at my Husband's request. He chewed cloves before the examination, as if he were to address me and wished not to offend! He had referred to my feminine anatomy as "tonsils" in the "mouth, precedent to reaching the neck and throat." "Do you know, ma'am," he said, clearly to distract me in my nervousness, "I have never seen two that were in all particulars exactly alike. They are as different from each other, you know, as our faces and noses."

This time he did not speak, and I did not regard his own face, for all about me was blackness and a spinning, and when I requested a cloth to bite upon that I might more obediently do as he told me, he bade the midwife place a folded table-napkin gently at my lips, and he went on with the tugging. It was a small matter, and I do not complain. No, it was a joy to me, all in all, it was. There was something small, some matter of your being somehow slightly turned about in the womb part-way, but all was straightened out and in a matter of an hour and a half, the midwife later told me, you presented yourself with a gay hiccough and a cry. I cried too, but I assure you it was out of joy. The organs are themselves the source of pain, the process one of greatest importance, and so the sensations are meant to be remembered and are therefore somewhat strenuous. I would welcome them again to bring you back. In a fashion, what I herein write is such a birthing. Would you could return because of it!

I laugh now, or pretend to, in remembrance. For such is what your Father said when my sister Mary passed away, and when we buried her, and for so many months thereafter. He proposed, indeed, that her grave be dug up and her corpse be moved, so that, when he too passed on, he might be laid beside her that their bones intermingle the more easily. He took her ring, that night, you know, from off her dying finger and he wore it long after as his own. He loved her as well as I who was her sister could ask, if I but thought to ask. Such was his composition and consideration that I never had to. He told me his dreams of her.

This was long before you came and then departed us, dear. He was writing his book about Oliver Twist, who did not die, but who was the occasion for the frightful death of a fallen girl named Nancy. Somehow, I think, she died for the little boy's sake. Your Father was very moved by her manner of dying, and thought it quite a triumph, and of course it was. He travels the countryside, performing that moment and to stunning effect—oh, the flare of the gas-light, his magnificent voice, the weeping that accompanies his Art! I have twice sat in St. James Hall to hear him. Everywhere there were women weeping, and I wept too.

In that time of our life, I was only beginning to recover from my confinement (Charles, who would be your brother, had been born), and your Father was searching for a London house. He was frightfully busy, as ever, having just finished his little play entitled *Is She His Wife?* and trotting over the streets with house agents. He found us our home at Doughty Street and wrote for *Bentley's Miscellany* and composed both *Pickwick* and *Oliver Twist*. My sister Mary stayed there with us, and the family circle glowed in the heat of his energies and brandy punches, the dinners I delighted to make for his literary colleagues, people I hoped to make my friends. I was quite nervous, I admit, but I did my best and thought it, actually, quite sufficient. And your Father was, already, nearly famous.

Mary had lived with us from her sixteenth birthday, and her youthful glow was added to my Husband's own. You may see her face forever in his Little Nell, for I think that is she. She was a beautiful girl, and she adored my Husband quite as much as he loved her. Returning in May, it was the year 1837, from our family at Brompton, she accompanied your Father and me to the St. James, and did we not return in the highest of spirits! Her face was radiant, and I put it to her pleasure over the most sociable of evenings.

As we lay in our beds, your Father said "Did you hear someone cry out?"

I told him that I had watched over little Charles for some time and that I was quite certain that he was well.

I heard his coverlet rustle angrily and he said "Someone called, Kate! Someone is calling!" He ran from the room without pausing for a dressing gown, and I followed. He did not go to Charles but rather to Mary instead. When I entered her room, she was in his arms, her face a deadly grey-white, her voice a trailing whisper.

She did not speak again. A doctor was sent for, and she rested a while, but continued to sink.

As if in the deepest of sleeps, she lay in his arms. Occasionally, weeping, he tipped a drop of brandy onto her dry lips, but there was no medication to suffice. He stayed by her, while I tended to him and to her and to Charles, and at three o'clock of the Sunday afternoon I entered the room and saw that my beloved sister was dead. But he continued to hold her while the largest saddest tears ran down his face and he sobbed aloud as if a child. He looked up to see me and a fury ran over his face, his face seemed to writhe as if touched by something deadly. From her lifeless hand he gently pried a small ring and, laying her upon her pillow, he put the ring upon his hand, and he wore it and wore it and wore it.

While arrangements were made by Forster and my brother-in-law, young Frederick, and while I tended little Charles and saw to the preparation of refreshments, your Father retired to his study, and there he worked, all of Sunday afternoon and the early Monday morning. He did not come to bed until dreadfully late. I was awake, and I transgressed. I stole to his study and lit a lamp. He had written a letter, doubtless out of his need to transmogrify the awful experience into an Art which might serve as poultice for his soul's sore wound. He had written a letter, saying words, saying "You cannot conceive the misery in which this dreadful event has plunged us. Since our marriage she has been the peace and life of our home—the admired of all for her beauty and excellence—I could have better spared a much nearer relation or an older friend, for she has been to us what we can never replace, and has left a blank which no one who ever knew her can have the faintest hope of seeing supplied. I have been so much unnerved and hurt by the loss of the dear girl whom I loved, after my wife, more deeply and fervently than anyone on earth, that I feel compelled for once to give up all idea of my monthly work and to try a fortnight's rest and quiet."

I did not speak of the letter ever after, but, the next night, after the trying funeral service, did simply pack our bags at his request and prepare for a rest at a small farm he knew of in Hampstead. He went riding there, and Forster came to join him from time to time, and the expected numbers of *Pickwick* and *Oliver Twist* did not appear. I had a miscarriage, dear, and your Father spoke to me admiringly of my strength in bearing two such losses with cheer and calm.

I took, I confess, and with much shame, to reading his letters at his working-desk. He never had let them lie about so, and I wondered at the interruption of his efficient working habits, and asked myself whether England was to lose its greatest writer in the bud. I read the letters. He wrote many. I saw this one after our return to Doughty Street: "The change has come, and it has fallen heavily upon us. I have lost the dearest friend I ever had. Words cannot describe the pride I felt in her, and the devoted attachment I bore her. She well deserved it, for with abilities far beyond her years, with every attraction of youth and beauty, and conscious as she must have been of everybody's admiration, she had not a single fault."

Yes. And he dreamed of her often, I think, for I often heard him moan in his tortured sleep, poor man. My mother sent him a lock of her hair, and he placed it beneath his pillow. I was pregnant again, and your Father told me "This confinement, Kate, will be a sorry time for me. It will remind me how we spent the last."

And when he rode to Yorkshire with Forster, thinking to gather material, months later, for another book, he wrote to me "Is it not extraordinary that the same dreams which have constantly visited me since poor Mary died follow me everywhere? I have dreamt of her ever since I left home, and no doubt shall until I return. I should be sorry to lose such visions, for they are very happy ones, if it be only the seeing her in one's sleep."

When he did return, he spoke to me of his death. I told him that he was too young to speak in such a fashion. He snarled at me and struck his thigh, and I retreated to my chair, awaiting the return of his disposition. He apologized, then, in his most gracious and winning way. "The desire to be buried next to Mary, darling," he said, "is strong. I do not think ever there was brotherly love such as I bear her, and I do not think that it will diminish. I cannot—" He was forced by his emotions to pause, and I lament to confess that I too was weeping. "I cannot bear the thought of being excluded from her dust" he said.

And it was later, seven years later, when we were in Genoa, in a dreadful-smelling and cold little old-fashioned palace, that he said to me at breakfast "I have dreamed of her again, Kate."

"I am sorry" I said.

"No!" he exclaimed. "I wasn't afraid. It was her spirit, after all. I was pleased, I was delighted, I was carried off by such delight that I wept, I saw my face in the dream, you see. I stretched my arms out and said 'Dear.' But it wasn't any help, she disappeared. I woke with tears on my face to tell you."

"I heard you" I said. "Your weeping awakened me, and I thought to comfort you but could not think how."

"No" he said. He looked at me as if in slow discovery and his face began to ripple that way. I stopped and his eyes grew softer. He said "I am so glad to share this with you."

I confess to looking away in the largeness of the moment's emotion. I breathed in the cold damp air and then told your Father "And I am honored that you choose to do so." She is in every book he afterward wrote, there are spirits in our words, Dora Annie.

I remember Genoa, the dankness and foreign language in the looks they gave me and the food we ate. Your Father was much with Monsieur De la Rue and his charming wife. I will not say the word I thought to apply to his relations with Mme. De la Rue, but I had suspicions. And I confess to speaking them, in the most delicate of ways, through the most circuitous of conversations. He listened to me, and then he shut me up. He leaned forward at the dining table and whispered to me "Madame, I will hear no more." I knew when to be still.

But, unfortunately, I knew not, myself, when to hear no more. And, passing in the long marble corridor and overhearing my name, I stopped, like a common scullery maid, to hear my Husband crooning pauses into his careful speech as the Frenchwoman's husband told him *"Ah, mais oui"* and *"certainement"* or simply *"hein."* I did not know what he meant by all that noise, but he was being sympathetic to my Husband, clearly, and my Husband was being rather desperately calm.

He said to De la Rue "So you see, sir, I haven't been getting on in latter days with a certain lady you, ah, are acquainted with. Alas, sir, worse! Much worse! Neither do the children, elder or younger, I am sad to say. Neither can she get along with herself. It is my unfortunate duty to confess to you, sir, that she has latterly obtained positive proof, some of it doubtless engraved upon stone, of my being on the most intimate terms with at least fifteen thousand women of various conditions in life. And this is only since we have begun to travel! The good Lord knows what I shall have to expect at home!"

My tongue grew thick in my mouth and I thought I would choke with myself and die at his door. I put my fingers on my lips and pinched them together, and pinched harder yet, until the pain made tears start from my eyes, and still harder I compressed the flesh which had kissed him and which, opening like an idiot's drooling face, had said "Oh" in delight when he favored me with toleration, sometimes admiration, often the affection—so I thought, Dora, in my woman's rage—one reserves for an especial, open-mouthed dog. The Frenchman made his noises, but I did not try to decipher them. I ran my fingers on the carving at the doors and waited for him to get to the point I was certain he wished to make. For he was placating an enemy whose pleasure he had decided to retain.

"So, sir," your Father said, "you will surely understand if in this lamentable context I utter the name of your admirable wife. Eh?" And without waiting he went on. "For it has recently been my poor wife's delusion that, despite your magnificent serenity, and of course my own decent comportment (that is, the deportment which is no more nor less than gentlemen by course expect of one another), that—er, oh, I shall say it out! She accuses me of dallying with your wife. *Not* that such dalliance is possible with a woman of the high moral bearing of Mme. De la Rue! We agree, of course, upon that. But, well, there you have it. She has made the accusation and I have chastised her, and there you have it. I, er, thought you should know."

The Frenchman laughed and made his noises and I fled to my room. No. I did not, it is only that I wish to forget what he said next, Dora. He was laughing as he said it. I had never heard that man whine before! Yet it was close to whining. He said "Why, what we should do, or what the girls would be, without Georgie, her sister, I cannot imagine. *She* is the active spirit of the house, and the children dote upon her, as you know, eh? I resort more and more to her sympathies."

And it was after that, further and further in the later years, that your Father began, with harsh regularity, after the fumblings and the dropped pots of tea, after my malapropisms (so he called them) and my general mistakes, after my tempers and (I do confess them) tears, to suggest that our marriage continue by law but that we be separated in physical fact.

Once he told Georgina to say to me that perhaps it would be happier if I went away and lived apart. I drove her from my room with language worthy of blushings and shame. He came to our room shortly thereafter to make the suggestion himself. I remember how cold the house was, then, and how cold my skin felt to my own touch. He stood, I sat, and he leaned away from me as he spoke. I could have borne it the more easily had he but leaned *toward* me. But his pretense at any intimacy between us had fled. My body felt overheated within, fiery, as if I had a fever, but my skin was icy cold. I remember wondering what I had done except to be a woman and be me. He said "You are not happy with our life, Kate. It is my deepest wish that happiness be yours."

"Sir," I said, "you do not want me any longer."

"Do you realize how melodramatic you are?" he shouted. "How like a wretched playhouse you are causing this room to sound? Do you comprehend what you *say?* What all of this is *about?*"

Against my will, I wept. I knew that my face grew swollen and sullen and red. "I know, sir, that you love other women and do not love me. I do know that. And anything I might say to you is bound to be the stuff of, as you say, the melodrama. What can be more the stuff of gas-light than a woman who feels herself scorned and despised? You wish to throw me away?"

After a long silence, during which he strode about the room and rubbed his chest with his hands—as if he were shining his waistcoat chains!—he broke the hush to cry "Not throw! Never throw! But mustn't there be an end to it, Kate? Must it not be resolved?"

I said "Tell me why."

"Our lives have become separated. It is as if the parallel lines of a railroad track have swerved away from one another under the pressure of flood and erosion of the earth. They are natural processes of which I speak, Kate, nothing sinister or hidden or cloaked in the raiments of shame. The tracks are apart. If an engine approaches now, it will hurtle off the bed and be shattered into hot pieces. Is that not reason enough?" He faced the corner of the room and stood there, like a boy in school I had punished.

My sense of his littleness overcame me, and I said softly "No, sir, it is not enough. But it is also all that you offer me. I accept it. I think that I do."

He turned around with a face gone white, all blood having left it. His bright eyes were glazed as if with ice—like the windows of a house grown cold and frosty, there having been no one home for a long time. "Would you?" he hissed. His shoulders rose and his neck receded, he was sinister as he walked across the carpet on his toes; I thought that he should hurl himself upon me and rake me with claws or fangs. "Would you?" he said.

"For the love of God!" I cried. "No!"

"No" he whispered, mimicking my ugly face. "No. For you forget, madam, that there are other people dependent upon us. You forget your children, madam. Must I shoulder every burden of the household and remind you of your children too?"

"But it is you who have proposed——"

"Proposed!" He pulled a chain from his waistcoat in a paroxysm of anger and hurled it past me at the dark velvet drapes; his watch hung there as if by its will, or his, before it fell silently to the carpeted floor. "Proposed" he repeated. He walked about and walked about, he paced the room from corner to corner and then in circles and when at last he turned to me, who had dutifully sat, like a fool, a dunce, an exhibit in a museum of waxen effigies, his eyes were warmer, softer somehow, and there was colour again on his cheeks. "No, my poor Kate, ah, no, we cannot do this, we must not do this, no." He approached me, then, and his scented breath, the cologne he wore, the smell of the lavender sachet with which his clothing was fragrant, all came down to me as a rush of memory floods upon the heartsick widow who opens and closes her solitary cupboards to remind herself that once she was someone's wife. He said, very softly, "The children must be the first consideration. Surely you agree. Their welfare must bind us in appearance, and we must fight this fight to its end. We must be brave, my Kate." He patted me on the shoulder, and I thought for a moment that he must bend to kiss my forehead, but he did not. He left our room.

It ceased to be our room. He took more and more to the production of plays, and the acting in them. It was at this time that he and Collins were putting on *The Frozen Deep*. Mrs. Ternan wept upon his Richard Wardour, and her daughter Ellen played a minor role. He gave further readings of his work, and was beloved of the public, more than ever, I suppose. Something occurred during the enactment of the play, and then during his idle tour of the country with Collins. He wrote home to direct the old servant, Anne, and Georgina, of course, to see to a certain remodeling of Tavistock House. His little dressing-room off our bedroom was to be changed, the washstands being taken into the bathroom and the doorway between the dressing-room and my room—once it was all called our apartment—separated from the dressing-room by a wooden door, and the recess filled with shelves. The dressing-room was now his bedroom. Where I had slept I once had designated our room, and now it wholly was mine, and mine in such a way as to be nobody's. In that house, then, we were many miles apart. I watched as the household staff moved my Husband's belongings away. I watched as I was watched by the staff.

He had always stayed away from the home as much as possible, it seemed, working with his journals—he had to oversee each step, from acquiring material to watching the printers—and going for five- and ten-mile walks with his friends. Forster still was his friend, but young Wilkie Collins came more and more to dominate his time, and Forster resented the intrusion. He spent much time with both men, now, but more with Collins, who liked to take him to Paris for God knows what awful purposes. And now he gave more Readings, *A Christmas Carol*, his *Chimes*, the foolishness of Sairey Gamp, the most affecting death of little Dombey. He was away with his public, and therefore not required to stay in a home grown rigid and, to say the least, unhappy.

He played in *Uncle John*—I think he loved to tread a theater's boards as much as he loved to write books, for it was the audience, you see, Dora, he loved the manner of their loving him—and therein was portrayed an older man in love with someone younger. Is it not curious how what is written may later come to pass? For shortly after the play was mounted—nasty word!—a pacquet came to our house and was delivered to me: a sweet enameled bracelet.

Clearly, I was not the intended recipient. I thought at once of Mrs. Ternan's daughter, who played in *Uncle John*, and I have to confess that lewd images swarmed my heated imagination. Yes, my mind was stung. I thought my brain had contracted a profound fever, and I said so.

He would not reply, except to say that I had the manners and the dreams of a slut, that I had insulted a pure young woman. He said "Whore is pronounced with a *w* so subtly rendered as to be quite nearly silent. And so, because such subtlety appears to be beyond you, my *wife*, my children's *mother*, I spell it: w-h-o-r-e—have you noted the silence of the final *e?* This is what you have just now named yourself. And I concur."

Katey, eighteen, the same age as Miss Ternan, entered my room that night—entered *nobody's* room—to find me weeping at the dressing table. She asked me why I was putting on my hat and I replied, as calmly as I could, that your Father had instructed me to see Miss Ternan and apologize.

Katey said "Why? Why *her?*"

I fell from motherhood and spoke as if she were my sister, and indeed I wished she were. My actual sisters were locked from me forever. I said "Your Father thinks I think Miss Ternan is his mistress. I am to demonstrate my confidence in him, and affirm her innocence, by paying a call."

"You shall not go!" my daughter cried, my sister. She struck her thighs with her fists, a feminine similitude of her Father if she but knew it. I wept the more to observe that.

I said "My strength is insufficient."

"But why, mamma?"

I pressed my fingers against my lips to keep from crying out, but could not bear the pain—I am a weak woman—and my lips flew open, fluids spattered onto the mirror, I disgusted myself and wailed "Because I will be thrown away and never see my babies again!"

Katey struck herself anew and shouted, quite in her father's tones, "No, mamma! No—because you will not be *treated* in such a way. Isn't that true? Please?"

I had to tell her "No."

Miss Ternan was most gracious. Crimson and confused, she introduced me to her mother and sisters. I told them I had called to congratulate them all upon their recent theatrical triumphs. Ellen could not meet my glance, and I found myself relieved. I opened my clasp-bag and offered her the newly tied jeweller's box. "This is from my Husband" I said. "A token of his admiration for your really splendid work, and don't you think she deserves it?" I said to her family. Little was discussed. There was talk of the theater, and of a certain Bealpost much affiliated, in undefinable ways, with things dramatic. Miss Ternan ridiculed his slightness of size, and dandy's attention to his costume. The talk then passed into inter-rupted silences. I smiled and smiled, it was as if my jaws took up my entire face and all I showed to the room were teeth. My face ached, and on my way home by cab I rubbed the sides of my face and cried until my gloves were damp.

My weakness led me to utter to my parents what a well of shame I thought to drown in. They told me I must leave. Georgina, who, it was evident, would never marry but would serve him for reasons I refuse to speak, told me she must stay. She had no sympathy for my dilemma, attributed it to female anatomy and various instabilities brought about by illness and the strain of running the household—which he and she refused to let me *try* to do—and she told me that she was in the process of seeing my Husband to new temporary quarters, in his office at *Household Words*. He left first, then, and my parents, who only tried to help me, I suppose, insisted I could do no less. I left him notes, and he left long letters of instruction for me—always *words!* So what was written came to pass. He gave me £600 a year and a house to live in. Charley came with me, my other babies remained at Tavistock House with their Father. Walter was over the ocean, the next three boys in school, and Mamey and Katey could fend for themselves, he assured me. He and Georgina would care for Harry and Plorn. Plorn was little, and when I wept, which often I did, it was for my boy, and for you, Dora Annic, as well as for myself.

There were feuds and statements, rumours and much dreadful gossip. My Husband forced my parents to publish a retraction of statements attributed to them, and poor Mr. Thackeray, ever a friend, was alienated from his colleague because of a misun-derstanding arising from certain public utterances. But my Hus-band was a great man, and famous, and one of his principal lessons to an adoring public was the sanctity of home and hearth. I sup-pose I cannot blame him for what he did in defense of his name. When I read it—for I always read his writings—I said to myself "Kate, you are called by your Husband a whore. Pretend that, like many a whore with finer impulses, you have retreated to a nunnery, there to serve as best you can. You are visited by your children. If they weep and are confused, it is what you must bear. If you think of your babies alone in their beds and weeping without your comfort and touch, you are bearing what you are born to pay. The world cannot touch you, for now you are locked away from it. And you must fight it out to the end, and do your duty to the rest, and show yourself worthy of their trust."

It was a statement he caused to be printed on the front page of the June 12, 1858, edition of *Household Words*. It spoke of a disposition he had made of a long-standing domestic difficulty. And then I saw why he had written the words: they said for him "I most solemnly declare, then—and this I do both in my own name and in my wife's name—that all the lately whispered rumours touching the trouble at which I have glanced, are abominably false. And that whosoever repeats one of them after this denial, will lie as wilfully and as foully as it is possible for any false witness to lie, before Heaven and earth."

I had agreed to its publication, Dora, although without carefully reading the latter portions. I had felt that I was paying a tithe I was intended to pay. Now I read carefully, and now I knew why: he was clearing Ellen Ternan of my charges, carelessly repeated by my parents, and some of their friends, and some of his. Once more he was punishing me, even at risk to himself.

And he survived. His fame was intact, perhaps greater than before. I made my tea and fried my bread and read the books my hands fell onto. My Husband traveled to Scotland, Ireland, the countryside of England. More than ever before, if I figure the frequency of the newspaper reports rightly, he traveled from Tavistock House to speak to a public who loved him more than ever. I thought of my babies alone in their beds. Dora Annie, I thought so often of you.

Katey came to me often, and we were like sisters together. I was pleased that she loved her father, still, but pleased, as well, that her face reddened when she spoke of his injustices toward me. She told me much, we were conspirators. And so I learned that her

Father had taken all the Ternans of Oxford Street under his protection, and that Ellen Ternan pursued her profession of actress in *The Tide of Time* (although her notices, I saw, were hardly the most excellent one might expect). Mary didn't come, and Katey told me she had turned a suitor down to remain with her Father. Katey said "She's like Aunt Georgy."

"Katey, what do you mean by that? Surely—"

"Oh," my daughter said, "I accuse neither one of anything." She grinned, and it was her Father's mouth. Then she slyly said "I mean only nasty innuendo, mamma."

She discussed her admirer, Charles Collins, Wilkie Collins' brother, and told me quite cold-bloodedly that soon he would propose marriage and that she expected to accept his hand.

"Your Father thinks not much of him" I said. "He has spoken against the color of his hair and, despite your Father's having printed his sketches in *All the Year Round*, he has spoken down about the quality of his cast of mind. He likes neither his being ten or eleven years older than you, nor his peculiar nervous health."

"Oh, I know all that, mamma," Katey said, "we've been round and round the course. I shall insist, and he shall yield."

I did nothing but weep, those days, I think, and when she left I wept anew. As I did when I looked out the cottage window to see her carriage, and her red-haired groom, pull into view on a hot afternoon in July. The carrot-top remained inside, although he waved stupidly at the house, and Katey in her traveling clothes came in to embrace me and hold me while the two of us wept, both in joy and sorrow, and the sense such moments give of total end.

Katey said "Why did you not come, mamma?"

I busied myself with cutlery and chinaware while I said "I was given to understand that my presence might be an embarrassment."

"By *who?*"

"By *whom*, your Father would say."

"And?"

"And I don't think we ought to talk on it further, darling. I want to know what you felt and what you saw and how he comported himself, our Mr. Collins."

But Katey told me, instead, of her Father's neuralgia, the pains and then numbness on the side of his face. She spoke of the flowers at the wedding and the champagne after, and how nobly her Father generated great good will among the guests. She told how, passing down the hallway for supervision of a last small portmanteau, dressed in her traveling clothes, she passed the room in which she had dressed for her departure. Her wedding gown lay spread on the bed, and her Father, on his knees at the bedside, sobbed "If I had not—if not for what I did, I would not lose you, Katey."

Her eyes were wet as mine, then. We sat in an old family kind of silence, though our hearts were sore. I saw her eyes close as I said "Which Katey did he mean, dear?"

Her eyes started at the lids, then, and opened wide. She stared at me, and I turned away. She whispered "Oh. Oh. Why, maybe he did mean you, mamma."

My voice was like a croak through my tightened throat when I said "No."

Did you know, Dora Annie, that shortly after we lost you I, too, turned to words? Indeed, although pseudonymously, I was the author of *What Shall We Have for Dinner? Satisfactorily answered by numerous Bills of Fare for from two to eighteen persons,* which I had the honour to have published by Messrs. Bradbury and Evans. I called the author Lady Maria Clutterbuck, upon the suggestion of your Father. I hope that in the eyes of History a single remaining copy might serve to show that, whoever Lady Clutterbuck was, and often I wonder, she knew how to provide for the sustenance of a household, if not how to cope with a household's words.

I dream, sometimes, as I trim the lamps here, or clean the coal dust from the furniture, or sit in the wide-lapped chair and read a book—and not infrequently it is one by your Father, with scenes of domestic harmony which waken pangs in me, and scenes of marital discord which give me to think that I have served as the artist's model all too often and unwittingly—I say I dream, darling, that one day I will nap, an old woman in her chair, and waken, then, to find that you have come to me. I will rise from my chair and say "Darling!" and then, quite properly and with no semblance of the histrionics which have often been my undoing, set about to make us a tea.

I will cook up the little cakes which so pleased your brothers and sisters, and even your Father, once upon a time. And the tea will be well brewed in a well-scalded pot, the cozy with its kitten's face planted atop it to please you as it once pleased Sydney and Harry and Plorn. And as if Kate and Mary were here, I will chatter—oh, partly to mask my nervousness: a visit, after all this time!—but partly from the simplest of joys. Yes, and the smell of baking and frying and steeping, the fragrances of a house, the crackling-pop of a hearth behind it all, and the sound of my singing at the stove, which I must confess to not having heard for many years.

I will explain to you, my girl, and as if to the other girls, how one sets out angelica, puts in a bit of cinnamon-stick, and perhaps a bit too much of sugar-in-vanilla bean—for it is a party, after all!—and how one arranges the table just *so*. It is all written down, you know, in my book, in the words I made to describe the kind of home I wanted to make for you, but I will say it all the same. And then I will sit at table and smile upon the house and say "Children, everyone, come now. Come to tea." Haven't I said this before? Have you not heard me saying it? I am certain I have called you often. Haven't I?

Half a pint of ale, along with half a pint of sherry,
boiled all together and sweetened, then flavoured
with grated nutmeg. In a covered dish, let stand by
the fire two or three hours. But we haven't a fire,
it's a cold ward tonight in the Fulham Infirmary,
and Moon is absent. Matron said she gave him the
sack, but I think that is merely her wish and not the
truth. Moon has let his facial hair assume the guise
of moustaches, wispy and delicate; it makes him
look like a little brown whiskery mouse. I believe
that Matron has taken offense, assuming that his
hair is meant to refer to hers. She is going grey, and
her own unfortunate moustaches are a mixture of
salt and pepper. She shaves them clean and covers
them over with talcum, but the dark hairs show
through the powder. She calls him a kaffir behind
his back, and "You" to his one-eyed face: "You:
carry those bandages out for the burning" and
"You: nip downstairs and tell them again that
man's been dead two hours. It demoralizes the patients when the dead ones are left about." Moon
never replies; he pulls at the corners of his
moustaches and shows her all his teeth.

Surely she's angry and spiteful, surely he will
return, or he'll come to work though late. Surely. It
would take so long to train another, and the risk!
What if the new one refused? Or demanded money?

I have no money and can get none. It must be the barter of words for wine and whisky. It has to be Moon. Lazy blackamoor! Moon, for the love of heaven, come to *work!*

Bloody excitement. Bloody because the man who paws through his papers and scribbles in the night is coughing blood again. It leaves the chest feeling like a cave of ice, at first. And then like a Dutch oven, heating redder and redder. And then as if the ribs have been stove. And then as if the heat and fluids are rushing out the hole. The feeling that night in the workhouse when I missed my gruel and coughed and coughed and knew I was through.

To oatmeal gruel add a cup of cold water. Pour boiling milk over it, return to pan and boil four or five minutes. Add ale or brandy or wine—why not add them all?—and sweeten. Add ginger. Boil. Use flour or fine-ground rice if you haven't the oatmeal. Use dust. Use cobwebs and pen shavings if you must. It makes a caudle, no matter what you add, and then you may sit, and sigh with anticipation, and lick your lips, and smile to the ceiling or the heavens—whichever you see—and drink it down.

THE REMEMBRANCE OF HIS FRIENDS

Back, then, on the loathsome boat from New York. A doctor on board, one of those silly detestable jolly types who intrude on one's privacy and are saved from murder only by the sympathy their utter social helplessness arouses, insisted upon examining the Chief, who could not hide long or deep enough to avoid the unwelcome scrutiny. The medical person insisted that the spring of 1868 was the very worst time for influenza and bronchial afflictions he had known in his career, and that he owed it to the Chief to prevent complications.

Lying in his stateroom, very pale, shadowed under his eyes, older than I had ever seen him look, and in great pain of the face and limbs and chest, the Chief nevertheless retained his voice, husky whisper though it was. And he said to me and Mister Fowler—spidery and red-faced and always smiling—"But complications are the stuff of art, my dear sir. Where would I be without complications?"

Fowler was not to be halted by repartee. "Words, my dear and famous sir, will not long stand between a physician and his patient. Nor, may I add, between a disease and its sufferer."

"If not words," the Chief could not refrain from adding, "what about *word?* I own a splendid selection of monosyllabic ejaculations, and make so bold as to offer this one: *No!*"

But Fowler was indecently obtuse, and something of an infection in his own right. For no sooner had he opened his mouth to reply at this point, than I was possessed of a great, almost unconquerable, urge to giggle. Watching his smile in the small shadowy room, and holding to an iron light stanchion for support as the ship rocked quite uncomfortably, I was forced to hold a hand against my lips so as not to laugh aloud. The Chief could see me from his recess of fringed maroon bolsters, and his eyes bulged mightily as he stared me into seriousness. "I am sorry, sir" I said. "It is not what you think."

"I pray not" he said, tossing aside the cover that lay on his sound leg (the other could no longer bear the weight of bedsheets). I saw the red and swollen great toe of his afflicted foot, which looked large, coming, as it did, at the end of a narrow white limb.

"Of course" Doctor Fowler said, beginning to prod. The more he investigated, saying "Sherry? Port? Rich meat?", the more the Chief was forced to grunt, so considerable was the pain. By the termination of Fowler's inspection, the Chief was paler than before, and in something of a stupor or fainting spell. Fowler rearranged the bedclothes and then motioned to me that we would speak on deck. He nodded, nearly bowed, to the Chief, said "A great pleasure, sir. I will prescribe. I will shortly prescribe."

The Chief whispered "Pray *briefly* prescribe, sir" and lay back as if to sleep.

And so, leaning onto the wooden railing, perched on the sanded deck, with smuts from the great smokestack showering us, the green hilly sea about us awash with the whiteness of its own turbulence, and with only sailors passing by because a drizzle worthy of London in winter had begun—the sun was only a nasty glare, like the wick of a dirty lantern on a foggy night—I was told by Mister Fowler that the Chief's "frostbite" was probably gout and perhaps a form of paralysis. "I lean to gout" he said, gesturing with his large meerschaum calabash, "because of the swollen joint, and its heat upon touching, and of course the attendant pain. Galen described gout, did you know that? Quite accurately. No treatment, of course. Oh, you might try elevation, though I doubt it will work. Steam's often tried. Not much use, I daresay. Lighten the diet, I suppose. Some have tried autumn crocus. The bulk of it is superstition, I suspect."

"It would be difficult to lighten the diet," I replied, "since he hardly eats as it is."

"Then there is no need to worry about that, is there? Of course, it could well be an arcane form of paralysis."

"And what would you suggest in that case? B-bleeding him?"

"My dear sir! This is the modern age! Few men on Harley Street would have that—unless it were a cranky dowager who insisted . . ."

"No, thank you" I hastened to reply. "C-cranky he may be, and even suggestive, perhaps, of a dowager. But if b-bleeding is to be prescribed, we shall have it done at home, and by his own m-man. No disrespect intended, naturally."

"Naturally. Though I doubt it will help in any case."

"What's to b-become of him, then? In light of your scientific expertise."

He smiled again, waved his pipe in the direction of America behind us. "If gout alone, and only the obvious neuralgia of the face, much pain. If paralysis, then death."

"D-death?"

"A logical end to it. Yes. Oh, and if it *is* gout only, you might advise nakedness of the foot for relief, or a light bandage. Certainly, no shoe or boot."

"Really! C-can you see him arriving in t-triumph from a t-tour the likes of which no writer and few k-kings have enjoyed, to luh-limp home b-barefoot?"

The doctor tried to light his pipe in the wind. I was pleased that he could not do it. "As you like it" he said around the wide stem. "Bit of a literary pun, eh? Quite suitable. Don't you think? One of Shakespeare's plays, you know."

"You have b-been most informative" I said.

But accurate. Pain, and then death. Though one would not

have known it to see him as we journeyed home, for the weather had smoothed the sea and calmed the air, and his lined face had smoothened too, and there was no hint of limp or other discomfort. We had arranged by mail, and against my advice, for a Farewell Tour of Britain to be conducted shortly after his arrival home. I went to Ross to see my new son, and the Chief returned to Gad's Hill Place, to see his children, and his Georgie, and his Nellie too. Of my family I do not wish to write again. I have forborne from doing so before. A writer must deal with the world outside. I do so here.

He worked doubly hard, since Wills, in a hunting accident, had damaged his brain, and *All the Year Round,* as well as his writing and rehearsals, required his concentrated efforts. But he was not too busy, although it was necessary for him to attend to family problems of some magnitude. And he wished to bring to fruit a poisonous idea: that he would do a Murder from *Oliver Twist,* the likes of which had not been performed in England or America, he claimed, by anyone so great as even Macready. Have I got this part right?

No matter. Yes. I've decided. I have got this part right.

We counted his money and estimated, after the conversion of currencies, that he could give his bankers £19,000. We were forced to except two $2 notes and a $20 note which had been forged. We counted ourselves lucky, since forgeries are everywhere, and the world—especially that of art and language—is endangered so constantly by unauthentic currency. And we arranged, finally, for Chappell's to pay £8,000 (and all expenses) for one hundred last Readings—of his will, you might say. And I do. No one cared less than the Chief for the actual possession of money, he said. I believe him. No one cared more for providing for his family, he said, and that was the motive for his killing schedule.

Do *you* believe him?

But there we were, then, preparing for the first Farewell Reading at St. James Hall, November, and the first Murder, too. And we prepared, of course, by turning old Dolby into an audience, a crowded hall, men in creamy collars and women in dark trailing cloth, the shadows cast on the high walls of St. James by the bright green-gold flare of the gas lamps, the shuffle of feet and rasp of clothing and sniffing-in of breath preparatory to holding it against the emotions known to be dragging their certain slow way among listeners who, like householders being robbed as they listened to the interlopers grope downstairs, were frightened, and thrilled by their fright. "It's in the sensations, Dolby," he said to me that afternoon at Gad's Hill, "it is not in the intellect. The heart's where I intend to strike. An audience *demands* that its heart be shaken and impaled. I'm their man."

And I was his. I sat at attention in a small chair covered in green, my buttocks draping over the sides, my back itchy, my nose needing to be blown but the time for such comforts well past; I sniffed as silently as I could and assured myself with the knowledge that, should I bubble too loudly through the nose, he would interpret the sound as weeping, and be pleased. The light made shadows of every blade of grass outside, so low in the sky was the autumn sun, and as it came through the large window of his study behind me, and over the slanted writing desk, it set each golden word on his books, each pottery figurine with which he decorated his desk, each bright thread of fabric in the drapes and furniture, to glow as if possessed of its own interior energy.

"I think it quite possibly too strong, Dolby, and you, the strong Man of Ross—remember that? do you?—will be my judge. If you are too shocked, or feel that ladies of the assembly will be adversely affected, you must tell me so. For we've an even hundred to do, and, though I suspect that the toll on my health will be considerable, I intend that half, or even three-quarters, of the evenings will show them the Murder. If the crime's too hideous for 'em, they shan't turn out. And then where would we be? *Sans argent* is where. That's French for—"

"Quite, sir" I said softly. "I cuh-quite understand." So I planted my feet, and held up a marked copy of *Twist* (it was not until later that he would have special, marked prompt-copies printed), and he pointed, as if showing me a pistol of especial bore.

Especial bore, indeed. " 'Fagin the receiver of stolen goods was up, betimes, one morning, and waited impatiently for the appearance of his new associate, Noah Claypole, otherwise Morris Bolter; who at length presented himself, and, cutting a monstrous slice of bread, commenced a voracious assault on the breakfast.' That's not in the book, Dolby, as you may recognize. As—do you, old man?"

"Oh, yes, sir. I've no d-doubt it will cause a little mirth at the Readings."

"Shed a bit of light on Claypole, eh? And, as we end with a 'voracious assault,' so we commence with one. Structure, Dolby. Design. That's the ticket, you see. Design."

Then he read without further halt, and his voice grew, swelled to fit the room as it could any room, no matter how large. He was moved by the swiftness of his tale and so was I—he had trimmed and revised so that it sped and jumped, and I listened again to the language I knew so well, pinned into place by the needles of prose he delighted in planting. He began to move about the room, into patches of fiery golden light, then into pools of deep shadow. I noticed that his health once more was ridden by the tasks he set himself to; healthy for a while, he now was clearly ill, and his pale face showed it, as did the limp, which had returned, but to the right foot instead of the left. I thought of Mr. Fowler's prophecy. But the language quickly pulled my attentions back where they belonged—to him. Where I belonged.

" 'At the instant that he brought the loop over his head before slipping it beneath his arm-pits, looking behind him on the roof he threw up his arms, and yelled, "The eyes again!" Staggering as if struck by lightning, he lost his balance and tumbled over the parapet. The noose was at his neck; it ran up with his weight; tight as a bowstring, and swift as the arrow it speeds. He fell five-and-thirty feet, and hung with his open knife clenched in his stiffening hand!!!

" 'The dog which had lain concealed 'till now, ran backwards and forwards on the parapet with a dismal howl, and, collecting himself for a spring, jumped for the dead man's shoulders. Missing his aim, he fell into the ditch, turning over as he went, and striking against a stone, dashed out his brains!!' "

He was panting, and his pale face was covered in perspiration. He looked dizzy, and felt with his hand for the top of a chair; he held on, the knuckles white, as if he suddenly felt the earth revolving beneath him. The autumn fires burned about his form, lighting him against the deepening shadows, and I heard him keening in a girl's horrified voice " 'For dear God's sake, for your own, for mine, stop before you spill my blood!!!' "

I watched him as if I looked elsewhere; he did not look at me; his language had separated us, and we were in different places, that moment, on separate planes—there are dimensions, I learned at that instant, when two people in the same place can witness the same act and see it as two wholly separate events. We were miles and years and thoughts and hearts apart, and yet were we not indivisible?

Then I heard him panting and heard the chair creak as he sat. I heard the rattle of decanter upon glass, and, as if forcing myself away from a dream in the cold dark morning, and back into the world—or as if the dream were deadly and I fell from the world back into the precincts of the mind—I made my eyes to stay upon him, and opened my mouth to speak.

In his low, strained whisper he said "Do not speak, Dolby. I can read your face. You are my book and I read you. God bless you for your thoughts and for your wishes, your invaluable assistance. Bless you."

I said "It is b-brilliant, sir, I must satisfy myself by saying that. And then I must d-dissatisfy you by protesting that one such

Reading, no matter half a hundred, will d-desperately com-compromise your health."

He was not listening. He said "Can you imagine, Dolby, if I had read it in America? Can you imagine the reaction of the crowds if I had read it to them in America?"

It is difficult to get this part right. But I have got it right, I assure you.

"Sir," I said, "it will k-kill you."

He turned to me slowly and said "Yes." He looked through me to the field outside his window. Then his face tightened and his head shook an instant, then snapped, like the whip in his voice, back and forth when he said "Never, *never* let me hear that again, Dolby! Do not come between me and the audience. Yes? *Yes?*"

I said Yes. What else does Dolby say?

I saw to the printing of the tickets and the handbills and the portage of his lectern and the gas-light equipment to St. James Hall. I watched him sit in silence, speaking in his mind's chambers the words of monstrous Sikes, my Chief writ large. I saw him, once, hobbling in the sere field behind the house, crying to choughs and bracken of the deaths he had made and which haunted him and which he would throw like a net over the select assembly with whom he would test the Murder and commence the tour. And throughout, I heard his voice describing Sikes, after the killing, as he fancied Nancy's eyes, seeing them glare from the bloody floor at him, and then looking up, " 'as if watching the reflection of the pool of gore that quivered and danced in the sunlight on the ceiling.' " And I asked myself, I asked again: whom had *he* killed?

Plorn was gone and the Chief's brother Frederick had died, hard upon our return to the country. His health worsened, and his introductory Readings, in Liverpool and Manchester, preceding the trial presentation in London of the Murder, though they had fared awfully well, had taxed his health enormously. His emotions were at low ebb, and I doubted he would survive the St. James evening.

Rather than limit the audience to a circle of intimate friends, as he first had planned, the Chief decided to extend the circle by inviting persons capable of rendering a more objective judgment, and so leading members of the press and others—upward of a hundred and fifty—were present as he strode from the wings to their hearty appause, set his book upon the lectern, drew breath and commenced. I stood in the back of the audience, as was my custom, and watched the usual paralysis settle over them—the stiffening of necks, tightening of shoulders, clenching of hands upon chair-arms. His voice rose and fell, muttered, yelped, screamed, whined, declaimed; he had as many faces and voices and tones as a church-choir in their highest public ecstasies, and I, too, was once again encircled, made his prisoner. I remember particularly the point when he said—in his book the lines became trebly underlined, with vertical lines, for emphasis, inked into the margin—"How those stains were dispersed about the room! The very feet of his dog were bloody!!!!"

A young man whispered "Ough!"

Simultaneously, from a woman farther to the rear: "Dear God."

I nodded, and knew. For he was witnessing their astonishment, and would be unable to resist creating such an effect again and again, and he would die for those words. When he finished, crying—doubly underlined—"dashed out his brains!!," there was a silence of the mortuary, the feel of cold stone and damp unhealthy air, and then they rose as if to rush the stage, cried *Bravo!* and applauded for all they were worth, those sophisticates of all the arts, cheering like conies in the music hall.

He walked offstage, to drink some sherry no doubt, and sponge his forehead; then, nodding and smiling, he returned to descend into the body of the hall to discuss the merits of the Reading. Stagehands appeared, and the screens and reading-table disappeared, and were replaced by a long table, arranged for an oyster dinner. A large staff of men served, and opened champagne. He later said, as he rehearsed his triumph, "Don't you think, Dolby, it was one of the prettiest banquets one could imagine? When all the people came up, and the gay dresses of the ladies were lighted up by those powerful lights of mine, the scene was exquisitely pretty. It looked like a great bed of flowers and diamonds, don't you think?"

No mention of Dolby, who helped to pour the champagne, and serve the oysters, and nod and smile and encourage the conversation. But no matter. It was "those powerful lights of mine" which turned the hall into day. He was the sun.

There was little conversation at first, all were unwilling to speak, or too awe-struck, and so he carried the burden of conversing, saying, as if to encourage them, "And the part where he actually strikes her—yes" or "I rather like that rope running up like a bow-string in its tautness" or "Pity about the dog, eh? Ha!" And then there was silence again as he drank at champagne, and an esteemed doctor, looking about him as if fearful of being overheard, cleared his throat and said "Professionally speaking, now, and surely not in your own profession, but in my rather unartistic one—I must say that I fear a certain epidemic of fainting. If but one woman cries when you murder the girl, one scream, there will be a contagion of hysteria all over the place."

The Chief smiled benignly, as if told that his cravat were attractive or his walking stick straight, and he nodded but did not reply. However, that remark seemed to open the door, and the air was filled with "Awful, in a masterful way, of course" and "Stunning" and "Brilliant, as ever" and "I was terrified, I must have torn at Ralph's fingers, poor dear, as if I were drowning" and "True shock." He looked through the chatter at a woman of strong beauty and equal reputation as an actress. Miss Ternan was not there. He stared down the table at her, and she stared back, as if they spoke in code amidst the plain-talk all around them. She, as if in reply—although I heard nothing asked—said in her deep voice "Why, of course you must do it. The public have been looking out for a sensation these last fifty years, and now they have got it."

"You are very kind" he said.

"Do you really think so?" she replied, staring levelly. "Or merely just? Merely . . . accurate. Are you *not* a sensation?"

"That, madam, I cannot answer."

"Oh? Then I shall: you are. You are."

I excused myself and went out for air.

And we went on, to Dublin, where he read the Murder again, and where he was received with the same acclaim given him in the *Times* and *Daily Telegraph*—that he was a genius, that his Murder was his crowning achievement at the lectern. And so in the provinces, thereafter, they insisted on the Sikes-and-Nancy, and he was on the rails toward death. He could not survive himself.

On to Edinburgh, and the Music Hall. We traveled on the Flying Scotchman, which went at a terrible pace, and as we sat in his compartment, he spoke again of Staplehurst, which, since his return from America, had come into his mind again to haunt him. The top window, next to which he sat, was open a crack, and the wind whistled in as if we were in a ghostly house, being enfiladed by the sort of storm which blows in frightening books. The northern country was a blur as we rode, and the sun was at such an angle that, as I looked out, I saw imposed upon the blur his face staring in as he tried to look at the scenery. I watched him gaze, as if he sought to find himself in the darkened reds and ochres of that autumn countryside. His hands gripped the seat on either side of him, and the stricken half of his face twitched as if he were an animal on whom the stinging flies had settled. He shook his head, finally, and turned to look in. Seeing only me, he looked away again, into the world, or his image.

"Do you know, Dolby, how many jolts the nervous system must receive on such a ride?"

"You are thinking of Staplehurst, sir?"

"I suppose that I am, yes."

"I think we're p-perfectly safe, actually."

"Oh? Really? Will you pardon me, good Dolby, if I fail you by not being comforted with your assurances?"

"No p-pardon required, sir. I cuh-cuh—I quite understand."

"You do? That's most impressive. For I do not. It is not something one really understands, you see, when the brain is filled with a roaring, and then images of terrific speed unceasing, and then the scream of iron being bent like damp straws, and the sensation of flying through the air with no control whatsoever. None at all. No control. And everything dark, and all motion." His head was moving as he spoke, and his eyes were moist. His voice cracked the whip again, and I could not tell whether he was trying to report his possession by that event, or provoke a similar horror in me. I can guess, and I did, and I stayed silent. Then, as if he were before his reading screen, his voice suddenly changed, and he forced himself to smile; it was like watching someone in a mortuary, as water spilled down upon the stern-faced corpse, brutally thrust his fingers into the dead man's mouth and shape a smile that ended not in placid composure, but in slyness. He said "I should say thirty thousand."

"Pardon, sir?"

"Thirty thousand nerve jolts, I should estimate. Do you think that's right?"

"Oh. Yes, sir," I said, "I imagine that's quite c-close to it. Quite right."

"Yes," he said, "I should estimate something quite like it. About thirty thousand, I think. Yes."

At Christmas-time, we were to suspend the Readings for a ten-days' rest, I at Ross and he at Gad's Hill. I do not know why I decided to send him the bird, except that one does give gifts, and I did wish to be represented at table during the holiday. And of course there is the probability that I loved the man. I am a person of strong emotions, in spite of my plain balding face and bulky design. So I bargained to supply the turkey for Christmas Day, and caused immense pains to be taken for the production of the finest turkey Ross could afford. It weighed thirty pounds and was packed in a hamper with other good things and despatched in ample time to reach Gad's Hill on Christmas Eve; I gave that information to the Chief and the ladies who would share that Christmas with him.

Of my family I will not speak, except to say that I was with them when I received a letter from the Chief, saying:

WHERE
IS
THAT
TURKEY?
IT
HAS
NOT
ARRIVED
!!!!!!!!!!!

I learned later that the turkey, and other gifts I had sent, were transferred to a horse-box at Gloucester and that this vehicle, en route, had caught fire and been detained at Reading. Well into the New Year, the Chief would catch me by surprise in bringing these words out of the blue: "What good fortune for the poor of Reading, Dolby, eh?"

I would have to chuckle and nod.

So that he then could say "I speak of the turkey, of course. They were able to purchase charred remnants of turkey and beef from the railway management at sixpence a-piece, *while the Inimitable went without his turkey on Christmas Day*. The tables turned, you might say." (Underlinings treble, in red.)

And I would have to chuckle and nod.

We had parted company at Gad's Hill when our Christmas Sabbatical began, but not before one of those incidents had transpired which never failed to excite both confusion and admiration within me. At the Higham Station was, during the daylight hours, something of a porter. He was little more—something of a man, perhaps, but one could descry his being only through the most astute scrutiny. For the creature was a toper in extremity, far gone into ruin. Upon his feet were ladies' boots, unbuttoned to permit his cracked and chafed and swelling ankles some little space. The toes were cut away to permit three of his soot-blackened cold-blistered digits to protrude. Their nails were yellow and thick, as if, with the decline in his civilized habits, his more bestial traits came into ascendency. He wore ancient velveteen trousers pinned to the hem of his bright yellow waistcoat, which I might have sworn I had seen once in a trunk of the Chief's. Around his upper body was a dun-colored horse blanket, held about his shoulders, under the arms, with a length of Indian rope. None did him any good in the winter weather, and each time that I saw him, he sat upon a baggage camion and shook with the cold, and drank when he could, and shook the more.

As our train left, this time, and as we stood to talk while the luggage was gathered and a carriage brought up, the Chief saw the creature in motley and beckoned him twice. Once would have sufficed. He lurched to his hooves and crabbed, edging sidewise in his ladies' boots, probably to relieve the pains his costume caused. When he drew near, he stopped, but not in sufficient time, for the cold Medway winds brought his odour to us, and we turned our faces away, choking. It was the usual smell of the streets, and something more—a corruption of flesh, as if the hard life ate him from without while inferior gin and Heaven knows what else digested him from within.

"Your excellency" he said to the Chief, in a deep hoarse croak or cough.

"Dolby, I should like you to meet an acquaintance of mine. His name is Pike. You may call him anything you please, for the price of something hot."

I produced the coin, was bowed to, called "Your excellency," and bowed to again.

"Pike remembers when I was a boy, Dolby."

"Surely he is not that old, sir?"

"He is older even than that, Dolby. He has lived here forever, along with the gargoyles at the Rochester cathedral, and the worms along the Medway banks. Am I not right, Pike?"

Pike hung his head, said "Excellency," and shivered in the cold.

"Pike's daughter was born a month before I was. We played at the docks together before my family removed to London when I was a lad. How is—er—"

"Helena, excellency" he croaked. His eyes ran and he wiped at his nose. "Dead of disease, excellency. Fever. Someat in 'er blood, we was told."

"Sir," I said, "I did not mean to imply, earlier in our discourse, that you are old. I beg your pardon. It is just that—"

"Shut up, Dolby" he snapped. His eyes were wet. His hand seized my sleeve as if to apologize and remonstrate at once. He stared into Pike's face and whispered "Dead. She is young, however old I may seem to my friend Mister Dolby, to be dead. Who cares for her children, Pike?"

Pike looked down to the cobbles.

"Charity" the Chief said. "The state. A poorhouse no better than it has to be. A house of things that crawl in the darkness and frighten children awake. Is that it, Pike? Of course it is. Cruel matrons and long stale days. And no tenderness for them, or comfort, or even safety when there's thunder in the night." Pike was shifting on his broken feet and weeping into his hands. Tears ran down the Chief's face and his nose bubbled in the cold. He moved nearer to Pike and touched him gently at the back of his neck, as one might tenderly cradle the slender neck of a child. And then his hand returned to his wallet and he drew forth coins which Pike had doubtless never seen in such quantity or denomination. "I expect you will attempt to ruin yourself further with what I give you now" he said.

Pike croaked "Oh no, excellency."

"I say I *expect* it, Pike. But not very much is meant for you. Do I make myself clear? I am not unconnected with the men in charge of such institutions as poor Helena's children suffer in. I shall speak with one such in, oh, a week's time. He will tell me—I insist that I be told—that you have brought them food, and have seen them bathed, and that a surgeon has looked them over lest they be infected with what removed my playmate from their awful little world. I will, Pike, in other words, *know*. I'll see you naked in a storm of snow if I cannot hear what I demand to hear. Is my meaning clear? Crystalline? Clearer than gin held up in the sun?"

Pike touched at the money. I wondered if he would know how to spend such coins. I saw the fury in the Chief's face and saw Pike remarking it, and thought that he would learn. Pike attempted to bow low and lost his balance. The Chief stared at me until I reluctantly reached an arm down and helped him to his feet.

"Goodbye, Pike" the Chief whispered, and Pike hobbled off on the sides of his feet. I wiped my hand upon my coat and wiped again, for his touch had been like that of a fish all covered in river slime.

"Think better of him, Dolby."

"Yes, sir."

"For we *are* no better. It needs but for the world to tilt and wobble an instant, and we are that helpless suffering man."

Before I knew what I would say, the words came: "I will learn it from you, sir."

He wiped at his eyes and shook his head as if to clear it. "Thank you, my dear chap. Thank you. And pray for Helena's children, if you can. They might be yours. Or mine. Or we, ourselves."

We had seventy-eight Readings left on the schedule, and were to be busy until the end of May, although the reoccurrence of the pain in his foot, and the occasional return of the True American Catarrh led me to doubt that we would fulfill the public's expectations. However, I rarely spoke to the point—that the Murder would shorten our schedule further—for he was far too adamant on the subject. And I rarely, to myself, addressed the pointier point: that his interest in the sickening crunch of blunt wood on fragile skull-bone, the explosion of brains and blood and cartilage across the room, the staring-up from the floor of a dead woman's eyes, the dead man's sway on the pendulum of his own rope—that these were too important to him; that they extended in importance beyond the confines of one man's fame or treasury, and into someplace smelling of graves and magic and despair. I tended, on the main, to be good Dolby—purchasing tickets and printing them, booking the halls and reporting to his sponsors and seeing that the journalists had their information correct. I posted his letters and wrote my own to the fish-mouthed, expectant audience at Gad's Hill Place. Can you hear the thump of my tail?

We returned to St. James Hall in January of 1869, where he delivered the Sikes-and-Nancy with a vigour rare even to me. I do not know if it is associated with Ellen Ternan's refusal to admit to him that she had been addressed, through the mail, by Bealpost who (so far as I could tell) was still in America. Whatever the reason, he was brilliant and, at the end, utterly prostrate. He lay on a sofa backstage and breathed quite shallowly and quickly, and could only wave his hand at me—the wrist quite limp and feeble—when I offered champagne to help revive him. The audience were equally exhausted, and uncertain as to whether they had witnessed an actual murder or simply heard a story read by a haggard small man.

The next day, at the apartments of a friend in London, he said "You will tell me not to go further with the Murder, Dolby, will you? Even before you say good morning and share my breakfast bread?"

I set my hat on a chair and said "Good morning, sir. What shall we have for b-breakfast?"

"Your wit's sound, Dolby, but not your strategy. I see through it, you're transparent."

"Hardly, sir. Me body's too b-big. May I pour c-coffee?"

"Dolby," he said, leaning over his empty plate, "the horrible perfection they ascribe to me in the Murder is opposed by what you see as dangers to my health. I have never been so dreadfully good and dreadful. They"—he gestured as if at an audience—"adore it. Adore *me*. My health be damned!"

I said "It will be, sir. With all re-respects."

"Beggar your respects" he growled. "Go send Telegraphs someplace."

I rose and left my coffee and retrieved my hat. I said "Good morning, sir."

"Dolby!" he called from the breakfast nook. "You know I didn't mean to insult you?"

"Naturally, sir. G-good day." You could not hear the tail thump for its being curled between my hindmost legs.

On to Belfast and Dublin, reading screens and reading-table, portable gas lamps and books of his words, the shrinking wincing Inimitable and his inimitable dogsbody, hurtling too quickly for the comfort of one mind, suspended and endless in the journey for the other. And into the Rotunda at Dublin, where, at the end of the second Reading, smoke poured down, greasy and nauseous, into the hall. The Chief still was followed by his fire, I thought. The hallkeeper rushed to my side to inform me that a disused grate in an upper room, in which someone had unwisely started some coals, was responsible for the smoke, the down-draught forcing it to the audience. I rushed onto the stage and informed the Chief and he raised his eyebrows, looked upward into the lights and seized the sleeve of my coat. "Ladies and gentlemen," he called in his calmest loud voice, "this gentleman is George Dolby. May I urge you to applaud him? He has kept my body, and sometimes my soul, each in its proper place and condition. That I am here is a tribute to this man, who now brings the information that where there is smoke there frequently is *no* fire. All's well, and safe, and Mr. Dolby begs you to resume your seats in tranquility." They did applaud, and I had no choice but to bow, my face as hot as the coals upstairs, before I could make my escape. He had held me up and bent me over like a stuffed doll: ladies and gentlemen, my Dolby, who seems to be almost alive!

To Belfast, then, and another success, and then on Saturday,

January 16, the midday limited mail bore us home by way of the Kingston mail boat, for which we headed at rapid speed in a plate-glass *coupé*. Something made the train shake, then slow, then speed ahead, then screech to a spark-blowing halt. A great piece of iron flew back and away, knocking down Telegraph posts, and the windows were rattled with large rocks and great gobs of mud. The Chief wailed like a child and hurled himself onto the floor. Thinking that the glass must implode, I threw myself upon him and placed my chest so that it protected his head, then covered my own head with my hands. We later learned that a tire of the driving-wheel had broken and had flown back over us, but that is not the matter now. What is, is his response to the crisis. He made little bird-like noises in his throat, and moved his legs upon the carriage floor as if he were a child who swam in a dreadful dream. I said "It is all right, sir. I think that we're all right. Don't worry, sir, don't worry."

His little hands shoved at me as if I were a great side of beef, fallen by accident upon him. I moved myself away and lay beside him, staring at the glass ceiling, which was still unbroken. The sun through it heated us, and the winter sky glared. He said "N-n-no, D-Dolby, I wa-wa-won't. Thuh-thank you very much.

I did not speak again for half an hour, certain as I was that I would imitate his imitation of the large bald man who, in stress, was known to stammer. He did not apologize until late that evening, and when he did it was like the other apologies: half-true, half-habit. When he did, I merely bowed and said not a sound, so much did I fear my own words. I sat up late and wrote a letter back to Gad's Hill about the hero.

A fortnight of readings at St. James Hall, Birmingham, Cheltenham, Clifton, Torquay, then Bath. His foot was worse, his body was in revolution and he, the monarch, could not control the rabble in his flesh. After triumphs and exhaustion, we arrived at Bath in the rain, which makes that city the gloomiest city in the world. Having seen to the ticket arrangements, I returned to the hotel, where I found him at the window, staring into the miserable streets. The Roman adventure stared back at him. He cocked his head and, like a clown, propped his hands at his waist. In a hoarse whisper, most melodramatical, he said "Dolby, I have a new idea about this mouldy old roosting-place. Depend upon it, this place was built by a cemeteryful of old people, who, making a successful rise against death, have carried the place by assault, and, bringing their gravestones with them, have contrived to build the city, in which they are trying to look alive. But it doesn't wash, it's a miserable failure, and not even Mrs. Gamp will give the place a semblance of life. We're in the finest graveyard money can buy."

Or at least with one foot in the graveyard, I thought a few days later, when, in spite of the success of his Readings, and the size of their earnings, his foot swelled, his face twitched and his voice was little more than a whisper. Still we continued, on to Edinburgh this time, where we were met by Mr. Chappell, who insisted upon sending for the celebrated surgeon Mr. Syme, who rejected Mr. Henry Thompson's earlier diagnosis, in London, that gout was indeed the cause of the trouble. Mr. Syme said that the problem was due to cold, to getting wet feet in long walks in the snow in America and then again in England. He thought fatigue might be a factor as well.

The Chief continued. Three Edinburgh Readings were scheduled, he said, and he would offer them. The houses overflowed, and so did he. Reading the Murder, he worked himself to such a pitch that, after the third Reading, when he went to his retiring room, reaching it only with difficulty, he was forced to lie on the sofa for some moments before he could summon the strength even to speak.

It happened later that night, at supper. I think I have got this part right. He joked about his "murderous instincts," saying that they deserved full credit for the success of his Readings. He then inquired how many Readings in advance had been advertised.

I said "You are advertised up to and including York on the eleventh of next month."

"That's all right" he answered. "Let us fix the Readings for the remainder of our tour."

I said "What if you require a rest?"

"Ah!" he said. "You see, that's the point. Once it's written down, and in print, then I cannot require a rest and therefore shall not take one. The pen is mightier than the physique, dear Dolby."

We went on with our supper, making notes of the Readings he had chosen for the various towns. When we had planned sixteen, about a month's work, and seeing that the Murder was taking precedence, I said "Look carefully through the towns you have given me, sir, and see if you note anything particular about them."

He looked away from me, and into his champagne. "I see nothing particular" he said.

"Out of four Readings a week, sir, you have put d-down three Murders."

He said to the champagne "What of it?"

"Sir, C-Copperfield, or Nickleby, or Marigold would produce all the money we could take, and would save you the pain of tearing yourself to pieces for three nights a week, and would keep you from suffering uh-uh—unheard-of tortures afterward. Think of your health, sir, w-won't you? Reserve the Muh-Murder for a few of the larger towns, but think of *yourself*."

"Have you finished?"

"I have—I have said all I feel on that m-matter, yes, sir."

He bounded up from his chair and threw his knife and fork onto his plate, which he smashed to atoms. "Dolby!" he exclaimed, "your infernal caution will be your ruin one of these days!"

"P-Perhaps so, sir," I said, "but in this c-case, I hope you will d-do me the juh-justice to say it is e-exercised in your interest."

I left the table and put my tour-list in my writing case. Turning round, I saw that he was weeping. I must confess, although I shall not bother to explain or wonder why, my own eyes were far from dry. He came toward me and embraced me, sobbing "Forgive me, Dolby! I really didn't mean it, and I know you are right. We will talk the matter over calmly in the morning."

As one of the Americans—was it Bealpost?—said, over and over: sure.

I think I have got this part right.

We did not talk the matter over calmly. We did not talk it over. We went on. Reading, London, Edinburgh, Glasgow again, then York, and on to Birmingham and Manchester, the great St. George's Hall in Liverpool, where Mr. Anthony Trollope came in staggered admiration and left in even a greater excitement, and then back to London, and on, then, from there to Leeds and the Lancashire manufacturing towns, or almost on—for Mold got in the way.

His health had worsened, but we did manage to get through Chester and Blackburn and Blackpool, and Preston was next, Warrington thereafter. We stayed over in Blackpool to rest, at the Imperial Hotel, as planned, and mail awaited us in the apartments there. He seemed to have shrunk still further, and I thought to myself that more than his health was catching up with him: his age marched quickly too, and death was taking him over, pulling in the ligaments and diminishing the muscle, rendering him an effigy of the Chief who had begun the American trip. He sat before an open window, gulping in the fresh salt breeze, writing letters, and reading all his mail—not really all, for one letter, much soiled by transit and in a familiar hand (though I could not recall whose), he reserved until much later.

He lay his writing case down with great care upon the table before him and rubbed with his right hand at the left side of his chest. I saw him study the left arm which lay on his lap; he reached with it, then, for the last letter, and did grasp it, but seemed unable to seize it wholly, the arm slid back upon his thighs. He angrily took the letter with his right hand, placed it near the left, and tore the letter open and read. I noticed that he held the paper off at a curious right-hand angle, and that it shook more than was warranted by the wind through the opened window.

It was shortly afterward, having rejected any dinner, that he permitted me, with only an hour's argument, to send for Mr. Beard in London. He arrived in the hours toward dawn, by a slow and uncomfortable mail train, barely spoke to me as he rushed to the Chief and only was cordial after a long examination when they joined me in the sitting-room.

"Shall I send for some sort of food, sir?"

Sitting in the chair again, and holding the letter, which he had folded into small squares, he said "Wait until Beard has had his say, then do as you think best."

"All I have to say is this" the surgeon replied. "If you insist on his taking the platform tonight, I will not guarantee but that he goes through life dragging a foot behind him. That is the least of the damage I warn of."

Tears rolled down the Chief's face. He hobbled across the room to me and threw himself upon my neck, saying "My poor boy! I am so sorry for all the trouble I am giving you! With all the tickets sold, and so late in the day, too!" It was sunrise. "How will you manage with these people?"

Oh, but Dolby's job is to manage, is it not? See how I manage this now. So of course I saw to arrangements for the return of the money through our local agent, once the banks were opened. I had men posted, and signs as well, at all the stations leading into Preston, thereby warning travelers that the Reading was cancelled. The Chief Constable was asked—by Dolby: who else?—to send a number of mounted police along the roads leading into the town. The Mayor was called to assist in the distribution of the returned monies. And a letter was written and signed, to be printed in the local newspapers, certifying that the Chief was unwell, and exhausted, "consequent upon his public Readings and frequent railway journeys." And I was despatched by Mr. Beard to take the Chief for a little rest in someplace peaceful, build his strength for the return to Gad's Hill, where, for several months, he was to do nothing but recover himself.

"Someplace in Wales, perhaps?" the Chief whispered.

I said "Why Wales, sir?"

I saw the doctor nod to him, a puzzled expression, perhaps even a helpless one, upon his face. I turned back to the Chief, and I saw him—I thought of that mortuary hand which stretched the stiff mouth into slyness—smile.

Spring was generous, as it almost always is in England, and even the north-west provinces bloomed bright as we rode in a fortress-like private coach toward Mold, a little Welsh market-town (the Chief informed me) about fourteen miles from Chester. I no longer inquired as to the reason for this backward-motion of ours; I became a passenger. We carried a brand-new leather case, made magically to appear before seven in the morning, with the coach, in which were all of the Chief's old medicines, and some new vials of curious fluids which a chemist had laboured mightily to produce before our departure. The seat opposite us was heaped with rich heavy blankets and waterproof cloaks and hampers of food, bottles of wine. There was a cudgel lying among the blankets, a lake-country walking stick of stoutest ash which was topped with a handle made of ram's horn, long and pointed, dangerous-looking; beside it was a heavy clasp-knife, also decorated in horn, the use for which I could not imagine. While the daffodils urged upward, and made bright yellows against the high ferns, a heavy fog dropped down from over the Pennines and slowly sealed in the carriage-road, slowing us to a walk. The coach and tack and horses dripped, the coachman stopped whistling, the cry of swallows over the rocky fields became muffled in cloud. We were dragged slowly into a thick moist blankness, and the Chief scratched at his face in irritation over the delay.

Sounds receded further, and even inside the coach itself there was a feeling of distances. The Chief said softly "Dolby, you remember our friend, Bealpost?"

"He cheated us, *insulted* us, I shan't forget him, sir, though I w-wouldn't mind doing so."

"He is in England."

"I thought he would not return. He fears you."

"He fears me in America, where his crimes reside. Though doubtless he has crimes to boast of over here as well. No matter—he's back."

I thought of the letter which had so provoked him. "You have heard from him, sir?"

"Mark Lemon has."

"But I thought that you and Mr. Thackeray and Mr. Lemon had feuded."

"Friends enough, Dolby. The whole regrettable gossip over Miss Ternan is responsible for a great deal of hardship and error. No, Mr. Thackeray and I did not address one another until the end, but we were friends. We had friends in common, and Mr. Lemon is one, and a true one. He spoke with a minor functionary at the firm who provide the paper for *All the Year;* he thought to mention the matter to Forster, who has transmitted the intelligence to me. One is always finding oneself in other people's talk, Dolby. If you want to know who you are, listen to your friends, and *their* friends, in your absence. That's the difficulty, you see—in your *absence.* If one could but lift the house-tops off and enter as a genie or agent of the air and listen . . . *Dombey and Son,* remember? No matter, though, the point is that Bealpost is back, is speaking foully of me and my, ah, personal life. Of things most interior to me. Do you understand?"

"Do you mean a young prot—"

"No names or characterization, please! They are fuel to odourous fires. Malodourous fires. The flames burn bright and high and foul enough. No names. Bealpost is back and seeding the earth with poisoned lies. He is, shall we say, approaching people in whose careers I take an interest and is tempting—is—" He held the wrist of his nearly immobile hand and flailed it against his thigh, as if half of him were an effigy which the other half made to jigger and dance at shows for children in the streets. "He is dangerous to me, Dolby, and is resolved to persecute my life. He seeks to work through those in whose careers I take an interest."

I pictured little Bealpost crawling up Miss Ternan. Then I realized that he was hardly shorter than the Chief himself, which led me to picture the Chief and Miss Ternan, and I dismissed the thought as unworthy and callous and liable to start me in giggling as well. I wondered if Bealpost were actually in England—now, apparently, in Wales, in a market-town called Mold. I wondered if the Chief were possibly, in the extremities of his illness, or in the furthest reaches of fatigue, imagining his worst and darkest fears to be actual. Was his language overtaking the facts of the matter? Did that place in his brain which made his books so real, and his characters to actually walk the stage before the awed, persuaded eyes, finally burn with a heat and light which overwhelmed his sense of what was true? I had lived in his language too long. I believed it capable of anything; sometimes I saw it making *me*. (Underlined for emphasis.) But here we were, being pulled by his mind into nearly impenetrable fog—the bright flowers were invisible now, everything was thickest mist, the air grew black—in search of a man (possibly absent) who sought to perpetrate iniquities (possibly made-up). Dolby along for the ride again. A character in an Inimitable play.

We stopped to dine, but remained in the coach. The driver mounted a lantern atop, and we continued, and as we came to Mold, the fog resolved itself to a misty rain, and there was visibility enough to see the small stone poultry cross, the crumbling ancient walls, the street the Chief directed us down, made of stone-fronted shops with wooden beams in plaster above, leading to a low-arched gate of rounded stones. The gate had opened, once, to a manor house or even castle, but all we could see through it were the grey and rain-soaked ruins, the uneven edges of wall, a staircase in a corner which turned twice and stopped, leading nowhere from nowhere. Cattle grazed about the remains, and sheep in the street ran from the coach and through the gate, into the fields surrounding what had once been proud design.

He told the coachman to leave us, to find a tavern and spend the money which the Chief offered as his gift. "Mind you," he said, "I want you able to drive with speed. But nothing more. My man will come for you when you're required."

The coachman, who wore wooden shoes and a greyish blanket about his shoulders, a scarf wrapped around his head and ears, clopped off like one of his horses. The Chief was whispering now, saying "Dolby, I am led to believe that we shall find him beyond this gate—in there." He pointed, and in the gesturing hand, the right and healthy one, was the walking stick or cudgel which had ridden with us. "I shall precede you, for it is my business we're upon." I wondered when it had not been, but said nothing. "I shall call you if I require assistance, and if I do set up a shout, you'd better come at once, for I shall be in trouble. He is the second most dangerous man in Britain, Dolby."

I could think of nothing to say except "Why, who is the f-first, sir?"

He laughed like one of his characters—say Quilp, the hideous dwarf who chased the sugared Little Nell through the Midlands. "The Inimitable, that's who, Dolby. He stands before you."

But he did not, for he was away. Soaked by then, and shivering, I followed past the horses—who needed to rest and feed and be warm more than we did, I thought—and went to the gate. I watched him drag his foot up the low hill toward the shaggy cattle, who moved away a bit, but did not shy too far. He went past them, and to the low shattered walls, which Puritan soldiers had probably delighted in crushing with their cannon-balls for the pure pleasure of the shooting and breaking up. He stood there, in the rain, wrapped in a heavy cloak, his pointed stick held at the ready as if it were a sword.

I do not know why, except as it may have been my truly being his man, in so many senses, but I did return—I saw his smoking pen above the page—and take the clasp-knife from the coach. I went to my post at the gate again and, with knife open and at the ready, although against whom I was defending, and why, I had no idea, there I mounted obedient watch.

He no longer was in view, and I peered, saw nothing—the soaked dark stones, the staircase winding toward noplace, the unexcited cows. From behind me an amused low voice said "Oh, aye, good to be ready i'n't it?"

I turned, hissing, and saw only a small wiry man in layer upon layer of clothing, all of it grey, undyed, some of it with sheep's hide still upon it, who looked at me with bright pleased eyes. He observed the knife, and I folded it and placed it in the pocket of my coat. "What's your b-business, sir?" I asked, in my most pompous heart-of-London tones.

"Not being stuck, I'd say. I'm off." He backed away from me, but in an imitation of fear, he was untroubled, he had lived too long on the land to worry about a man who mounted watch on nothing with a long bright knife. "Now, don't ye hurt ye'self, now" he called as he disappeared into the rain and darkened air.

I turned back to the ruins. The cattle were gone. There was no movement. Everything was chilled, as if the cold old stones could still give winter off from their frozen interiors. There was no sound save the movement of the horses and a steady drip of rain from eaves and sparse trees. The ruins were a painting, or the painted curtains of a stage.

Then: "Dolby! Dolby, in the name of *God!*" Faithful Dolby reacted like the hound he'd been trained to emulate—as I started, then ran, I sought to open the knife on the trot uphill. I held it wrong, then pulled it wrong, then carried it wrong; as I panted, quickly breathless, I drew the cutting-edge across my open palm and bled quite nastily down my sleeve. I lowered my arm and shook it, as if to send the pain away, but could not, and was gasping with the shock when I arrived at the nearest piece of wall. No one was about. I ran along one side, saw nothing, then ran to the far corner, and then the next, tripping once, nearly stabbing myself again, covering my face and clothing in thick red mud. I arrived at the corner with the stairs and kept running, around to my left, and then to my left again. I had rounded the entire square building like a trained mouse at the fair—nothing. I struck off down the far side of the shallow hill then, holding the knife, and my bleeding hand, well away from me.

That was where I found him, at the bottom of the hill. He was lying on his side, his feet tangled in the hairy roots of a great turned-over tree. His arms were deep in mud and one of his hands was vanished into the river he lay by. He had lost his cap, the stick floated on the little river, and he sobbed in his fury like a child. When I reached him, I flung the knife away from me and, planting my feet near his head, dragged him by his shoulders from the riverbank. I helped him to his knees, and then, with his good arm alone, he pulled himself to his feet and held fast. His weight pushed me deeper into the mud, which rose to my ankles, then above. I pulled one out with a great sucking sound and shook my foot. When I put it down again, I sank in deep at once. We stood there, gasping and heaving, our faces and hands a dark silty red, our clothing filthy and wet as the river.

He caught his breath and the sobbing stopped. He stared into my eyes, and a question rose to the surface of his own, then sank as he dismissed the thought. He panted "Why did you not *come*, Dolby? That was out of character, old man. Failing me in such a way."

I held my bleeding palm to my mud-soaked side and did not reply. I asked no questions, he said nothing further, and I helped him to drag up the hill and to the carriage. He was shivering, then, like a child with the influenza. I packed him under a mound of blankets, still saying nothing, and poured brandy for him in a metal cup. Only his face peeked from out the blankets, small and drawn and white; the eyes showed nothing but exhaustion, as if he had just enacted a scene with all his strength. I went for the coachman.

He was in the first tavern I tried, round the corner from where we'd stopped the coach, a wooden-fronted place with no window or sign. I opened in the door, which hung on leather straps, and stood there until I could descry the faces in the darkness. There was low talk, and the smell of rum and a sharp taste of ale and sausages. One by one, the faces turned, and the coachman's turned too. The room fell into silence, even the clatter of pottery ceased, and then someone laughed—Dolby in a red mud mask, looking like driftwood at the river—and then everyone laughed, and laughed louder, louder. One man staggered from his chair to spin in place, so great was his mirth, another held his cheeks which seemed to ache from the hilarity. The noise was like thunder. I said through it, to the coachman, who held his hand upon his mouth, "Yu-you are wuh-wuh-wuh-*want*ed."

And so we returned to Gad's Hill, in clean clothing and washed skin, a faithful assistant and his Chief, triumphant and weary and sick, and filled with news about the trip, and never mentioning Mold.

Within months, his surgeon celebrated a return to health, and twelve Farewell Readings, in London only, were set in motion by that loyal, efficient chap, good Dolby. Thump.

He spoke to me, during his healing months, of a voyage to Australia. Limp and listless, and bandaged in black silk, unable to do more than read, and not much of that, he spoke of sailing around the world to a colony of convicts. He missed his sons, he said. He also said that he had been offered £10,000 and all expenses. And then—perhaps the crux of it—he said that he was restless for a subject, he'd been long between books, he was slowing down in his production, and perhaps the inspiration of a new and startling place would provide him what he needed. A reason for more words. But his health was still miserable, and his son Charles had replaced Wills at *All the Year Round*, and wanted some watching for a while, and he dared not separate from the family so soon again. So he stayed home.

But not in Gad's Hill. Frequently, in spite of his pain and fatigue, he and I were to be found at the Blue Posts in Cork Street, or at the theater, making plans for the next Readings. And in May, to be near his medical man, and to avail himself of invitations from innumerable friends, he secured apartments for himself and his daughter and sister-in-law at the St. James Hotel, in Piccadilly. From there, he entertained the Fieldses of Boston and the Childs of Philadelphia. He and I drew up plans for their entertainment of the most meticulous and calibrated sort; it would have taken them months to see what he wished them to. I was his amanuensis, though, and, no matter the logic or possibility of the endeavour, I helped him design their forays.

There were visits to Gad's Hill, of course, and picnics with hampers of rich food and excellent old wines, and for the gentlemen only, excursions into "Horrible London," the worst of the slums. From the start of his career, he had inveighed against the wretched places, their poverty, disease and crime; so now, to titillate his friends, he led them at night, escorted by the largest of policemen, to thrill at how the paupers struggled and died. His conscience, you see, was rather wholly at his disposal, and he used it as he used his pen—for his sake.

How they whistled low to themselves, and murmured at the wretchedness, and shook their heads. Especially in the neighbourhood of the Ratcliffe Highway and its opium dens—the short crazy streets which gleamed as if with slime at midnight, and across which maddened victims of the world would scurry like awful insects. We walked through the rooms which smelled of sewage and despair to see the men—and women, too!—lying curled around their charcoal burners, pipes in their mouths like long hard teats, dead to us, who stalked among them, gawking, tall, nourished and superior, like men from another world. He clapped his hands together softly and muttered to himself, made notes, and waded in the ocean of the poor. I will tell you: it was the real world; anything else was verbiage, illusion, and still is.

He should have known that. Cast, at a tender age, upon his own devices while his family were in the workhouse, he should have known that. He used that history enough, in story and conversation, and it did affect him truly. So he should have known what the grindingest poverty, and the surrender of will which the work-house commanded, and the utter despair of actual helplessness—he should have known the meaning of what we witnessed. But he was thinking of a book.

He could not be still. As his health increased, the round of parties, evenings, theater and excursions increased apace. He took the Fieldses and Childs and several others to Rochester, the cathedral city near which he had been born, and to the marshes at Cooling, where Pip had been seized by Magwitch, then along the old Royal Dover Road, in carriages turned out with postillions in bright red jackets and buckskin breeches, as if time had been rolled back.

And during these outings, and in the long nights when he sat up late and read—pages from *All the Year Round*, and his own early books, which made him laugh and weep as if he'd never seen them before—a book was bubbling like deep springs under yellow mud. In the early pages of this book he used the visit we had made to the Ratcliffe Highway opium dens: all those shrunken souls were food for him and never knew it, or would know. He called it, early on, *The Mystery of Edwin Drood.* He had told me, at the start, that he would write of a very young boy and girl, pledged to be married after many years, but separating. The book's interest was to rise from the tracing of their separate ways. "It is a playing with impossibility, Dolby. The impossibility of telling what will be done with that impending fate by the dangerous vortices of a cruel life, which—which—" I remember how haggard he looked as he stopped, then went on as if he had no cares. "Which often forbids the most desired, even most fervently promised of loves." And I thought of Ternan, whom we saw less, and of whom he spoke, even in his indirect and proper way, with a tone of hopelessness one usually didn't think to associate with him.

The conception of the book quickly changed—I would hear him, sometimes, read the finished parts to Forster—and a note of darkest dread took over, superseding the love story, and plunging him into the profoundest explorations of despair. However, despair was insufficient to move his mind from having his way; when it came to publishers and contracts, there was no one able to drive for the bargain harder. He was to receive £7,500 for the copyright, and a half share of the profits after a sale of 25,000 copies, and an additional £1,000 for the advance sheets sent to America. Furthermore, it was he, himself, who demanded this agreement—that, in the event that he could not complete the book, or in the event of his death, the publishers agreed to arbitration to determine how much of the money should remain in his estate.

As the writing progressed, with some difficulty, and as the demands of *All the Year Round* increased, he became fully absorbed, and began declining all social invitations; he would give the twelve final Farewell Readings, and would speak at Birmingham, when he was inaugurated as President of the Midland Institute; he would see some friends on rare occasions at Gad's Hill; but he would mostly be alone with his book.

And, again, without cause, he redecorated his house, enlarging the dining-room, building a conservatory and spending much money unnecessarily, I thought. But he always had to change things round, didn't he? He could not live in the world—in any world—as it was.

The writing went on, and the Readings began. He started them on January 11, 1870, and continued through March. He did the Murder, of course, and what improvements he had made in health were soon vitiated. He declined. Exhaustion set in, and the limp worsened, as the pain did in his limbs and then chest. One side of his face was rigid, soon, and he read just half of any signs he claimed to read out whole. But on the stage he was a decorated panther, and he stalked, all giant eyes all-seeing, and hunger ready to spring. I think I have got this part right. We took his pulse, under doctor's orders, and it varied with the art he performed. Its ordinary state was 72. The Copperfield brought it to 96, the

Dombey to 114. Toward the end, one Murder registered 118, another 124. The wrist was very thin and ropy, the pulse beneath beat like bone at the skin of a drum.

And then, admitting no decision, and giving me no warning, he ended it. The girl screamed, the man roared, the weapon rose and fell, the rope ran out, the dog went in circles with its bloodstained paws, the eyes stared up from the roseate floor, and women wept, and men, and the gas-light flickered, the reading-table shook, and then applause and shoutings, and then the silence as he walked offstage like a healthy man, then declined to a hobble and the prostration of ultimate fatigue upon a sofa, and then, before there was time to have properly rested—though he did permit us to register the pulse—he was back upon the stage and standing, in the smell of beeswax and gas and perfume and excited perspiration, and he spoke. He told them at last goodbye, saying "I have thought it well in the full flood tide of your favour to retire upon those older associations between us which date much farther back than these, and thenceforth to devote myself exclusively to the art that first brought us together." There were tears on his face, and tears fell in the audience as he waved a hand gently and said "From these garish lights I vanish now for evermore, with a heartfelt, grateful, respectful and affectionate farewell."

They cheered for the emotions he had wrung from them, then wept the harder as they saw him slipping not just from the stage but from the world. We, backstage, cheered too. I forgave him. But he limped through us and into a small room I had prepared for him. The audience sat, as if expecting that he would return; when they left it was with a child's disappointment. But I did not watch for long. I slipped from the assembled staff and went softly to his room. He sat quite comfortably before a mirror and, his face bathed in moisture, his feebler arm supported in his lap, his face lit brightly by a single gas lamp which left the room a well of shadows, he wrote in his note book. He wrote!

I tapped at the door and whispered "Sir?"

He quickly closed the book and pushed it away. He looked into the mirror—all I could see in the glass before him was my own subservient face, the eyes made orange by the lamp—and he said "Come, Dolby. Come. It's utterly fit that you and I should be alone together at the end of this longest of roads."

I entered a few paces and said "Thank you, sir. I feel p-privileged—"

"Your companionship, your plain hard work—it's *I* who should feel privileged, and I do, Dolby. Thank you. From whatever's left of my heart, I give thanks."

His back was still toward the door, so I addressed my reflection in the mirror, as if he were shown there: "You are a g-great man, sir, and, if I dare say it at such a time, a greatly admired f-friend. As to your f-farewell speech, there aren't w-words, at least for me—"

As if from the mirror, as if from my face, the ragged and whispering voice of the man in his final fatigues returned, crooning: "Got them, Dolby. Didn't I?"

Moon asked me why Forster so served the Chief, and for what rewards. I replied that they were, simply, friends. Whispering, of course, our heads together in the light of the lamp at night, Moon declared that as I wrote, and as he so served and encouraged me, he was not unlike friend Forster. I giggled at the thought of such similitude. I wished that Forster, instructing the world about his famous friend, now dead, could have heard. I wished that his famous friend could have heard. And I said "Yes, Moon, you are my Forster. What have you got I can swallow?"

And I wonder if Miss Ternan, married and become Mrs. Robinson, actually *did* have a daughter in the flesh and blood. I am certain that she wished that her husband, member of the Clergy ordained, would require of her a certification of purity and noble relations with the Chief. I am certain that Robinson, himself, wished to require one. But they could not speak on it, could they? They were British, after all.

For those who cannot sleep, I recommend—and wish, this moment, to partake of—the following. Half a pint of strong ale, simmered to the point of boiling, *but not boiled.* Half a quarter of nutmeg grated, a teaspoon of moist suger, and from two to twenty tablespoons of your French brandy. Mix all.

Drink just before getting into the bed. Sweet Jesus in His glory, let me blaspheme long enough to pray for such, and hard enough to have it, here, right now! Speak to me, Ellen Lawless Ternan Robinson, and I shall write you down. I hear you, my disappointed darling. I hear it all.

SIN OVERRATED AND ABANDONED

I, George W. Robinson, member of the Clergy ordained, school-master, Member of the Margate Council and Husband to Ellen Lawless Ternan Robinson, do hereby offer this affidavit as true and verified, on this second month its twelfth day of the Year of Our Lord 1879. To wit:

That my wife's relationship to her deceased, lamented and great Protector was in the form of that which a daughter bears to her father, a niece to her uncle;

That my wife has sworn the facts appended herebelow as true, and that she has sworn on the Bible which my family have used since 1760;

That I do believe my wife's statements to be true, her purity requiring no proof, her virtue no testament, her nobility of character no witness; and that she is often fully supported in her testimony by witnesses of such spotless repute as Miss G. Hogarth, and Mister G. Dolby, *bona fide* observers to some of the events to which my wife has sworn;

That I do believe that which I herein present, for keeping in the vaults of my bankers, Messrs. Coutts, to never be opened by any hand but mine, except in the event of my death: whereupon my

133

wife, Ellen Lawless Ternan Robinson, or our issue, should such blessing eventuate, retrieve said affidavit.

George W. Robinson

I, Ellen Lawless Ternan Robinson, swear that what I say is true, and that I write this for the sake of my adored husband and for the sake of Truth.

My Protector was as considerate of my womanly feelings as it is possible for a man to be. To say that he worried overmuch about them, and about the effects of our friendship upon my reputation, is to understate his almost obsessive concern for what the world might say of me or us. To speak only of outward results, I was taught as if in a College of the sublimest and most charming literature of our age; I was introduced to some of the most accomplished dramatists, actors, actresses and journalists of London and the Provinces; I saw aspects of modern life I might not otherwise have suspected to prevail; I came to understand the poetry of the most seemingly mundane people and places England could boast.

Of the unfortunate circumstances of the ill-fated marriage of my Protector and his virtuous wife, I will say nothing, since it is not my place to gossip, nor is it ever becoming of a lady, especially the wife of a schoolmaster.

Except to say that I am favoured by the affections, attentions and household visits of his daughter "Mamey" and his adored sister-in-law, Miss Hogarth, and that their kindnesses reflect no blame whatsoever, my relationship to the disruption of the marriage comprising matters of mere coincidence and misunderstanding. It was not a marriage built to last.

Lest I be unclear about matters so indelicate as to bring a blush to the cheek of even a married woman, I must hastily, and with much reluctance, insist, for once and for all, that, had I been fortunate enough to then be married to Mr. Robinson, my relationship to my Protector and Mentor might, with my Husband's permission, even have gone on, and changed in no wise.

For example, so concerned was my Protector that no tinge of

ill-repute attach itself to me, given the Public's willingness to believe the worst, that he did report this incident to Miss Hogarth, who, years later, thought to inform me of his tender considerations. He was in Paris, at a production of the opera *Faust*, by Gounod. He was, he told Miss Hogarth, much moved when a blue light was made to fall upon the garden of Marguerite, who was beloved by an elderly lover who had presented her with jewels. The blossoms and leaves of her garden faded, withered and fell. And, according to Miss Hogarth, my Protector reported "He could hardly bear the thing, it affected him so, and sounded in his ears so like a mournful echo of things that lay in his own heart." Had he not been worried about misunderstandings—interpretations of friendship in the most scurrilous light—would he have said so tender a thing?

There is the matter of his reading tour of America and the Telegraph messages, the "code" some ill-thinkers have seized upon; apparently, his pocket diary, despite Miss Hogarth's efforts, has been seen and rudely used—perhaps (although I bear no malice toward them) by the same Hogarth family, Miss Georgina, of course, excepted, who thought to blacken my name because of the marital *contretemps* which so embarrassed their family name, and their daughter, once his wife. It is said that my Protector left with Mr. Wills of *All the Year Round*, his employee, instructions as to my whereabouts; this is so. I was with my sister Frances, and her husband, in Florence, at about the time he departed for America. Evidently, he was concerned that I be seen to, and he had instructed Mr. Wills to take all precautions. I am grateful for such thoughtfulness; a woman who travels alone on the Continent can be glad for such manly protection, if even from a distance.

From this point, however, rumour and truth are horridly separate. It is said that my Protector instructed Mr. Wills that he would send a Telegraph from America, and that Mr. Wills was to write the contents of that message to me, and to my Protector's home at Gad's Hill, and to his friend Mr. Forster. If shame were in his mind, and I insist that such an interpretation is impossible, why would he have told Mr. Wills to send the same message to Miss Hogarth at Gad's Hill, and the esteemed Mr. Forster? Quite clearly, he intended merely to inform his friends, and there were many of us, that he had arrived safely, and was well.

But rumour! Rumour insists that in the back of his diary is written something along the following lines:

Tel: all well, means you come
Tel: safe and well, means you don't come

—but would I not be unable to profess even knowledge of such a construction if there had been a shameless conspiracy among us? And Mr. Forster, and Miss Hogarth, and Mr. Dolby and I are able to swear, as I do here, that no such eventuality was discussed, no such plan put into motion. We were friends and were concerned, all of us, and there the matter stops.

Yes, I received £1,000 in his will. His estranged wife received far more (eightfold more, I can say), and his household servants were generously treated too; my legacy was that of a child, or, say, a niece. And, yes, I was favoured by Miss Hogarth with the presentation of the pen with which he had been writing his *Edwin Drood*; but so, too, were the staff of the house repaid for their devotion with such *mementos*. My husband and I still discuss the possibility of encasing the pen in glass upon our mantel, and perhaps one day we shall. And, indeed, I did hasten to Gad's Hill upon hearing of that saddest of occasions, his death. I was summoned by Miss Hogarth herself to see him lying in his dining-room, surrounded by blue lobelias, and musk, and red geraniums, his favourite of all flowers. Would Miss Hogarth, than whom there was or is no one more devoted to his memory, have summoned me if she but suspected the faintest tinge of dishonour in the relationship between a Ward and her Protector?

There is a certain Miss Barbara, a Jewess, once employed at Gad's Hill as a maid of all work, to whom friends have attributed certain infamous and unkind rumours concerning me and a Great Man who no longer walks among us. While I will not suggest that he might have hired on a woman of fallen state and thereby taint his home, I must report that rumours hung about her like unrefined cologne, and that her character, not to put too fine a point upon it, was hardly said to be of the best. All who are friends to me, and to my Protector, will pay her no notice. It is said that she died in the sea when she could have saved herself, and that her child, whose father is unknown as the ancestors of creatures painted in aboriginal tombs, must look to the State, now, for parentage. Of a woman who abandoned her own moral state, and then her child, no matter the state in which he was conceived, I shall say only that her word is not the instrument through which another woman's soul ought to be examined. That she was a Jewess need not be mentioned, I suppose.

That I am a Christian, and the dutiful wife of a Christian shepherd, *should* be mentioned. I am a daughter and a wife. I had a Friend. It takes all my heart and courage to say no more. Mister Dolby believes me, he has written today. I pray that I might be believed around the world and in those Precincts which interrupt the lifelong passage to Heaven. In that Place, there are Ones who know, for They shared with me this little and momentary World.

One Mister Bealpost is to be given no credence, as a witness or as a man.

Signed, sealed and delivered by the
    above-named George W. Robinson.

    Edward Marjoribanks
    Sampson Brass

Yes. A document. A proof.

If he would but require a legal document of me in some place besides my dreaming hopes. If he would but demand it, force from me what he needs for his rest. He has no rest, nor do I. I would hate him for the asking, since a man must trust his wife that she repose her trust in him, but I would gratefully write such a testimony to myself, and on my own behalf, and his. For George does not sleep when he sleeps. His smooth face screws and then loosens, screws and loosens, and somehow, instead of looking like a husband, member of the Clergy ordained, he is a little boy in misery, and I know why.

I will not confess to fault before him, though I will damn myself forever in Heaven for the sake of some peace on the earth we share. Is making stories for the sake of a gentle reader really, now, such a sin? Perhaps. But I would fabricate the stories, and even suffer the torments they might merit, if he would but renounce his gentleness and delicacy with me, and enter my bed, and let me enter his life. I bear his food to table, and since I must I do willingly bear the contumely of his forbearances. But I would give much to be treated like a woman who is real, instead of what I am to him—his idea of grace, and not that truly. I am the form he makes his prayers assume. I have not heard him, but I dream the hearing: *Dear Father, let it be that she is pure. Let rumour be untrue. Let her be mine.* Aye, Ellen Lawless Ternan Robinson cannot be yours, George, unless you be hers. And that you will not be without the necessary guarantees. And you cannot accept them. Nothing short of a sign from the Lord will do. And you see no sign. And your faith is rocked. Will you lose your Trust in Him for me? Or let me die while waiting for your faith to flower?

Flower, and petal plucked, and at eighteen in the cold coaching inn, he in his ridiculous frock coat and clergyman's collar and countryman's shoes, whispering that he was hoarse because of a latterly bout with the influenza. Did I not know what was about to happen? I did not, finally, care. I was flushed with him, his words of endearment, of adoration. He, the greatest man outside the Government, perhaps, kissing the tips of my fingers in the coach, and saying that prayers were answered because I was with him. And his laughter as the coach rolled like a ship in storm through the pagan countryside of Hampshire toward the New Forest and the rooms he had reserved. I did not care. I was exhausted, from the currying and grooming I had seen him reduced to, from my embarrassment on his behalf, and my own knowledge that a man felt it as his greatest necessity to seduce a young woman as young as his daughter.

At Moor Park in Surrey I had decided. Oh, I had been certain long before. But in Surrey I agreed, though I said nothing to him, for he was rarely silent enough to permit reply. "My wife," he said, as we passed the South Downs, and the greenness died away as if a fire had just consumed the underbrush, and all was long and flat and yellow, "my wife does not understand me, you know. She is a dedicated woman of such recent nervous extremities that we no longer know what to say, the one to the other." He looked past me, past the leather curtain, and out on the shabby cottages and the road which smoked with dust as if the countryside burned. "I do not denigrate her, you understand. She has carried our children and has done her best to rear them. And yet, if it were not for Georgie, whose zealous cares can never be rewarded—indeed, they never *have* been!—I would be master of a household so strongly resembling the workhouse that only a beadle could distinguish them from orphans." He interrupted his own instant of silence to add "And I, of course. Their father."

I had decided. I no longer cared. It received its value from his desire. His was the currency I knew. I knew little else. There was, somewhere in my mind, a sense that I soon was to be blessed, or that my body was to receive. I had no sense of giving, for I knew not what I might give. I was eighteen years old. And he had taught me, already, that we live in the mind and the soul. Our bodies were our accidents, I had learned. Burdens of death we drag behind us, is what he called them. I assumed that I would receive a life. But I no longer cared, for I looked beyond the coaching inn we rode to, and saw myself, alone, in a theater or a promenade, cherishing to myself what I had gained. One doesn't believe in loss at eighteen. It happens, but one doesn't believe.

The clergyman's collar slid and he adjusted his disguise and we laughed, I remember, and then he pulled the curtains, for the coach was filling with clay-red dust, and he continued to tell me "Catherine cannot give me what I need. I am a man who needs, and I am determined to—my God, Nellie, you make me feel like a boy. No, a knight! I wish there were a hill out there, with a dungeon in it, and by God a dragon of inestimable proportions all covered in slime and breathing more than flame—molten lead with fires on it eight feet high. Yes! And you were captive there, and I came riding up to leap from my shying horse and carry a lance for you! Do you know that I actually *feel* that?"

The coachman called back "What's that, mate?"

He pushed at his moustaches and whispered "A bit of cheek, that one, eh?" And then he said "And I don't care. I don't *care!* It isn't dignity I'm after, Nellie. We are hunting love, it is the rarest of flowers, we are stalking with silken gloves and soft words. Oh!"

And then the red tile floor, the skewed steps up, the rooms which were chilled and which we never managed to heat, despite the coal and tending he demanded. My room, next to his, was dominated, of course, what else?, by the bed. It was four-posted, curtained, raised, and had to be climbed to on a two-stepped ladder. Its little dressing-room was three marble steps up, and was colder than the bed chamber. I never saw his room. But immediately the innkeeper's father had left us alone, he fell to his knees, like a supplicant knight or a gouty man in his wintry middle years, and he kissed the tips of my fingers.

I said, and I do not know why, "Oh, sir."

"No," he said, "there is no Sir or Miss between us any longer. We are married surely as Heaven looks down upon the earth. I must call you wife."

"Only Nellie, just that."

"Nellie cannot be only Nellie. It must—I must . . . oh, Nellie, I *must.*"

It was not what I had thought. I did not care that his thighs were small or mottled with veins against their whiteness. I did not care that the skirt of my traveling dress was torn, nor that light came in between the shutter and the casement, nor that a fire did not burn yet in the hearth, nor that on the wall a wooden crucifix hung—I am not superstitious. His organ was a great red sausage and I wanted to look at it and hold it in my hand, for I had never seen one before. But he would not permit my handling him, nor fondling of any sort. The fondling, he said, was to be done by him. "I owe this to you, Nellie, this is part of a much-beloved's education. For example, this crevice, here, this, I do not know its name, but it—yes, you see? Ah! No, I do not want you *hurt!*"

I cannot remember it all. It was undistinguished, I know that now. And even then, after my eyes slid from his shoulders to the wall to the ceiling, after I smelled his breath and then expelled my own at the first pain and the dry long pain throughout, and after I bit my lip so as not to cry lest he feel responsible, and after he collapsed upon me like a child at my breast, I remember thinking that if, as my mother insisted, damnation should follow, then sin was overmeasured and torment a hasty judgment. To suffer so much for so little, I thought, makes the Lord a mediocre judge of pleasures in the flesh He so reviles.

It was cold at the inn, and cold too in the coach on the long, interrupted ride home, his moustaches riding his face like the flies which rode our horses. But it was colder in his mistress, and grew colder, and I watched myself from outside, like one of the bodiless voices he made on the pages of his books.

Aye, Ellen Ternan, I, Ellen Ternan, turned to *she*. She was ice, and she watched his flame lick her blue surface as his tongue had licked her blue-white neck. She did not suffer remorse, as he thought, and the pain itself was quickly replaced by some bruises, and a little ache, and then nothing. Oh, she went with him and talked with him, and always he spoke and instructed her, and, as before, he was the knight and she was his rescued maid. But the maid, she learned, had been made to rescue the knight. She was his errant idea, and though he worked to salvage its shape, his long-fingered hands could not contain it. Seeing his weakness at his moment of strength, she understood that nothing much was better than anything else. His strength was his need, and she, to give him sustenance, was only needed too. She was back where she had begun, and the folly, not the shame or the fall or the friction itself, but the folly, froze her.

He pursued her anew, sent her baskets of flowers and canvas sacks of wine and food, delivered to her home by puzzled manservants. The frequency of his notes increased, and she was larded within by his generosity, his helpless prayerful giving, and oiled without by his words. He spoke so often, then, of "begging" and "asking" and "praying" and the supplications hardened, like those minute northern plants on icy stones, until she was crusted against him, and by him, yet so much by his side.

He cupped her and kissed her and fumbled with his tongue on hers. Teeth snapped on teeth like pebbles in a pocket, and he read to her aloud and told her what she ought to know. He grew boyish in his slow calm grief, for he knew her always, that he did, and she grew to feel more tall, and heavy at the breast, more womanly, and more divorced from the sense of womanhood he sought in her. He did not know that she'd grown old, but he knew full well how she was cold, and he could not refrain from rubbing at the chill to give her warmth for his own need of heat.

She permitted because he needed her and because she owed it to herself—not out of a "fall" or any such nonsense, but because such stupid great expectations as hers deserved their punishment. A woman would know this, she thought. And he stayed for the simplest of clod-foot reasons: he needed to live through a woman again, and she was there, and his, and the right punishment for his self-permitting needs.

Driven to her and driven by coldness away, he naturally turned to language and sought to turn her, through his words, into an effigy he might shape. He wrote a book. He named a character Estella, to stand for Ellen, and described her as a princess carved of ice who says "So I must be taken as I have been made. The success is not mine, the failure is not mine, but the two together make me." And then again she says "It seems that there are sentiments, fancies—I don't know how to call them—which I am not able to comprehend. When you say you love me, I know what you mean, as a form of words; but nothing more. You address nothing in my breast, you touch nothing there. I don't care for what you say at all. I have tried to warn you of this; now, have I not?"

But she has not told this truly. Such immortality may confuse a woman's sense of time. They were long together, before and after the acquisition by him of his prize which signaled his loss. And he wrote these words before they heaved on a coaching-house bed with a player's moustache curled in the cold air on a dark gleaming bureau. Is it not curious how what is written may later come to pass?

And so, she went to Europe while he traveled to America, and she awaited his Telegraph signal, knowing as she did that no matter the code which was forwarded, *all well* or *safe and well*, little was as good as that, and absence at the time was plenitude, and they must be far apart, as indeed they were growing to be while together. She never, since the inn of the New Forest, had permitted them to mock the Lord with the tininess of what He set such weighty stock in, and their chastity was grim but survivable, like the pain of a wrongful marriage's open secret.

He complained, upon his return, of one Bealpost. And, as he limped the more, and as his face twitched, as one shoulder rose and a stiffness spread upon his features, as his pallor increased and his voice sometimes dropped to a ragged whisper, he complained of this Bealpost the more. He asked her if such a man had written her, and she said no. He asked if she had heard reports of such a man in the district, and she said no. He sent her baskets of delicacies and on the anniversary of Staplehurst a great shaggy man in a leather apron carried in a crate of champagne, to which was attached a card. It said *Remember?*

She remembered. And each bottle retained its cork.

He drew her on journeys, that they might be part of something larger, such as motion, she supposed. And they saw the Wapping workhouse. There were no whipping racks for her to see, or treadmills, or the closet-like cubicles for those condemned to silence for their crimes. The crime this workhouse punished was poverty, and his family had been such prisoners for such a transgression. His face became pinched and curled, not unlike her husband's now in sleep, and he said nothing. He listened to his guides, and when they spoke a point capable of moral underscoring, he pressed her elbow, or nodded, or lifted his clasped hands in the air and let them swing back against his little belly, as if to signify to her: Aha, you see? My parents and their children endured this. I worked in a blacking factory and lived in a rented room and had to feed myself with pennies among the workingmen while they, in here, together, without me, lived like this. Without hope. But in truth he said nothing. He watched it all and assented. Yes, his silence said, this is what it was. This is what it is.

Aged people were there, in every variety. Mumbling, bleareyed, spectacled, stupid, deaf, lame; vacantly winking in the gleams of sun that now and then crept in through the open doors, from the paved yard; shading their listening ears, or blinking eyes, with their withered hands; poring over their books, leering at nothing, going to sleep, crouching and drooping in corners. There were weird old women, all skeleton within, all bonnet and cloak without, continually wiping their eyes with dirty clusters of pocket handkerchiefs; and there were ugly old crones, both male and female, with a ghastly kind of contentment upon them which was not at all comforting to see.

She was not comforted, nor was he, but, for a time, at least in his eyes, they had lost the issue of themselves in the greater issue of continual loss unredeemable. A woman spoke of "the dropped child" and sobbed and sobbed, and he moved away from her, then back, and finally he stood nearly close enough to touch her and he watched. Finally she urged him away and they rode off to supper. They dined, she did not speak, he would not eat. At last, blowing at a candle, urging it toward extinction but refusing to extinguish its flame, doing that over and over, he whispered "No one appeared to want to live, but no one complained. Is their patience not extraordinary?"

And she replied "Not really, no. It can't be helped."

"Of course not" he whispered. "How could it be?"

Upon returning from a jaunt to France with Mr. Collins he once had written this: "Whenever I am at Paris, I am dragged by invisible force into the Morgue. I never want to go there, but am always pulled there. One Christmas Day, when I would rather have been anywhere else, I was attracted in, to see an old grey man lying all alone on his cold bed, with a tap of water turned on over his grey hair, and running, drip, drip, drip, down his wretched face until it got to a corner of his mouth, where it took a turn, and made him look sly."

She recalled those words, the utter singularity of his insight and his friendliness with death, when he begged her attendance upon a soiree at Gad's Hill. She was to sit behind the closed carved sliding doors of the parlour while, in the sitting-room, he would read a bit of his justly famous *A Christmas Carol* to the Carlyles and some others of equal importance. His note had said *Will you come, Nellie?* and she had sent back the reply *Safe and well.*

He himself appeared, instead of the manservant whom he used for the portage of champagne and Continental delicacies and sundry notes of love, and he said "Ah, Nellie, I should read it so much the better, with so much deeper a note of conviction, did I but know you sat behind the door and nodded and wept with the words."

He was very very old, she understood at that moment: she bore responsibilities. Nevertheless, she said "Your secret audience?"

"Most secret, alas" he answered. "But also most audience, the one to whom my words shall be directed, if you would but humour me."

"Do you ask out of need or desire?"

His face was crimson and he wrung his gloves. He said "You, of all, must surely know that my needs *are* my desires. You of all, Nellie!"

So in the little dressing-room at the Kensington flat she dressed as if for special company, and stayed before the mirror as long as if someone besides the coachman would see her face. The ribbons just *so,* and *thus* the bonnet, and *there,* new shoes. She could see in her mirror the great bedroom cabinet he had ordered delivered, all wooden scrollwork and insets of silk and golden hinge, and the tall blue urn from Messrs. Wedgwood on which a plump woman, most unlike herself, though with hair worn the way she often wore it, danced beneath the head of a ram with oiled coiled horns. "You of all" she said to the mirror.

The driver who had been sent for her was wrapped in a dozen cloaks, it seemed, and in the darkness he gave no sense of human shape. He was a troll from her dreams and made her shiver as soon as she saw him. "Do not get down" she said.

He answered "As yer like, love."

She stood as if to reply, but did not know what to say. His answer was a kind of scorn, and she thought she might merit it. She stepped up, and was delivered to the servants' entrance, as her Protector clearly had commanded. Miss Hogarth met her stolidly, her light blue eyes cast down, sharing her embarrassment. They did not speak, but smiled at one another in the dark antechamber as men, surprising one another in the hallways of a brothel, must do. She was goods, delivered, and Miss Hogarth set her in the prearranged place. The furniture looked unfamiliar in the darkness, but she had expected that. For she herself was unfamiliar to her own emptied mind.

So she sat in the lightless room and, as a child upstairs listens while the grown-ups have their party, she heard the foam of fluids and the ring of ladles on glass, the half-formed words of muted conversations on the wooden doors. All went still, and he performed, and he was naturally the great success they all, so separately, had expected him to be. And then, suddenly, wrapped in the darkness which grew darker with her tenure in its folds, not lighter as one might expect, hearing his voice and envisioning his limp and drag, the growing paralysis on his features, the protrusion of his cheekbones, hearing even the smallest children fall into fearful silence, she attended his description of Scrooge's vision of the death of wilful Scrooge: the vulturous old woman cackling "This is the end of it, you see! He frightened every one away from him when he was alive, to profit us when he was dead! Ha, ha, ha!" And she thought not of Scrooge, but of the grey-faced, grey-haired man in the mortuary, old and swimming in place beneath the drips of water, and looking sly, and all alone. And she wept for him. She bit the skin at the edge of her wrist to keep herself silent and she wept on his behalf. And then his voice thundered louder, and she understood his reasons for wanting her there, a wall's width away, and in the darkness, sobbing to herself, and she went on the tips of her toes by feel and recollection and let herself out and called the carriage over.

The driver woke and moved his horse. He said "All done for the evening, love?"

She said, quite mildly, "You would do well, sir, to keep in mind your place." But the driver laughed, and she was still.

Her husband keeps her in her place—away. But she swings toward him, like a boat that is moored upon a tide. He thinks of her, and so do I, and we brood in our separate places upon a past which lives, a little at least, within his books, and which moves, like the silver surface of the Thames, beneath the language he has left. George stirs in his sleep. The sunlight falls into his bedroom where I stand, and he wakens, to see me silhouetted at the window, a dark figure looming into his life. He says "Yes? Yes?"

And I cry "George, I am innocent!"

"Yes," he says, "certainly. But what—why are you—"

The small boy's face squints into the bright shore light, and he holds a hand before his eyes, such a sweet child's gesture of defense. I walk down the stream of early sun, I feel myself grow large, still shadowed, before him. "I have always been" I tell him.

"Been what, Nellie?" he asks.

And I stand still. "You have never called me that before. *You* call me Ellen."

He closes his eyes and the sunlight burns on his thin blond hair. It is as if he hides from me. In his darkness he says to my darkness "Now, then, it is only a word."

A long time since I've written at this table. Its top
feels gummy, and the inferior paper adheres, as if I
spend my evening hours in pasting labels on a damp
black box. The patient prepares his coffin for
shipment. And it did nearly come to that, it was a
long hard pull between whatever seems to want me
and I, myself, who wish to remain in what's left of
my pale bodily tube of soft bone and bitter fluids.
Matron said it was the mildest strain of influenza
infection and that I was fortunate, what with
healthy people dying in fine homes during the
epidemic. She said I truly must have wanted to live.
Well said! She said it must also have been the care I
received. I did agree, and why not? She does work
earnestly to keep us breathing on the earth. She is
not, like so many of her number, merely waiting for
our deaths. She cheers us on, in her way, her bulging eyes bright, her shadow of moustache a-jump
with the excitement of our not dying. I am alive. I
want to be. I am working.

Moon was not sacked, by the by. He was detained
at home, it eventuates, on account of the birth of
his son. And then by his son's nearly immediate
death. It was infection killed the little thing. And
then his wife, who lingered a week and then followed her child, to leave poor Moon alone. The
pestilential vapours of his neighbourhood may be

held to account, though such an accounting will give him no comfort. He is a small dark stranger in the solitudes now, and he has shaved his moustache in a type of penance or protest, but the solitudes remain upon him like the darkness of his skin. Whether from sympathy for his losses, or because she was relieved by the absence of his facial hair, Matron kept him at work.

But poor old Moon has taken worse to drink than ever. It occurs to me how little he is paid, and how much of his livelihood has gone, this year of our acquaintance, to my precious potations. How much more he must be spending, now, on us both! He drinks not a little. I drink all I can. Moon, then, must be thieving for our appetites' sake. I wonder what he steals. I hope it's in endless supply.

Now comes the part of my work I have waited to do. I returned, to put it accurately, from the land of the dead; I fought not to die in order that I write what comes next, and Moon! let me hear the dainty drag of your feet and see your humpy shadow on the wall! Let me hear the unresonant peal of well-filled vessels as you bring me what I need!

WHO, OF ALL, MAY SPEAK?

Alfred, Charles, Dora Annie, Plorn, Frank, Harry, Katey, Mamey, Sidney, Walter. And Kate, their mother, yes, who was my wife. And Micketty, frightened by her grandfather's tears at the final Reading. And Fanny and Frederick, Alfred, Augustus who was "Boz," Letitia, Harriet, the first family I knew. Dear Mary Weller, paid to care for me but caring more than that, and her childhood tales of talking rats, of murderers and poison and all that a boy wants to hear.

These are names to dream on, they call up days and nights to dream. There are other names. They are Wood Street, Cheapside. Bayham Street, Camden Town. Somers Town, Kentish Town, Canning Town, Hackney. They are Dukes Place and Houndsditch and Bevis Marks and Goodman's Fields. I have walked them all, I have walked, some nights while a youth, twenty-five miles, to think my thoughts or to flee them. I have smelled the smells of Limehouse and Ropemaker's Fields, Newgate Street and Seven Dials. St. Giles. I have heard the screams of tortured animals at the Smithfield Market. At night, in Saffron Hill, Rotherhithe, White Chapel, Bethnal Green or Spitalfields, I have watched the coughing child, eyes wide and not surprised, search his drunken father out. I have watched that child witness his mother accosting men in hope of selling the wretchedest use of her body for money enough to buy his gruel, her rum.

And Jacobs Island, past Dockhead in Southwark, where the houses decayed and fell, where floors rotted and whole walls crashed to the streets, where every repulsive lineament of poverty, every loathsome indication of filth, rot and garbage lined the banks of Folly Ditch. Where the cholera started in '32 and '48, where the smell was of the graveyard, where animals burst with their death-gas in the water beneath the bridge and where human filth eddied among heads of fish in the thick and iridescent water.

And the cleaner, and yet worse—the worst—of Hungerford Stairs, off the Strand, where a little boy worked amid the coarsest company at the cruelest time of his life for 12 shillings a week and all the nightmare solitude he could swallow, and where the man who survived that boyhood crossed the street to avoid the blacking warehouse at 30 Hungerford Stairs, and where that boy, alone at night after visiting the Marshalsea in quest of his parents' comforting, always wept, and where the man, in later years alone there by chance, did continue to weep.

Fit subjects, all, for an old man's summing-up dreams. Reveries I have had and sometimes hated, places and people I have heard and felt again at night within my heart. Yet one, unless he write them, and only then with perseverance, and good fortune, and much pain, can never will his dreams. They do not come as they're bid.

The old man's heart is a leathery pouch, and whether it will burst with blood from the excess fill of his accumulating hours, and explode his life away, or thump through his slumber with a weak and stupidly steady motion undisturbed, filled with nothing but his dreams, will be determined by powers other than my own. I can dictate only the dreams of others, and not always then. There are those reported to recall that my sister resembled in her youth the young, and dead, and tragically mourned, and always unforgotten, sister to the woman once I called my wife. They are not correct. When Mary comes to me in dreams, as sometimes, still, she does, she wears her own face, and I know who she is.

I recover my health, according to the surgeons and those about me—children, faithful Georgie, the wagging dogs about the house who wait to journey noplace in particular beside my stiffened knees—and I work. I receive the visits of friends. I venture to London on business, and to the Blue Posts in Cork Street for pleasure, such as it is. I am given awards. I dream of Mary, dead quite nearly as long, it seems, as I have lived. I mourn my children while still they breathe. I write my Will.

I, who do reside at Gad's Hill Place, Higham in the county of Kent, hereby revoke all my former Wills and Codicils and declare this to be my last Will and Testament. I give the sum of £1,000 free of legacy duty to Miss Ellen Lawless Ternan, late of Houghton Place, Ampthill Square, in the county of Middlesex. I give the sum of £19/19/0 to each and every domestic servant male and female, who shall be in my employment at the time of my decease, and shall have been in my employment for a not less period of time than one year. I give the sum of £1,000 free of legacy duty to my daughter Mary. I also give to my said daughter an annuity of £300 a year, during her life, if she shall so long continue unmarried; such annuity to be considered as accruing from day to day, but to be payable half-yearly, the first of such half-yearly payments to be made at the expiration of six months next after my decease. If my said daughter shall marry, such annuity shall cease; and in that case, but in that case only, my said daughter shall share with my other children in the provision hereinafter made for them. I give to my dear sister-in-law Georgina Hogarth the sum of £8,000 free of legacy duty. I also give to the said Georgina Hogarth all my personal jewellery not hereinafter mentioned, and all the little familiar objects from my writing table and my room, and she will know what to do with those things. I also give to the said Georgina Hogarth all my private papers whatsoever and wheresoever, and I leave her my grateful blessings as the best and truest friend a man ever had.

The skin stretching tight across the face, the tautness of wet linen draped on bone and baked in the heat of a cholera summer's sun at noonday in Leadenhall, where the children die in the streets and where the sun, unmindful, continues in perversity to shine. The skin aching across the bone, as if flesh were an organ, and pulpy within from disease, yet hard-baked without, like the chitinous eyelids of those long-dead.

I give my eldest son Charles my library of printed books, and my engravings and prints; and I also give to my son Charles the silver salver presented to me at Birmingham, and the silver cup presented to me at Edinburgh, and my shirt studs, shirt pins and sleeve buttons. And I do bequeath unto my said son Charles and my son Henry the sum of £8,000 upon trust to invest the same, and from time to time to vary the investments thereof, and to pay the annual income thereof to my wife during her life, and after her decease the said sum of £8,000 and the investments thereof shall be in trust for my children (but subject as to my daughter Mary to the proviso hereinbefore contained) who being a son or sons shall have attained or shall attain the age of twenty-one years, or being that age or be previously married, in equal shares if more than one.

The final Reading. The hall at St. James a blur of coarse faces, some that are reddened from the shedding of tears. The violet screen stretched behind me, taut as the skin of an old man's face. The glow of the lamps increasing as I wave my finger and point with it, on their behalf, to Death, who smiles with evil pleasure in the box above them, stage right. Death is not made in the form of a skeleton or skull. Death is a well-made woman barely twenty years of age. Her porcelain skin which gleams in the gas-light's glare and glowing. Her fine white teeth which are large and, at the canines, long. The crimson of her lips, the flare and hunger of her nostrils, the lids which never, in the course of the performance, blink. And I cry in the voices, and murmur in the words, I move my finger toward her in warning and salute, and still she does not blink, and no one sees her.

There is no sound to hear save my voice, which echoes in my skull which, like a stony crypt in darkness and damp, gives back my voice enfeebled. Her long pink glistening tongue slides slowly out. It laves her lips which do not love me. They are lips I know. I cannot hear the voices I cry in, but only the rustling of the cloth which lies against her bosom, and the sound of the slick tongue licking lips. Then there is nothing to hear. I see her open hands, in gloves—but not gloves, but a brown and oily unguent which coats them, they are reaching to me. And the reading table to which I hold now is loosed from the platform, and it carries me forward, it is my ship, and I sail, stage right.

I give my watch (the gold repeater presented to me at Coventry), and I give the chains and seals and all appendages I have worn with it, to my dear and trusty friend John Forster, of Palace Gate House, Kensington, in the county of Middlesex aforesaid; and I also give to the said John Forster such manuscripts of my published works as may be in my possession at the time of my decease. And I devise and bequeath all my real and personal estate (except such as is vested in me as a trustee or mortgagee) unto the said Georgina Hogarth and the said John Forster, their heirs, executors, administrators, and assigns respectively, upon trust that they the said Georgina Hogarth and John Forster or the survivor of them or the executors or administrators of such survivor do and shall, at their, his or her uncontrolled and irresponsible direction, either proceed to an immediate sale or conversion into money of the said real estate or personal estate (including my copyrights), or defer and postpone any sale or conversion into money, until such time or times as they, he or she shall think fit, and in the meantime may manage and let the said real and personal estate (including my copyrights), in such manner in all respects as I myself could do, if I were living and acting therein; it being my intention that the trustees or trustee for the time being of this my Will shall have the fullest power over the said real and personal estate which I can give to them, him or her.

This my Will. Yes, with the heart knocking inside at the ribs and wall of the breast at the darkest moments of the night. When I awaken because my heart and not my will decree it. When my sack of death, this mouldering and voiced dust mound, decrees that

155

I shall sit up on the perspired bed linen and look into the blindness of the night and cry "What? What?" A mad old man who states *his Will*, confers his *fullest power*, and who has so little control over his rags of skin and clicking interior bones that his body is a runaway horse, but one that gallops as if upon the wet sand, as if somehow beneath the water, as if in a dream; and still the palsied rider will be shaken off to fall away, and knows so. Barbara, the whore and Jewess, knew so, and told me so with her lewd eyes. Georgie is instructed to provide for her, and we know why. They tell me, and I let them, that it is the gout. Let them call it that, and paralysis, exhaustion. They prattle of chemical solutions and the ebb of fluids in the veins, and they know nothing. It is a foot which bears no weight, a leg which twists against itself, a numbness in the body which feels too little to begin with, a blindness of the peering wetted-over eye. Hands which cannot hold. A cold perspiration over everything, and the hammering heart before dawn. Knocking to say it is time.

On, then, with the Will. The money and rents and annual incomes, the applications of same to the person or persons in the manner and for the purposes to whom and for which the annual income of the monies to arise from the sale or conversion thereof into money payable or applicable under this my Will in case the same were sold or converted, yes, et cetera, and the trusts and trustees and they shall pay my just debts, funeral and testamentary expenses, and the legacies. And my children, provided always, and their needs, and hereby I do appoint. Yes. My Will.

I have seen many men hanged, and two women. I have seen the corpses of countless drownings, and of hunger, and disease. The emblem of our days is a child whose bones have torn from the skin, quite nearly, first from hunger, then infection. This child, repeated a thousand times in a fortnight during the summers of disease in our cities, resembles a blue-brown skeleton, a little rotting doll, an insect of awful proportions—but with the eyes of a small person conceived, perhaps, in joy and even hope, and beloved of a woman in a foul moist bed whose pain informs her that she will not live to protect him—if she could!—from his fate.

I have drawn this child, his short life, his animal's death, so many times. I have been faithful to the stenches and indignities and dangers of his days. And yet I have not been true. I have delighted, and I need to confess it, in the drawing as well. In the location of the just and only word. In the dreadful music of his despairing cries. In the aptness of the motion of his sister's plunge to the silt and sewage at the bottom of the Thames. In the incandescence of the fire in which his gin-soaked father has roasted, like any meat. This my confession: I have loved him, and mourned him, and called for his rescue, in my name more than in his. I have enjoyed my work.

And now I do fear that a fire awaits me. Perhaps in the spontaneous burning, beneath the ground, of my own corrupted coffin. A blue lambency of death-fire surrounded by worms which writhe as they cook, and cannot escape. Or a death by accidental flames, say in a carriage at Pall Mall, bursting alight inexplicably, then drawn all afire by fear-maddened horses through the black night, the driver on fire and screaming, the tack and harness on fire and the horses bellowing and rolling their eyes and biting at nothing, running on and striking sparks with their hooves, the whole a behemoth of burning motion which vanishes into darkness and is recovered miles away, days later, by a rotting pier beneath which the stinking water laps—my body within the charred wooden frame, a shrunken ashy doll forever sculptured black, forever arrested in his open-mouthed shriek, which is forever unheard.

And I desire here simply to record the fact that my wife, since our separation by consent, has been in the receipt from me of an annual income of £600, while all the great charges of a numerous and expensive family have devolved wholly upon myself. Wholly upon myself. I emphatically direct that I be buried in an inexpensive, unostentatious and strictly private manner; that no public announcement be made of the time or place of my burial; that at the utmost not more than three plain mourning coaches be employed; and that those who attend my funeral wear no scarf, cloak, black bow, long hatband or other such revolting absurdity. I direct that my name be inscribed in plain English letters on my tomb, without the addition of "Mr" or "Esquire." I conjure my friends on no account to make me the subject of any monument, memorial or testimonial whatever. I rest my claims to the remembrance of my friends upon my published works, and to the remembrance of my friends upon their experience of me in addition thereto. I commit my soul to the mercy of God through our Lord and Saviour Jesus Christ, and I exhort my dear children humbly to try to guide themselves by the teaching of the New Testament in its broad spirit, and to put no faith in any man's narrow construction of its letter here or there.

For the church may crumble while the spirit climbs. The spirit too may crumble as do the churches it has built. All may fall down. As in the cathedral at Rochester, the city of my birth and near environs of my coming death, the workers in the crypts of the cathedral are excavating, sifting, searching, seeking the antique truth of whence emerged the most unlovely church. Sometimes at night one can wander there, limping, and sniff the damp, and feel the reassuring coolness on the hot skin. Drift silently in darkness past the wooden chests with dirty glass windows where they've hung the coats and ammunition canisters left by some of Cromwell's crew. Walk on the quiet feeble feet of the introspective wanderer who seeks little else on his way except some phenomenon to reinforce his mood. And, by the light of the lantern, in a cellar nook, surrounded by the damp stains of the labourers' urine, and leaned over by the low arches of the lowest levels of the church, find, staring back in stony gape, the open-eyed decapitated chiseled head of a bishop, lying on his granite ear: what one seeks. With his one ear open to the world, he would make for most Americans an adequate, though overly shallow, spittoon.

Or in daylight, one can climb the eroded steps to the top of the nearby castle keep. And once up, panting old man, the chest pushing too hard at the shirtfront, one can look down and see the cathedral. Or see, in the other direction, the River Medway, winding to the Aylesford paper mills. It is greasy and green. It goes to the Royal Naval Dockyard, where my father worked and took me to play near the boats. I must thank him for that, and I do. I learned the mysteries of water there, or started to; saw first how it may bear up so much weight, a ship of many tons, yet suck under and keep there for days the body of a frail child or woman weighing not one-hundredth of what it sustains on its surface; cast up, finally, what it has devoured, leaving those on land to contend with drained white human meat eaten by the crabs in pocked patches, the glistening bone come through.

It has been a long recuperation. And I do not heal. No further Readings now, I am without a public though I labour for them at a book. It shall be about a man who kills. It shall be named *The Mystery of Edwin Drood* and it shall be my final work. A man besotted by opium, the very medicine I take too much of for my pains. Who has done the murder? the readers shall ask. And I shall not tell them. Let them think what they will. But at the end, there shall be chapters of the most astonishing originality, written in the condemned cell. The presumed murderer to review the murderer's career *by himself*. As if, not he, *but some other man,* were in the cell and condemned to die. As if he stood outside himself. His own Crown's Prosecutor. His own accuser. His doubled self. A stranger, yet himself as well.

I work too slowly upon the final book, my hissing villain crushed by the monotony of Rochester's groined arches and cold stones. My life, now, is postponement and so is my murderer's, and I strive to keep us both alive. By force of will. My will.

By my dear heavens, I blush and tremble to think how little that Will may count for. To think how, for an instance, when I took the apartments at Hyde Park Place, so as to hasten my recovery while enabling me to be near the paper's offices and still see friends. To think how—yes, as if I stood outside the events, to think how I sent the letter by messenger to Nellie when she visited with relations at Kensington. How I waited for reply. How I sent the porter to wait in the road lest a messenger miss the house. And the old man's voice, its tremor of suspicion at his own folly, as I told the chap "You are to wait at the door, do you understand? You are to eye each messenger-looking fellow, whether he is afoot, or mounted on a horse, or driving in a postillion behind a white camel wearing crimson harness. If but one hesitate—and by that, I mean slow his pace, look twice at the house, scratch his head or pull significantly at his nose—you are to hail him.

"And how do I mean *hail?* I mean by that a lifting of the arm, a furious motion of the hand, a hearty *halloa* from the very bottom of the lungs. You are to *stop* him, in other words. You are to breast him, dear fellow, confront him, you are if it is necessary to *seize* him. And you are to say 'Do you bring word to my master?' Is that clear, absolutely pellucidly with marvelous transparency *clear?*

"A letter brought to me earns half a crown. No: a *crown.* You can retire for life on the virtue of your imitation of a sergeant of police if you but arrest a certain messenger and bring to me what I require. And now I require, my dear fellow, that you desist in your goggling wait upon my words, and you *go!*"

Spindly-legged old man in a silk waistcoat, a limp, and one burning eye. Dear God in His endless skies, the senility and foolishness of it! And the lambency of lust. The worming appetites of the worser need, that which eats at the entrails because one needs another's *need.*

I did not write further that morning, or that afternoon. I sent for coffee and could not drink it, then sent for tea, which would not go all the way down my throat. I drank off brandy, which caused me to sputter, and then I began to sit. As if guarding a tomb for some caliph, I sat. In a chair, all covered in pink, and harsh against the tender part of the back, I sat. I sent the woman away when she inquired as to luncheon. Dear Georgie, faithful and welling over with a sister's love, I even sent *her* away from the door. And the afternoon sighed on, I extended my swollen foot upon a stool, but sat where I was. At two o'clock, I drew my foot in, made as if to stand, but did not. At half past two I did stand. And, several moments later, with a walking stick and light cotton cloak given me by Longfellow in America, I went outside without giving notice to the servants, to Georgina or to the boy, sent by the printers, who had awaited outside since late of the morning with queries about corrections on the proofs.

And I did limp in the streets without watching what I passed, or whom, and at four o'clock, by the Palace of Westminster, was staring into the Thames. It was greenish brown and crowded with craft. Heat danced above it, the clocks tolled the hour, the carriages rolled, and I looked at the dazzle on the surface of the river and saw what lay beneath—the bones of dogs, the limbs of babies, the sewage of a civilization.

I leaned at the Embankment and whispered, as if to myself who were then another such as I, "Bealpost, do I imagine you here, in my city? Have you followed me once more? Why, you are such an *insignificant* fellow, with your sharp dark ferret's face, and your gleaming hair, and your little legs which barely can reach to the floor. Is it your youth attracts her? Her knowledge of my detestation of you for a common criminal? My disgust with those who betray me? Does she require that, like some handsome knight, I prove myself by clashing broadswords with you? Are you *worthy* of me, Bealpost?"

There was, of course, no answer. For I interrogated myself. There *had*, once, been a Bealpost in my life, when Dolby and I were rattling through America. And at Mold? Yes, and was he the man I spoke with now? I wondered what I had in mind. I watched myself as if an observer and not the love-besotted man, now limping on, watching for passers-by who might recognize me, and who failed to, of course.

I paused where the mossy worn steps descend to the poisonous waters. It was in their murky race that Gaffer Hexam and his virgin daughter Lizzie fished for drowned bodies. The book was *Our Mutual Friend*, wherein they wrestled with their lives and where I proved myself, again, a murderer, and man of too many parts. At Westminster Bridge, limping upon its iron frame, I stood again. The sky was oceanic, the clouds too white, the carriages rolling too perkily, the pedestrians' chatter too redolent of contentment. I slumped upon my own frame, growing sulky with fatigue and the confusions, stood between the Houses of Parliament and the City Hall, both of which shone amber in the sun. A black barge of coal wallowed down in the tide and passed beneath my legs.

I cried, of a sudden, "Oh, get me *home!*"

A clever high voice ingratiated itself from behind me: "Why don't yer excellency clamber on board and tell old Arfur where yer lives?"

I turned to the cabriolet which had paused at the curbing behind me. I did not chastise the fellow for his insolence. I was too weak, of a sudden, with the exhaustion of walking overmuch with noplace, really, to go. I shook my head, but then I slowly nodded with the new idea—new feeling, really; I thought with my body, then. "Higham" I said. Then the confusion: I said "Or Hyde Park Place."

"Ow, it's a world of difference, excellency, miles and miles apart, if yer didn't know." The narrow white face and its heavy eyebrows, small bent nose, all screwing into a great yellow smile which floated before me. "Would yer like to fink abaht it a minute, excellency?"

I thought, then, but of Bealpost. Why Bealpost? I observed myself performing the fool. Saw me strike my stick upon the paving and heard me shout, as if in triumph—why triumph?— "Yes, then. Higham! Yes, at once, Victoria Station, driver, at once!"

And that is how, fawned-upon and sneered-at, I came to be in a first-class compartment as the sun was setting, looking out upon the city and seeing myself looking in. I did not enjoy what I saw, and that is probably why I turned to the man who sat near me in spite of an otherwise empty compartment. I said, most reasonably, "My dear sir, may I point out that this compartment is relatively unoccupied? And that the seats across from us are *wholly* unoccupied?"

The passenger drew from a shining leather case a long and nearly black cigar. He slowly clipped it with a golden clipper, brushed tobacco crumbs from his light grey flawless trousers and then struck a vesta, made coal and delicate ash to appear. He sighed, then, and reached into his bag on the floor beside him, withdrew a book, rolled the cigar about on his lips, sighed again, settled his shoulders, opened the second volume in the cheap edition of *David Copperfield*, found a center page, blew smoke from the right-hand corner of his mouth, which settled about my face. Then he said, in a deep and satisfied voice, "I, sir, unlike those seats, *am* occupied. Pray pardon me now, grant silence."

The train shook and rattled and I gripped the window ledge and the edge of the seat, stuck the swollen foot forward for balance and for comfort—though of that there was none to be made—and leaned my head back and, because I could not tolerate the sight of his spittle soaking the end of the cigar and making it gleam like something horrible and organic, but not, probably, human in origin, closed my eyes. But I could not keep still, the fellow's rank insolence and inconsideration rankled me, and the train was shaking severely as suburbs and fields and shacks and long factories were united by the rush and rattle and roar of the train, which bellowed through them all at a speed which made the settlement or peaceful poise of anything so very unlikely.

I did not know that I would speak, but I did, observing, as if an outsider, the tremble of my voice, which the motion doubtless caused, as I told the passenger "I wrote that book."

The passenger did not look up from his page, but rolled the wet cigar upon his lips again and, in the flare and hiss of the lamp, said "Do watch my jaw muscles, won't you? I am informed by those of my family and circle of friends that I become angry when molested, and that anger makes those muscles move. Do you see them moving? Why not watch for that?"

I was not surprised to hear myself say, the voice now shaking like dice in a cup, like bones on a drumhead, "I say I wrote that *book!*"

"And then I clearly *am* molested" the passenger said.

I knew what I would say to him next. I did say it: "Sir, do you know who I am?"

The cigar came out of his mouth in a long strong hand—it could not have been Bealpost in disguise, then, for the limbs were far too long and well made—and the cigar, still lighted, was dropped into my lap. As I jumped and brushed and patted lest I burst into flames, as I grinned with fury and sputtered like a fuse, the passenger said "Have a cigar, then, in case you are important." Next came the book, which arced and fell with a whisper of pages: "And have something to read while you smoke." The passenger took his bag and ticket and, before I could reply, slid open the door, went out, slid the door to with a solid thump and left me to brush at a still quite possibly igniting lap while I clutched with my free hand a volume of the book in which I had set so much of my misery down.

And when the train came into Rochester—Higham was not on the schedule at night—I was reading *David Copperfield* as if my life depended upon it. I had to be reminded to disembark at the station, to limp downstairs to the hut, just off the High Street, where the cabs waited. I paused long enough to send off a Telegraph to poor old Dolby, in Herefordshire, and then went along in a cab over the squat Medway Bridge toward Higham and home, still reading what was, after all, a most remarkable achievement, that book. It was true! So much of it was *true!*

But I had not forgotten Bealpost, or the message never sent by Nellie to me. One does not forget. Bealpost, whom Dolby thought a figment of my imagination, a fiction, a friction produced by the rubbing of my sad mind against the harsh realities of the day— messages never sent, ill health and so forth—and a heat, in sum, of a mind which burned with fancies, Bealpost, nevertheless, was not forgotten.

The Telegraph had said

WHO, OF ALL, MAY SPEAK?

PLEASE ARRANGE COME GADS HILL
AT ONCE URGENT BEALPOST IS
ABOUT I NEED YOU ONCE MORE

and I am sorry to recall that Dolby sent no answer, and for days was not to be found at my side.

But the family found me, the house at Higham was full of sounds, though not of conversation about my hasty retreat from London with no notice. The foot of course flared up and flared worse still. I drank more laudanum off, cursing my weakness, sat in poultices with my leg stretched before me, fretted at my work and waited for word. And still none came.

On the next Sunday in that—to me—most unlovely month of June, Katey, who was the best of daughters, and I, not the best of fathers or men, went for a little stroll. I fear the pain was more severe, though I refused to show it, and I made myself to offer the pantomime enactment of a healthy man. We prattled of politics, of which she knew much, and of the price of berries from France, over which we muttered and shook our heads, laughing at our own mock-seriousness. She wore her mother's face. And after eleven o'clock that night, when Mary and Georgina had retired, when the lamps made the shadows of the house both soft and enormous, when we sat on an upholstered bench, I heard the rapping of my heart, as if I had been lying on a hard pillow. And then I felt it, felt my face pound as if it were lower in my body, and noted the inclination of my seated thighs to rattle in place; I restrained them. But I could not keep from looking about me as if I had just then awakened. And I tried to remember of what we had been speaking when my heart had knocked to summon me conscious; I tried to calculate how long I had been dead or sleeping or dumbstruck or paralyzed while sitting in place, conversing with a daughter I soon must leave. I wished to sob and hurl myself upon the carpet at her feet, to beg that she see I were kept in the world I had laboured so long to entertain.

But I merely patted her hand, and, as if it were part of the conversation, which I couldn't recall, I said "I wish I had been a better man."

The furrow appeared above her nose, the same furrow as her mother displayed in bewilderment, dismay. She saw my loss of bearings, I am certain, and spoke as she thought I needed her to: "Surely, father, you are a good man. You, of all!"

"And that I had been a better father" I said.

"You have been—you are the best." It was her mother's face, her mother's voice, leaner, though, and wrenched with sympathy, I suppose, for my pain. She waited for me to speak, but I could not. For I did not know precisely what I mourned. And again, as if observed from a distance, but in darkness, I heard me say "Not even you are the medicine, my love." I felt my hands upon my face, heard my voice say hoarsely "I say in all truth, I wish I had been *better!*"

I rode, next day, to Rochester to mail letters; I said that I was well, and knew that I was not. I walked a small measure with the dogs. I wrote, but not enough. I was looking at the silly precious necessary figurines atop my desk when Dolby was brought to me, at last, by Georgina.

How tall he looked, perhaps because I felt so close to the ground, so nearly beneath it; and how slender he seemed, compared to the burly man who had shepherded me through the wildernesses of America, and the illnesses of our Britain; and how distraught, in contrast to the able man with large hands and slow manner who had dealt with journalists and physicians, innkeepers, gas-lighters and ticket-sellers, all on my behalf; and how rapidly his hands moved about, from pocket to cheekbone to receding hair to eye, to ear, then, and back to pocket, to stay there an instant at the waist like a giant spider on a heap of decomposing matter, and then to wander on; and how moist his eyes, how husky his voice, how wet seemed his large strong nose, now much larger-looking by virtue of the pallor of his face and its new slenderness. This was not my old Dolby, and yet it was, for he half-bowed, smiled something like the old energetic smile and said "You have required my p-presence, I believe?"

"Ill-said, my dear fellow, but accurate. Was that, let me think, was that last month?" He waited, as I knew he would, for I was snapping the whip, though gently, as he knew would be my wont. "No, no, of *course* not—last *week*, I suppose it was, eh? Dear me. It was but a mere four or five days ago. *Was* it? Was it really? Ah! Well, I knew it was some good time back that I sent the urgentest of Telegraphs. It *was* something near to a week, I suppose, was it not?"

May I say that I don't know why I smelled a Bealpost on the wind, in my dismay? May I say that I know not why I sent for Dolby, nor why I needed so to put him in his place—which, so far as I knew, he never wished to leave?

Of course I may say. This is my will.

But Dolby, apparently, exercised his own. For he held onto his dignified hat, and with his traveling coat folded beneath his arm, his free hand moving as if in opposition to the portrait of composure with which he clearly wished to present me, he said only "I am here, sir." Something about his speech sounded wrong, and I could not put a name to it.

We looked upon one another, we who had traveled so many roads together, who were master and servant, and yet something more—that was my hope, at least—and I said, in as calm and gentle a voice as I could muster, "Very well, dear chap. It couldn't be helped, I suppose." So much could not be helped.

Dolby made no reply.

He studied me as I smiled as best I could, and then I said "Right. We're off." And then with insufficient urgency, with Dolby bearing a cudgel at my request, we set forth against Bealpost in a small carriage drawn by a creature half-mule, half-Shetland pony, away from the broad brick front of Gad's Hill Place and down the Higham Road, past the Sir John Falstaff and through the final fall of dusk.

167

Dolby spoke not at all, but murmured assent as I spoke, or grunted acquiescence, as we entered the grounds of Rochester Cathedral. Then we made no sounds save those clumsy noises men make as they bear their sticks high, their bodies low, pressing themselves against rough crumbling walls of an ancient keep while wandering worn-down stairs. Each ten or fifteen feet, the stairs inside the walls made a turning which brought us in the closing darkness to a cul-de-sac created by virtue of there being no place to go, at its end, save down and into the black bottom of the keep. We pulled at each other's coat, then, for safety's sake, retreated on the tips of our toes, hushing each other, stumbling without light into one another's back, bumping into walls and tripping upon steps, until we found a tributary stairway which led once more directly up. The moon was hidden by cloud, the inside walls of the keep were black as ink. There was a general thickness to the moist night air, and a sense on everything of old cellar stones and walls of wells. Onward we staggered, advancing, retreating, helping each other, hindering each other, seizing and releasing each other, as if we strove to exchange places in the other man's body. And then, heaving harsh gulps of humid air, we emerged, soaked in perspiration and covered with the stains of ancient stones, onto the keep's open gallery floor at the very top.

The ground seemed farther below than I knew it to be, at night in such darkness, and the boats which were moving in the river seemed farther away, their lights more gassy and feeble. I had to stop and, like a secret stork, stand on one foot while the ailing one throbbed and beat as if with a heart of its own. I saw nothing, really, and then everything at once—lights on the river, houses below, hedgeworks, roadways, river, the huge open plain of sky and dark cloud, and I saw each imposed on the other, as if the plates in a lantern-show were all displayed at once. I rubbed my face and blinked my eyes, I held my breath, and then, as I softly exhaled, the land and air and buildings slowly retreated, each to its proper place, and I whispered before I really looked for him "There is no one *here*, Dolby!"

"I beg of you, sir," he said, the old and comforting note of concern in his voice, and something alarming and new, "do not go too near to the parapet's edge."

"Dolby—Bealpost is not here."

"No, sir" he said.

"Then where? *Where?*" I could not look into his face as I spoke.

"You had firmest intelligence that he was here, sir? At Rochester? Simultaneous with your own presence?" There it was again, in his voice.

I spoke with severity, but not at his eyes. "Would I require you here otherwise, Dolby? Now, really."

"No, sir" he said. "Of course not."

I sat upon the stones, involuntarily groaning. I leaned back at the low ledge, rubbed the thigh of the swollen foot, I could not help myself. I did think—I owed him something—before I said "Go on, Dolby. Question me. You've a right to. Who else, if not you?"

I looked up at last. He was a shapeless hulk in the darkness, a voice. He said "I've no questions, sir. Shall we go down?"

He frightened me, then, with his silence, his air of wise coping, his dreadfully rational calm—and something more I still could not name. I wished to cry out at him, to heap his broad shoulders with abuse. But he had shamed me, and I could not speak. We went down, Dolby regulating his own pace so as to accommodate my own severely hindered hobble. I knew he sought not to embarrass me, and was embarrassed. And so I talked, I well-nigh chattered, as we came lower, of the crazy rushes made by the wind across the close and at the cathedral doors, the smell of the Medway, the shape of the sliver of moon against a cloud above the town. And then there was silence, and no reply, and then of a sudden I said, without meaning to, I hope, "Here I was born, Dolby, or nearby, and here, or nearby, shall I lie down dead."

And Dolby merely said "Yes, sir," leaning above me as a parent might lean above a cranky and fatigued small child.

I stopped. I said "You accept my death, Dolby? You do that?"

And he, placatingly, replied "I do not wish it, sir. I do not desire to think on it. I pray the matter forgotten and the actuality delayed. But I acknowledge death as my master."

"I thought *I*, at least some of the time, was your master, Dolby." Why had I need to *speak* so?

"Yes, sir, and you are. But death, I think, always is. Might that be so?"

We paused. I thought on him, on me. The roar of wind round the oldest of stones, some cemented in rows, others perpendicular in the churchyard. The sense of the waiting river underneath the black hill's lip on which the castle keep is poised, preserved like a huger upright stone. I had heard something, again, and still could not name it. And then I understood that not only was it something I heard, but something that was missing. "Dolby," I ventured, "there is a *something* in your turn of speech—may I say elegance?"

"I, of all, could not tell, sir."

"And a certain—*panache*?"

"I, of all, would not admit to it, sir."

"Yes. And on your lips and breath a certain *parfum*. Something perhaps imbibed in the dark of the recent ascent. Port wine?"

"Sir, you suggest between the two apparent phenomena a coincidence? A relationship of sorts?"

For I knew, then. I said "Sir, I do."

Another long pause. More wind. More weight of unseen river somehow felt. "We do not need to speak of it, sir."

"Do *you*, my dear Dolby?" I asked him.

And then, in a rush, as of dark wings or a larger darkness, Dolby, losing his moment of majesty for once and for all, cried "I am on my wuh-way to bu-buh-b-being a t-toper. A d-drunkard, sir. The-uh-wretchedest of men!"

I said "In America? Did it start in America, Dolby, with those taverns and hotel lounge bars? Yes. And the separation from home, the knowledge that at home there was—oh, say it, Dolby! Trouble?"

He whispered, like the Dolby of old, "I w-will not speak of it, sir, with your p-permission. Wuh-with your permission, I m-mean to leave it at that. Sir: even wuh-without your p-permission. T-trouble at huh-home, y-yes, and o-overmuch drink, and t-trouble in muh-my heart, and that is enough."

The third long pause. I was smiling. Like the tolling of a haunted bell, there was the third long pause in silence. Like the crowing of a cock upon a haunted eve. The rush of darkness about us. The river we were on or in. The time which poured about us, black. I smiled and gently held the cloth of his sleeve, asked "Is it another man, Dolby? Is it your good woman and another man? I understand the dilemma. I under*stand* it. Let us speak on it, Dolby, and exchange our wretched news."

But he was walking away over that pocked and darkened medieval ground, and though we spoke again that night in the house, he drank not at all, and spoke on everything but his problems, doubtlessly drinking nevertheless while I slept, then stealing away with the dawn to walk to the station and journey home to I knew not what. I could guess, and I did.

I wrote. I constructed my final murderer for my final book—that it would be the last, I knew full well. And I wrote at my Will, binding up the future with my wishes as best I knew how. I was conscious as I did so that someone in a sorry room would read it aloud, and my voice would come upon the air through his, and I would speak, then, to those who mourned me. I spoke to them as tersely and with as much strength, as little self-sorrow, as I could. I was, after all, providing for their lives. I did omit Dolby from my Will, I confess. His own will proved too great, and I have given him gifts.

I did not think of Bealpost. There were occasional letters from Dolby, which I answered with all my grace and affection, for he had given me years of his life. I chatted much with Georgina, whom I knew I soon would leave. My Nellie stayed away, and I thought myself to be served quite fairly in this; she sensed my departure, had doubtless wished something like it long ago, though not, to be fair, my actual death; and she was preparing to live for a very long time in a world I never would know.

I woke, once, at my desk, and did not know how I came to be there. I had not been writing, the papers were neatly piled, the ink-well stoppered, the fresh pens dry. I had been sitting at my desk and then had been elsewhere. My heart had knocked me into waking, and I sat at my desk and listened. I did not love the dreadful music it made.

I sit here now, and I wonder what I might have done to prolong a not unsuccessful career and a life not without its share— although a small one—of love and delight. Had I lived in the harsh and teeming life of the streets, afoot all day and much of the night, drinking rough potation and eating meager, enduring whatever the weather might bring, might I now be tending toward another fate? How close I came to that, when my parents set me loose in the prison of impoverished London, wrenching me from a school I loved and the learning I thrived upon, locking themselves in the Marshalsea prison for their stupidly won debts, and leaving me, a tiny boy, to fend for myself in the blacking factory, and to live alone with the terrors of the night in a stinking room that was little more than a cell. Without a will of oak and iron, I might still be there.

But, of course, I would be old, enfeebled, in truth. I would be coughing, more than likely, in some gaspers' charity ward, pouring out my blood upon the coarse and yellowed sheets. But would I be a man more pleased with where he has been, more ready for where he's to be? For all my life, and even now, especially now, there is the sense upon me of entrapment. I am cloistered in my life, and still not wholly free. Always, from my young manhood, and each success withal, a sense has come crushing upon me, as now it does too, of one happiness I have missed in life, and one friend and companion I never made. And it may be that the man whose blood pours upon the sheets of the charity ward, whose life is sputum and gagging for hours, still does not complain as I do.

The morbid thoughts of an old and dying man. Ellen is far

from me, and Georgie as close as she can be but to no effect other than the loyalty and comradeship she always has offered. The children, scattered, helpless, little more than children still. I shall leave them money, at the least. I have broken myself upon the Readings for that, have I not?

Have I not?

Kate, wife, child though woman, we could not have grown any older together. Was it wintry passion, as you said, which drove us from the consolation of our former tenderness? Or was it simply another savage mistake in my life of mistakes? Whom did I love? Whom *now?*

I love my children. I love Georgie as my sister. I regret the loss of Nellie, whom I barely possessed. I love myself, but not enough now. And I am an old man making lists of loss and writing a Will to serve my history forever, sleeping through my wakeful hours, waking from rest at night, waiting for my death. It has been a life, I think that I can say no more. Except this: that, like every other man, I have often been a fool and did not want to be, and hate even now that I was.

It will come. It will come, say, at dinner, and soon, for the anniversary of Staplehurst is nearly upon us, and I feel the tumbling of the railroad carriages, the metal's shriek, the dreaded helplessness of motion. It will come in this month of June, in 1870, my final year. We shall be dining, Georgie and I, and she will watch me—yes, and now I feel her gaze, I return it fondly, although the bud vase, the gaping glass mouth of a fish in which a little flower is set, does merge with her own round mouth, and I cannot separate them. She stares, now, and her mouth drops open wider, she makes no pretense to eat. My face has changed, I can feel it, and I push the chair back and sit at a distance from the table, seeing everything in wavering shapes as if underwater, where the bones are.

I hiss at her "Continue the meal!"

Poor Georgie weeps.

I whisper "I never thanked dear Dolby sufficiently. Oh, I did shed tears when we bade one another goodnight, those days ago. And he did too. I think we know each other. But I never told him, Georgie, how much, truly, he has meant to me. The difference in my life. The immensity of his importance and it was five years ago, you know, Nellie and I at Staplehurst, you know, five years ago tomorrow——"

And now the chair lies upon the carpeting, I have stumbled to my feet, although I can stand on only one, and I tell her "I must go to London at once."

Georgie holds me now, but cannot bear the weight. She cries "Oh, do lie down!"

I snicker—it is the only word for it—and relish my words as I reply "Yes, I will. On the ground." My heart is a stick that bangs on the bones inside my chest as I lie upon my left side, feeling nothing except the drum inside me which beats, there is no pain, though I find that my teeth are clenched, I cannot force them open. I lie down, I stare down, I hear the motion in the house, footsteps on wood from a great distance, a hollow thump going muffled, now, which is my heart that beats against the walls of the house.

And then the Telegraphs to Mr. Reynolds the surgeon, the grunting of the gardeners who, summoned by Georgie, lift me to the sofa, where I hear, and slowly breathe with clenched teeth, and then become another man, *he,* the one who at fifty-eight on the sofa no longer breathes, whose jaws have fallen open, *he,* who is the subject of Telegraphs to Forster and Dolby, poor Dolby, the best of men. He does not breathe, that one on the sofa, and there is a tear on his cheek which has taken a turning to make him look sly.

And the to-ing and fro-ing in the house, the weeping, the bandaging closed of his mouth, and the death mask, the sketches, the washing and dressing of his negligible body with its thin blue thighs, the shrunken progenitative apparatus so long useless anyway, he is in body a little brown-blue boy with the head of an old weathered man.

And the days of lying before the stares of weeping men and women, Nellie among them, silent, shocked by what she knew approached, and then the long ride, hauled like freight by defecating horses, to the trench dug in the unselective earth. Being trundled to the boards, the ribbons threaded beneath the simple coffin, the boards removed, the swollen Christian words which guarantee so much and mean so little, they are only words at last. He is lowered down as the people stand in a ring above the trench to see him put in his place. The sound of pebbles and heavy wet clods which rain upon the little room, the cell, which he so long fled, from his childhood in London. He is in the cell, and he knew he would be. His Will is in the light, is in the wet trembling fingers of pale men who count his money.

Is this not just? Am I finally not the only man, of every man, who can speak so of his dying and interment in the fields which one day must grow crowded with the dead? Cannot I, of all, tell how the dead will mount up as the brutal age progresses? How his coffin will vie for space in the shifting snake-swarmed ground with other boxes until, like little ships in a slimy sea, they coast and bump and crowd one another, thrust one another up, and away, until the prow of one break the graveyard's crust and the gases of corruption within force the lid up, squeeze out rotted green and purple portions of a nostril or toe, a finger perhaps, and a terrier at play seize upon it, scrap of maggoty meat, to drop at his master's feet, and wag in pride above the redolent toy?

I, of all, may speak of him thus. I booked his halls and all but blacked his boots. You know who I am. And they are all of them here with me. Moon especially, thank God. It is the autumn of 1900, and whoever reads this book shall read our lives. It is night at the Fulham Infirmary. Sometimes I think it always is night. Soon the Matron will come and tell me that the smell of paraffin from my light unsettles the other patients. And what she will mean is I'm a charity patient, latterly come from the sewage and streets, and were I healthy I would still be wandering, and those who require the beds and medicine and iron hospital courtesies should have no call for a lamp, and these extra hours of the night alone with paper and cheap ink, a charity, like the hours themselves.

Of my family I shall not speak. We sold the Shetland pony he had given our daughter, and the silver gifts he had caused to be sent from America when George Charles my son was born. My son is in Paris, now. He is becoming an artist, I know. He wanted, always, to be one. I think the Chief may have given him that. His mother is dead of the influenza and with no one but her daughter to nurse her. I gave them that. Our daughter emigrated to America, with no one left at home to nurse.

I have committed all these people—Barbara, Ellen, Kate and Bealpost—to the previous pages while resting from my travels through Lytton Grove and Eel Brook Common, and into and out of the doss-house, the workhouse, and this, my final house above the ground. I think they think I drink the paraffin. And probably I would, if it would but consent to consumption. Still, there is Moon and his ingeniousness, and I, who saw my best days as a great man's middling amanuensis and high groom, have consumed the drinkables, and those people whose voices you have heard. I am consumed by them, in turn. I spit them out upon the page. And they spit me. *Low laughter*. No mean feat.

Fitzgerald and Forster wrote their reminiscences of the Chief. So did Georgina. I, George Dolby, did so too, before drink completed my ruin. It was entitled *As I Knew Him*. T. Fisher Unwin published it to the greeting, in *The Saturday Review*, that it offered "an excess of trivial detail." The first edition, brought out at 6 shillings, and the popular edition, following at 3/6, earned me less than £200, and all of them gone.

In Ross, where I was a boy and almost a man, there was a market square made of red Heresford sandstone and low wood cattle stalls inside, below the second-story village offices. It stood before the wood and plaster home of John Kyrle, the Man of Ross, whom Pope wrote a couplet about and after whom my Chief once named me. In our little church of St. Mary the Virgin, after

Kyrle's death, early in the last century, at the window under which he always prayed, two elm shoots grew up through the floor, inside the church. They slowly burst through the stones and, clinging to the walls, grew toward the light. I pray, here, where no one prays with any hope, that I might somehow similarly be remembered to the world. However, I also recall that the trees died; their trunks remained and spread a dry rot; they had to be replaced by live trees which the parishioners planted. I haven't the cost, nor have I survivors available to foot the bill. I'll end up lying in a pauper's field, and the growing green commemorations to my presence here will be the horizontal diggers children catch for bait to use on a string off the docks at Lime.

Coming into Ross on market days from Bishops Wood, we used to run through the narrow cobbled passage called Pigs' Alley, low branches whipping our faces, down the hill and round the turnings, past the small gardens and into New Street where the jail sat. It was like the last remnant of a castle, or the brand-new fakery of a rich builder who thought that Gothic horror was just the thing for someone with much money and a love of the awfully damp. Squat tower and low outbuilding, all in red, like everything of stone in Ross, its narrow barred windows seemed the best of targets for stones and pried-up cobbles. We made stories for each other of cells inside, and leg bones stapled to the walls left hanging three hundred years, and subterranean passageways lit by candles in skulls beneath the streets of Ross, and scenes of slow torture and drawn-out torment. We never went inside. Although I might as well be in there tonight. It is difficult to believe that I once conceived a building for incarceration, any place where men are locked, as proper for a game.

There *was* a Mr. Caldecott. Remember Barbara the whore, and her wholesaler? He haunted my children at the house, I was told. He sometimes took them, on market days when I was away, to watch the Gloucestershire Forest People come over the nearby border into Herefordshire, and Ross. My son George, as I dream him, can remember a day in early summer, June I think, when

177

the hawthorn was blooming brilliant white and the sun was harsh on their necks; Mr. Caldecott, who hated Italians because they were susceptible to Catholicism, and because they were swarthy and dirty and smelled a bit—rather, in effect, like him—told George and his mother that he was put in mind of his days in Siena. George didn't know then where Siena was, and thought that perhaps his father and the Chief were in that place. The plants along the Wye, and, more strikingly, upon its surface, bloomed a brighter white than the hawthorn, and Ross seemed surrounded by a great brilliant flowering vine which traced the municipal dimensions. It was one of those days when the insects seemed to come individually, so that one heard the interior engine of each. Between their arrivals, one heard the daws above the old jail, and the rooks at the church, swooping to surround the mass grave from the plague days. And, above all, there was the laughter of children—George heard, then saw, his sister running with her friends while he sat, young gentleman, a bit too close to the touch and breath and great bee's buzzing of Mr. Caldecott, and listened to him and Mrs. Dolby speak politely, and wondered where I was and, if I were here, and if I were rubbing his head, or tickling his chin, or reprimanding him, or giving him sweeties, what he might say to thank me for my presence.

They were out of the sun, then, at a municipal bench in the shade of the cattle stalls at the market. George was tucking one ankle beneath the other and then reversing the condition. He was edging from the casual and accidental and insistent touch of Mr. Caldecott's hand, those flat and bitten dirty fingers. He was wondering what his father thought of the neighbour who so adored his little son. He was wondering a general *why*—to cover, like a law that should work but didn't, his solitude with my wife and daughter, the presence of Mr. Caldecott, the heat of the market day, my devotion to the Chief, the mystery of such a Chief's great nature. As they sat, the Forest People began to drive their stock up Pigs' Alley, which was doubtless named for its function. They had been granted the perpetual right to graze their animals, and water them, and drive them too, on any land near the Wye. It did not matter who owned the land: their right was to use it. That was the price for the peacefulness of these once bellicose barbarians.

I suppose they drove their stock for sale and slaughter up the alleys as they did so that everyone should see them come in their long and bleating smelly file. They wore the shaggy skins and dirty jerkins of a hundred years ago to remind the men of Ross how rude and frightening once they had been. They could come severally or singly, but they came all of a pack. They could come in any direction, but they all chose the same. They could be silent, but they whistled and shouted and splashed in the turds of their great pink pigs and shaggy cattle. They reminded the people of Ross that the recent rising class were descended from such peasants as now they beheld. It was a dun-coloured, smoking, high-odoured, loud-sounding affair that approached, and they did it for the audience and probably didn't know quite why.

And I dream George Charles Dolby, my son, thinking, then, as he stood to walk round to the other side of his mother so as to interpose her between Mr. Caldecott and himself, that he was learning something about his father and his father's Chief. The Chief as the jolly barbarian. His father as his Chief's pink pig.

Well, I have snuffled severally since then. I've run through a good many years. I have been in lodgings near Spitalfields Garden, where for 4 shillings a week I was permitted to live between wet crumbling walls beneath a ceiling black with damp and peeling down upon me. There were holes in the floor for the easier, more convenient passage of the vermin, and the smells from below of the fish and cabbage which the street vendors stored in their quarters at night, along with six or seven children and perhaps—with some luck—a rotting chicken or goat.

Upstairs, above me in the attic, I heard the howling of a child one night. It grew so deep into the bone that I could not mind my business, which was the nursing of a pint of wine to keep me warm. I thought of my children, you see. I went slowly up, in the darkness, picking my way through the holes in the stairs. Something made me stop. It was the ending of the stairs, there was a need for several more to reach the open door I peered in. An infant lay as if dead, wrapped in dirty rags. It merely slept, though, and the weeping emanated from its sibling, brother or sister I could not tell. A child of three or four years, filthy and wailing its despair—a watcher, set by its parents to mind the baby didn't roll through the open door and through the gap in the stairs and to its death below. The child had probably sat there all night, fearful of the beating it was promised if it moved. And now it was thirsty, or had to relieve itself, or had merely understood how from that moment until the end of its life nothing would change: a deathwatch in life its legacy. I wanted to hold it and give some comfort. Have I not been a parent to small scared children? But I could not hold it forever, and that was the least required. So I gave it a drink of wine to stop its weeping, and then went down again. Soon its crying commenced.

I have watched, in a sawdust pit in Hanley, while a shrunken man, his bare chest writhing with scars, sank to his knees to fight a starved white bulldog for a bet. If he won, his family would eat. He was quite cocky, since he got his living at the work. And if he lost, he would never know the difference. Covered with blood and saliva, rocking back and forth with pain, as if in prayer, he finally felled the dog with a blow delivered beneath its chin. The creature was unable to attack again for the count, and he collected his wager and then, very slowly, in an underwater motion, lay down in a faint.

People die daily in the worst of conditions and are buried even worse. Their coffins in the crowded fields soon burst and the mud and water running off through footpaths and felled old stones and sagging iron gates carry the excrescences of rotten glowing ancient meat to the neighbourhood of the standcock, hard by the house-drains, where all mingle together and provide the drinking water which a short bony child will come to collect in a pail used recently for slops. And King Cholera strides through the dark brown streets, putting a stop to the noises of the children begging food or torturing dogs.

We poor are told that if we worked we would not live so badly or die so wretchedly and young. I once lived, if that is the word, in a district known as Collier's Rents on Long Lane at Bermondsey. Shortly after I came there, the bodies of nine infants were found in a large rough box at the foot of some stairs in an undertaker's shop. The court was eighteen or twenty yards long by little more than nine or ten wide, and there leaned twelve houses, each of two or three rooms—but the owners, in their mercies, refused, utterly refused, to permit more than forty families to reside there. What Christian concern! Oh, the odour of the dust bin which we shared! The four water closets we cleverly managed among us! The smell was like a wall one's body always was frayed against.

In the Cradley Heath district are manufactured four-inch mooring cables and fine-gauge wire, crane-cables and dog-chains and handcuff-links. I made links for 10 shillings a day, so hard did I labour in the heat. Unfortunately, the furnace is rather terrible, and one becomes thirsty and cannot swallow, so buys beer by the pint, which a boy fetches. And then one has spent his money or owes it to the factory. At 3 shillings a day spent for beer, I owed 11 shillings by the end of my second week. I hardly could move my body, but still I reported to work, making do with seconds, which is what my employer called the milk left several days at the dairy. A woman there who worked at making spikes carried her infant with her so as not to lose a day of work; she wore him in a sling, she said, because another child, left untethered, had rolled over into the furnace to be cooked, in an instant, black.

I could not live without the work, but could not live with it, either in the conditions or the indebtedness. I paid my obligations back and with a few pence in my pocket after purchasing supplies, I set about the making of matchboxes for a time. I started slowly, on account of the dead baby, the second in a month in that family to die of the pestilential vapours in the air. In the room next to mine where its parents and brothers and sisters lived (that is, ate, and slept, and engendered more of their kind), and because the parish boasted no mortuary and no room, even, for post-mortems, they cut the baby open to examine its lungs and liver while the children sat round it and watched. The father could fortunately faint away. The mother looked the while at her babies who still lived. It was difficult to concentrate on matchboxes.

I lost my lodgings, one usually does, and started in to wander. You might as well ask me about Bealpost as why I drank the claret or rum, gin, whatever I could cadge or steal. Oh, I worked when I could. I hauled fish heads in Greek Street and helped the dustman tip barrels of night soil up into his cart. I pushed a broom, once, after a parade of American cavalry who had come to London to ride past our Queen, saluting. And though the Chief would never have believed it, I worked at helping to clear out a blacking factory; I pretended all the while that it was the same he had been trapped in as a child, and which he had hated, and which had turned him into a man of will, sworn never to be required by the world, but always to compel it on his own behalf. And I thought of what he might say, to see me so reduced. He would have raged at my conditions, for he did truly hate the abyss in which the poor must dwell. And then he would have raged at me. For insufficient energy. For giving in to the world. For being *forced*. For lying at night on the Embankment as Big Ben struck a late cold hour over the Thames. Bodies about me, contorted against the crushing winds, struggling with their own skin as if they wished to pull their flesh up and over their heads like woolen comforters. Some lying upon scraps of waste paper. Some having removed the hat, replaced it with a bit of rag, as if it were a night cap and they were at home still, and had not fallen.

I had the cough by then, and had just left the Camden High Street Infirmary, having vowed to never drink. No one would employ a man with a swollen nose and bowel-deep rolling cough. But I drank. Near me, a woman and child were sleeping. Her arms were about her four- or five-year-old son. I could not lie above the river and watch them. I left my coat over her shoulders and his. It was that or roll myself into the river. And I thought of him, the eyes and nostrils wide with indignation, the body swaddled in comfort, and delicate fingers opening and closing, or made into fists and beating at his thighs. I thought of him at Dublin on our Farewell Tour, as he bounced upon his toes, one finger pointing at the upper air, as he read from *The Chimes,* that New-Year's cautionary tale of his, in which the distraught impoverished father, Trotty, is given a visionary dream of the Chimes, the bells which the Chief intended to ring the music of Hope. Trotty, seeing his impoverished daughter, now a widow with an infant, driven beyond hope, is forced to follow her in his imagination as she runs to drown herself and her hopeless baby:

"Putting its tiny hand up to her neck, and holding it there, within her dress: next to her distracted heart: she set its sleeping face against her, and sped onward *to the river.*

"To the rolling River, swift and dim, where Winter Night sat brooding like the last dark thoughts of many who had sought a refuge there before her. Where lights upon the banks gleamed sullen, red, and dull, like torches that were burning there, to show the way to Death."

And, strangely, for the first time since I had read the story or heard his performance, I did not think how cruel it was, how vicious in its smug beliefs, that a father must be driven mad with such a vision—I have been a father too, and of a woman named Barbara and with my own visions—in order that he bend beneath the torture and cry out his admission: "*'Spirits of the Chimes! I know that* we must trust and hope, and neither doubt ourselves, nor doubt the Good in one another. I have learnt it from the creature dearest to my heart. I clasp her in my arms again. Oh Spirits, merciful and good, I am grateful!'" No, I did not think of the savagery, the utter tyranny of such generousness. And it was the first time that my feelings had seemed clear.

Standing above the sleeping woman and child who now were under one more layer of futile cloth, my own, I thought instead of his brilliant indignation, and his penetrating ability to watch, to

understand, and then to *make*. I thought, as the smells of the
Thames and the chime of the clock and the deep disturbed breathing of the little boy all mingled about me, that he had been
great. Yes. Great to make us ache and sigh and fear for that
woman and her child. Whether or not he had enjoyed that
mother's terror as he made it, felt the pleasure of the craftsman at
his craft. Whether or not he had thrilled to the devastating fear of
the penniless father. Despite his own needs or nastiness, he had
sensed the slime on the stones at the Thames, and the hopelessness
slick upon the souls at the Embankment. He had captured a part of
us, and had said our name. He still was alive.

I thought to walk all the night to stay warm. I thought that in
the morning, my cough would ease, and I would find a gill or two
of drink. I thought of my son George, in Paris, working as an
artist or a writer, I wasn't sure which. I wondered what he would
think of me; I thought I knew. And I wondered why it was that
people ended their lives alone. The Chief had died in the loneliness
of his language. Ternan had been distant in body and mind, Kate
away in her own dark solitudes. And what would become of
Georgina now? And crotchety Forster? And me? My distant daughter, Barbara. The son who, born away from me, now required that
he live away from me too. It ends with being alone.

I thought of my son, and I dreamed him in Paris, remembering
this: The fourth or fifth day he was in London, having left the
valley of the Wye to make his way to Paris and there become a
kind of artist—any occupation, he thought, in which one made
another place to shelter in. He was at the inn in Southwark, the
George, where the Chief had set some scenes. He had come there
from the Boot and Flogger, craving something of a sudden besides
wine, which was all they served, and was at the stand-up bar
opposite the entrance, bowing his head beneath the low ceiling,
eating meat pie and drinking strong ale, and feeling too young to
be so drunk and solitary and in such a quickly moving stream of
conviction and purpose and his own vague hopes. He was thinking
of a rutted narrow track in the valley under Wotton to which he

once had walked by himself with a knapsack of books and sandwiches. It was called Ozleworth Bottom, a little cul-de-sac which two meadows ran down to; there was a fast brook behind a small stone cottage, and the wind, the sound of water, and a slate which seemed to wait for his arrival before sliding from the roof to crash behind the house onto stones.

After no more than twenty or thirty seconds—he stood in the track, merely listened and watched—the great wooden door opened in and a tall man in spectacles hurled himself out to move first in one direction, then retrace his steps and aim his body in the opposite direction, then, seeing George, stand violently still. After another few seconds, he placed his hands in the pockets of his trousers, let his slumping shoulders slouch further, lifted his patrician's nose high—like the sight of a rifle being placed for the kill—and he called "What?"

George called back "What?"

He answered "I said it first: *what?* What do you want? What do you want to make all that *noise* for? What are you doing at my house? What *is* it?"

George said "I'm sorry, I didn't make any—I was just walking, sir—for the noise, I mean. But your roof—"

"You're an articulate fellow, aren't you? Listen: do you know what I was doing?" He smiled, then stopped smiling and glowered. George thought of the Forest People of Gloucestershire.

"No, sir" he answered. By then he had taken his cap off and was stepping backward.

"I was writing a poem. I was writing a *poem,* and you hurled something, you made some sort of *noise* and I had to stop. I no longer am sitting at my table, writing a poem. I am speaking to you on the subject of your noise. But I would *rather* be writing a poem. Do you understand?"

"Oh," George said, "oh, are you—" and the names raced between his ears, and he remembered and forgot all the work by all the men he had been worshipping—"are you Mister Matthew *Arnold,* sir?"

185

The man very promptly, very quietly, said "No, I am not. Not yet."

And George understood him, and didn't feel a fool. He said "I may become a writer also."

The birds and bugs and water and wind filled the pause in their conversation, and George waited for the man to encourage him, or tell him whom to read, or show him his work. He looked at George with eyes which could laugh, though now they didn't, and he brushed a fly away from his long face. Then he nodded. And then he said, softly, "You know, we work in quiet. We need the quiet, you see. We work alone." He raised his eyebrows and nodded, tried to smile, then nodded again and waved his hand and went inside his door. George stood a while and listened to the silence which was necessary, and somehow also frightening because it implied a solitude so dense, so irrevocable, which no one ever might share. He waved at the door and went away, wishing that he were old enough, and accomplished enough, and interesting enough, so that the poet might have taken him in to show him his implements and artifacts and the general mysteries of the trade.

And, abuzz with port and ale and London and the George, and with the sense of how terribly alone and at the beginning of things he was, George remembered the cul-de-sac at Ozleworth and was beginning to slowly shake his head and sip at his pot when the door which was still on leather hinges opened to the failing afternoon light and admitted the ghost of Dolby the elder. He was taller than George had remembered, his remaining hair was longer, his clothing, never the neatest, was shabby at best. He held some coins in his hand so that the landlord might see at once that he was a patron and not a beggar. He went to the little window in the wall, no more than ten or twelve feet away from George, and said "A p-p-pint, p-please, best b-bitter."

He stammered under stress, and George wondered if his life in general were now the cause. He soon found out. He watched him, then closed his eyes, then opened them again. His head felt covered with perspiration, and his back. He could not eat his pie. He turned to look at the corner in the wall. He heard his breath heave in and out as if the air were water and he no longer could use it for staying alive.

Then George turned, he told himself to turn, and he watched his father draw himself up and brace his chest out and lean against the wall and look about the room with a little grin—he remembered the grin—and then take two steps on his very long legs and, a few feet away now, he heard his father, looking elsewhere, say "Hallo, George. How are you, boy?"

Into his mind came scenes—whole ones, long ones, quickly moving, but complete in their wished-for detail: his father and him at a restaurant in Holborn, their heads together, talking together, laughing aloud and simultaneously; his father and him at a park, listening to the children call; his father and him in a quiet inn, drinking brandy and making careful plans; his father telling his life, his secrets, what George required to know of his inner world and outer events, and George in turn telling him of what he must do, then hearing from his father how he must go about it.

But instead George actually saw, too close for the focusing, how quickly his father lifted his pot and drained it, and let it slip to the floor; how his neglected teeth and coarsened skin leaned in toward him and how, amid odours of charcoal and onion and general lack of care, his father's head came close to his, and he kissed his son on the cheek and whispered "Goodbye, laddie." And how, then, his father was gone through the door—the brilliance of an instant's dying sunlight, then the customary dark.

George stood where he was, against the wall, paralyzed by the sudden appearance and then disappearance, and rooted by the public exposure of his private shame and wish. He did not move. He was too painfully conscious of how young he looked, and how much of his story had been told to strangers for whom he was nothing but diversion. None of this came as thought. He felt it all, as one feels the air hiss in his trousers-seat after a loud fart among genteel company in a small room. There is nothing to *do* but feel, and wrinkle the nose.

So he did not pursue his father. He continued to drink his pint, and he finished it, though it tasted by then like a coal-tar infusion. And *then* he left, walking slowly in order to demonstrate to the company of the George that he was commander of his soul's journey, undaunted. Outside, near the urinal across the cobbled courtyard, in the smell of damp and waste, he looked about as if for clues. There were none that London could offer which it had not offered before, and he was glad to soon go to Paris.

He walked from the ancient slippery alleyway of the George, and out along the dimming streets of Southwark. It was a moment of smells, and all at once he was filled, like a child's balloon by a rush of gas, with cabbage and horses and chestnuts and coals and mildew and excrement and awfully old fish. He staggered as if drunk with port and ale. But it was the city assailing him. The cocksure, bitter city, unafraid. People called and smoked and lounged, their dark clothes—sodden and crushed-looking, some of them merely projections of the shadowy walls and wagons they were near. A woman with a long narrow weasel's face, in bright red skirts and a soiled white shirt, stood near the channel of urine and feces, vegetable leaves and chickens' heads, which ran in the curb, and unbuttoned the blouse from the neck, a button, another, another again. She caressed her throat and, even in that hastening darkness, he could see that it was grubby and streaked, sooty, like her knuckles and nails. She smiled. He wept harder and went past her. She didn't laugh at him, and he was grateful.

He wandered, but in haste, and therefore seeing rather little went to the Westminster Bridge, and went nearly half the way over to the Houses of Parliament and the pier at which some pleasure craft were anchored, probably while their owners were sipping champagne on the veranda of the House of Lords. He stood on the bridge, between the shabby side of London and the slightly less shabby, looking down at the dark Thames, which was growing darker but in which veins of orange from the sunset were glowing, going redder, becoming, before his eyes, bloody. And he thought at once of his father's Chief, who saw blood in so many places, under so many circumstances, and to whom his father— perhaps hating him much of the time for the servitude's harshness: who can tell?—would have given his life. Certainly, he had given much of it. *And some of it was mine,* he thought. And as my son watched, the sun glowered more crimson, and it, and the world, and the place where he stood, and the pull of the moon to shift the tide, and everything in the world which might conspire to create a vision one sees but once and inexplicably, all clicked into place like the greatest and tiniest cogs in a marvelous machine: he saw the Thames run red as far as he looked. It was a river of blood, and its reflection on the hulls of the barges and the oars of the shells, on the stanchions of the bridges and the slime-deep steps of the Embankment, all were red as well. Blood was everywhere in the world, then, and my son felt like a creature of his father's Chief, seeing what only *he* could have invented, and written, and made convincing. George was in his bloody mind, along with Mary-le-Bow, and the Treasury, and St. Paul's, and the Haymarket, and Covent Garden and the flowers at Kew. George saw them all, then, with his eyes closed, rippling reflections of the blood tide in the Thames. He held to the rails before him and shrieked inside himself to open his eyes. He did. The moment had passed. His father was gone. The Thames was a dark muddy river, quite wide. He was in the middle of it, alone, on a bridge, and he was going to Paris. Nothing could be explained. It was like the matter of Bealpost, who was either a symptom of the madness of my Chief, or who in fact was a secret stalker of his life and mistress. It was like the matter of a life gone over into the sewers of poverty and drink, I like to think. Call it all Bealpost, the ferret-face of facts, the secretest tick of events, the reason with no name: the truth in what he wrote.

My son, above the Thames and understanding nothing, re-membered from when he was three or so—merely a vision, an

instant. Two horses coming up the hill to Bishops Wood. The
martins diving in great circles away from the eaves and out and
back. The sound of their shrill cries, as if something were the
matter. His mother working the door latch and appearing within
the martins' jabber. His father's bald head in the sun as he removed his hat. The mourning smile of the small man beside him
in the carriage. The deep uneasy eyes, pale face. His father calling
over the little pond, through his mother's voice and the shrilling of
the birds: "Georgie! Look, laddie! Look who is *here* with us!"
Nothing could be explained.

I continued to walk through the city at night with no coat. A
crawler dossed in the doorway of a house. She was twenty or
thirty, looked sixty. Homeless, too weak from exposure to work or
even beg, she depended upon beggars to drop some old tea leaves in
her pot, or leave her some old bread scooped, wet and mouldy, from
the waste bin behind a restaurant. When she was given enough
money, which was infrequent, she would crawl, for want of the
energy to walk, to a gin-house or cocoa-house, and for a moment
revive the remnant of her body. As I stood before her, she tilted in
the doorway, and slid around the doorpost, and started to fall. I
stopped her and wedged her back in. She didn't waken. My cough
didn't cause her to stir.

In the morning, I thought as I walked on, she would be paid by
a prostitute or honest mother, to mind an infant while the parent
worked. She could sleep while the child in her arms was sleeping.
And if the child didn't catch her diseases, why then it might also
survive.

I have committed to memory, and proudly recite, the solution
to the crawlers and those others of us said to be erect. One aspect of
it was written by Henry Austin, a brother-in-law of my Chief's.
He addressed this report to the General Board of Health, under the
title *Report on the Means of Deodorizing and Utilizing the Sewage of
Towns:* "In towns of rich and of poor population the quality of the
sewage may also materially differ. The excess of animal food

consumed by the classes in easy circumstances manifests itself in nitrogen, which is discharged in the faeces. The value of the refuse of Belgravia would, no doubt, exceed that of Bethnal Green."

It is the age of numbers. And so the Commissioners of the Exhibition of 1851 reported that at the Crystal Palace, the apotheosis of *things*, there were 54 urinals for men and an additional 22 convenience rooms; for women the total was 47. There was a consumption of 33 tons of hams at the Exhibition, 20,415 savoury cakes, and 5,350 bottles of Masters' Pear Syrup. There is compiled by Mayhew, in his famous book on the London poor, the following: "TABLE SHOWING TOTALS OF EVERY DE-SCRIPTION OF VEHICLES PASSING PER HOUR AND PER DAY OF 12 HOURS THROUGH CERTAIN STREETS WITHIN THE CITY OF LON-DON." And the very well-meaning Mr. Charles Booth has let it be known that there are in East London (of which by now I know a little) 900,000 inhabitants who may be divided into eight classes:

A. The lowest class of occasional labourers, loafers and semi-criminals.

B. Casual earnings—very poor.

C. Intermittent earnings } together, the poor.
D. Small regular earnings }

E. Regular standard earnings—above the line of poverty.

F. Higher-class labor.

G. Lower middle class.

H. Upper middle class.

Perhaps it is of some interest that A, the lowest class, which is said to consist of some occasional labourers, street-sellers, loafers, criminals and semi-criminals, numbers 11,000, or 1¼ per cent of the population. According to Mr. Booth, "Their life is the life of savages, with vicissitudes of extreme hardship and occasional excess." We are not considered a danger to the civilized world and we will not rise in revolution. "They are barbarians," Mr. Booth concludes of us, "but they are a handful, a small and decreasing percentage: a disgrace but not a danger."

In fact—a word I have come to hate—my Chief did fear that the barbarians who constituted the poor might one day rise. He was all John Bull, and he loved his comfort, and he hated the mire his toes, for a while, had sunk into; he would not fall back to it, nor would he countenance its reaching up to him. And yet, he never once said 1¼ per cent. Because, whoever he was, his heart *was* great some of the time. Because he knew whom to blame and therefore hate. He took the world most personally. That counts for something, I thought as I walked. I thought that ought to count for something. Even if I did not.

Once upon a time, in the borough of Higham, outside the English city of Rochester, a young man employed by the payroll office of Her Majesty's Navy walked with his very young son. The young father was of decent heart and spendthrift habits, and he spent his way, beyond his means, to the poorhouse. The son who walked at his side was to leave school for a basement factory room in which he labeled bottles of stove blacking; he later was to leave the family itself, to continue his work, while the family remained otherwise whole in the Marshalsea, the only house the very poor were permitted. As the son survived his childhood and grew famous and wealthy and even more troubled, the profligate father (and mother as well) came to rely—against the son's wishes—on his private treasury. He set them up in housekeeping, once, in the country, so they might embarrass him no further with their letters to his merchants and publishers, begging, in the name of their child, for help. But that was later. Once upon a time in Higham, they walked, father and son, and probably held hands.

Selecting a house at random, the father paused near the Sir John Falstaff to point across the road toward a high brick building with mullioned windows and chimneys enough to warm a hostel. "Do you see that?" the father said.

Because he could not help but see it, the boy nodded that he did, said "Yes, father."

"If you work like a man, and live like a *good* man, and come out as the *best* man, you may one day own a house just like that, lad. Do you think so too?"

The boy said "Yes, father" and looked away.

When he was forty-four, he bought the house at Gad's Hill Place. The house his father had, and doubtless at random, pointed him toward.

I knew as I coughed that I would not be able to stay afoot all night. I gagged, nearly, at the thought of the workhouse again. But I knew, too, that I had no choice. So I kept in the direction my feet had chosen long before, and I came to the door, and lifted the knocker and, when the high door was opened, I went in.

A small stone room. A tall thin clerk who had a little fire to warm him. A plate of Her Majesty upon the wall. Gas lamps and rush mats, and a sense that all was well. How I wished to live in a world of such clean colours for a time! The man who had opened the door stood behind me, taller than I, and bulkier, and of course without my cough. He wore a black woolen shawl about his shoulders and looked lugubrious enough to match it, with his pointed nose which was slowly collapsing in from syphilis, and his hooded eyes and the great bird's-wings of hair upon his brows. He simply stood while I spoke to the clerk, sometimes shuffling, as if to remind me that he was something of a guard as well as something of a host.

The clerk, who looked like every man in England with a good job and a home in which to boast of it, said "What do you require?" Between three and four in the morning, with cold winds over the waterways and down the alleys, a shaggy, ragged man in snuff-coloured vest and trousers, in a once-white shirt which is now the colour of old walls, and shoes which look made of paper, and which, certainly, are reinforced with same—this man, with hunger in his eyes and illness in his cough and a tinge of grave mud to the complexion, comes to the workhouse where you greet the men in need of lodgings for the night because they cannot afford to buy it for themselves in even a doss-house, and you inquire what they need. If such is true, then you *must* be a servant of Her Majesty's Circumlocution Office, and possibly a pensioner of the Anglo-Bengalee Disinterested Loan and Life Assurance Company, and how I wished my Chief were with me, then, and simply for the sake of his comments on the scene before me.

Within me, as well. For he almost always knew a bit of that.

I said "I want a night's l-lodging, p-please."

"You're late then, aren't you?"

"I *feel* late, but how do you m-muh-mean it?"

"The doors are to close at midnight. Never mind, though, everyone's late here. It's the neighbourhood, I think."

I raked my teeth over my lower lip to remind me of humility, for that was what the clerk was clearly requiring, and I said "Muh-may, may I stay for the n-night, sir?"

"Sleep in the shed."

"Yes, sir."

"And have a bath."

"Sir" I whined, thrusting my wrists clear of my foul shirt so that he could see them, "I'm c-c-uh, I'm c-clean. Really, sir, I am."

"And have a bath" he repeated, looking down at his book.

I said "And have a b-bath, sir."

"Then what's your name, poor fellow?"

"George Dolby."

His nondescript, forgettable face looked up and he screwed it into a horrible map of torment, he scratched at it, he furrowed it up and down, then said "No. No, I thought I knew it but I don't."

I said "No, sir."

"No. And your occupation?"

"None."

"It says here *Occupation*. Now, you may be out of work, and you may not know any work, you may not be able to *get* any work.

I will give you all or any. But it says here *Occupation* and I will fill in the blank or you'll be dossing with the crawlers tonight."

"Tour m-manager."

"That's more like it, isn't it? Yes. By the by, who was your company? Who did you arrange for?"

"Boz." I looked at the floor and waited.

He said "Why not tell me old David Copperfield himself? And did you work for whatshisname Twist? Oh, fine, splendid. Yes. Boz. Indeed. Thank you. You're a rich one for such a poor one, do you know that? Well, tell me: where did you sleep last night? For the form, now."

"Camden Town."

"How many times have you been there?"

"Once before."

"Where do you mean to go when we turn you out in the morning?"

I coughed and we had to stop and wait for it to pass. "I d-don't know, sir. I—" His expression had changed, and it looked to me as if that were the unacceptable answer, so I said "I mean buh-back to Camden Town, sir."

He nodded and said "Long journey. Well, they all are, aren't they?" He told the porter to take me through and fetch my bread as he went. The porter took one from a basket of equal-size pieces and, unhitching his keys from his belt, led me through a series of wandering passages, all very dark, but clean-smelling. We went out a small door and into a narrow dirty yard which smelled of rotted squash. At another small door, on the other side of the yard, we stopped and my porter called "Sonny! Sonny! Here's another!" Sonny opened the door out, and enough of his gas-light bled into the yard to show me that Sonny was taller than even my porter, weighed in the vicinity of twenty-five stone, had carbuncles on his face and earrings of brass wire to show where his ears had been before the lard grew over them. He smiled quite like an angel and groped inside himself like a dying man for his breath. "Come in" he said, and I felt, for a moment, welcome.

I said "Thank you, sir" and he smiled again and patted my back. It was like being stroked by a ham.

In his little office, really an anteroom not much larger than he, the smell of his perspiring body warmed the air and was not at all unpleasant, combined with the glow of his fire and the pictures he had hung—our dead Prince-Consort, an engraving suggested by *Hamlet* and a colour map of the area close by Coniston in Lancashire.

"Pity you've come so late" he confided. "It's well past the time for skilly, of course, and even a man who swears to me his hatred of all forms of gruel would want it on a night like this one, eh?" I nodded. I had not hoped for a hot meal. I wanted to sleep and not dream. "Well, then," he said, "we can't cry over skilly spilt, come along." And, laughing at his own wit, he led me through a door, and then down a little corridor, and through another door, into an apartment in which were three great baths.

I fear that I retched, which brought another bout of coughing on, and we had to wait for my noise to cease. He very solicitously patted me upon the back. Each bath was some ten feet long and almost as many wide. Each bath was the color of old weak mutton-broth, a cold-looking greyish-brown. A scum of grease lay on the surface.

"Take off your clothes," said Sonny, "and tie 'em in a great big knotty ball, and I'll save 'em in a cubby till the morning."

"All of my c-clothes?" I knew the answer.

"Oh, yes. All. You know as well as I do, don't you, that whatever of your own you take in will be nailed by one of those hooligans in there. No, it's safer for you here. And, besides, you've to bathe. It's the rules."

I knew the rules. I took everything off and tied a bundle and gave my clothes to Sonny. I had the one gold button I had kept for the worst of the worst of emergencies between my cheek and my teeth. I closed my eyes and held my nose and jumped into the broth. It was the temperature of iron bridges in winter. It clung to me like silk. I scrambled up as soon as I was in, for I feared that it would enter at my pores and poison me, that *soup du jour* of filth. Sonny gave me a scrap of cloth, once white, now black, and I wiped at myself, but only smeared the human silt on my body. He gave me a blue striped shirt from a pile, a ticket so that I could reclaim my bundle, a rug to sleep on, my bread, and the warning that everyone in the shed would nail whatever I had, so take care.

I wore my rug about my shivering shoulders as he led me, my feet still bare, into a flagstoned yard which was open to the air. He pointed, patted my shoulder, told me to make myself comfortable and locked me in or out. My naked feet seemed to stick to the icy stones, then burn. I followed where he had pointed, went in at a lighted doorway and was in my home for the night. A space perhaps thirty feet by thirty, enclosed on three sides by whitewashed wall. A low roof of roughest lath and tile, on which the cold seemed visibly to cling. A fourth wall, made of one-third unfinished boarding, and two-thirds canvas, which swayed like a sail with the wind and showed all over at its margins the dark cold night outside (and, really, inside as well). A floor of stone. One might think it at first a floor of earth, but one learns quickly that the stones are covered with vomit, saliva, excrement and dried urine, although there were whole feet of it clear. Iron cranks protruded from a wall, like the crooked arms of men long stiff and dead.

Men and boys, and creatures of some condition in between, lying on the flagstones, separated from them by narrow bags barely stuffed with straw, and separated from one another by very little besides their shirting. In several cases, two and three and four men lay with one another, sharing pallets and rugs. Those who slept or pretended to sleep were rolled in their rugs, head and feet tucked in, so as to be completely enveloped; it is the usual way, and it makes a man appear a corpse about to be buried. I never grew used to any of it. I thought of Staplehurst, and bodies littered about the railroad wreckage, and my Chief running to and fro, being brave, at least by his own good lights.

I found an empty space of crusty flooring and laid myself down.

I kept the button in my mouth for when I should need it, and tucked my bread between my body and my pallet, then rolled in my rug. I waited and watched. It was as usual. As filthy as I, and filthier, reeking of the streets and the daily pollution of London, and worse, they squatted, some quarter of the company, perhaps more, and sat in various simian positions, and picked at themselves, and laughed at little, and smoked disgusting pipes, some naked, seeming to enjoy their display, and showed their yellow fangs and waited for someone to victimize. I saw a few who eyed me, but I still was a rather large man; they preferred the old men and boys. They roared the very old song about Lushing Loo—

> "The first I met a cornet was
> In a regiment of dragoons,
> I gave him what he didn't like,
> And stole his silver spoons."

—and the Ratcliffe Highway song about Black Sarah:

> "The lady with diamonds and laces,
> By day may heighten her charms,
> But Sall without any such graces,
> At night lies as warm in your arms."

One of them said his prayer to gin—"Christ's blood, I'd like a beaker of the old blue ruin!"—and bellowed his favourite nursery rhyme:

> "There was a young man of *Peru!*
> Who had nothing whatever to *do!*
> So he whipped out his *carrot!*
> And buggered his *parrot!*
> And sent the result to the *Zoo!*

He was a very short and wiry man, the dangerous kind, with a head of dirty red hair and the features of a child. He looked a killer and he probably was. He would do.

I whistled as the pimps and slum bosses did, and his head turned, in spite of his latter effort to control the motion. He was a runner in the dirtiest districts, all right, and now, staring at me with his pale blue eyes, he knew I knew. I leaned on one arm and held my bread in the air. He saw it, and so did his friends, and he moved quickly to be there first. The others stayed where they were. The sleepers slept, the coughers coughed, and I kept myself from both by dint of great will because there was something first to do. I noted that I nearly was used to the smell, and then shifted the gold uniform button as far back in my mouth as I could.

He was completely naked. His penis was very long, and black with dirt. He lowered himself, not quite into a squat, so that his organ would wobble near my face. He had been summoned with a whistle, like a dog, and he had now to show me that he wasn't one. To do so, he acted as an ape. He let the organ hang near my eyes and nose, and I had its fullest sight and smell. Then I struck at it sharply with the hard-crusted bread, and he sank away and down, in some pain, though making every effort that his fellows not see it. Men walked past us, constantly, to the drinking-water bucket and the three pails in the corner which were to serve (but frequently didn't) as toilets.

I whispered, clumsily on account of the button, "You want your blue ruin."

He looked at my eyes, then nodded. Then he laughed, saying "And I'd like a frow who's flymy too."

I continued to whisper. "I can't get you a whore who'll do anything you ask"—his eyebrows went up; he was surprised that I not only wasn't impressed by his archaic flash language, but knew it as well—"however I can do something about gin."

He said "You got the posh?"

"Could you use it well if I did?"

"Stay 'ere. Right 'ere." He went away, and I lay back, suppressing a cough, but knowing that one would soon come.

He returned, nudging my shoulder with his bare foot, but

keeping his privates to himself. He lay a small flask on my pallet; he had one for himself in his hand, pressed by it against his stomach, hidden by it, so small was the portion.

I spat the button into my hand, wiped it against my rug, then tossed it to him. "Will that do it?" I asked.

" 'Is sit-me-down's not long for the rest of 'im if 'e says different."

"Good night" I said.

"Want to doss together?" he asked. They always wanted a chief. I knew the mentality.

"Good night" I said.

He shrugged and went off. I lay back and closed my eyes, then drank down the whole small bottle of cheapest gin, perhaps a gill or two; I wanted to be rid of it before someone tried to take it from me, for someone would. I inched the bottle away from my pallet and underneath that of a sleeping man hard by me, winced as the shock of the drink continued to roll in over my organs, then again closed my eyes and listened. The nasty singing went on, and shouting, and the desperate deep snores of the ill and the very exhausted who could sleep through it all. The slap of feet as the interminable rounds to the buckets continued. The noisome sound of bowels letting go, the awful stench as all varieties of internal infection flew upon the air. The cry of a man at the singers to sing a decent song.

Their laughter, and the general din, and I felt myself to be falling farther back each second, my hands beneath my head, and a kind of comfort within me, and then the man, again, crying out "For God's sake, can you not comprehend? My son is here beside me! He is six years old!"

And the voice of my accomplice: "Oh, is 'e for 'ire, then?"

That was when I started in coughing. I kept my eyes shut and saw the cough as a red rivulet, beginning in the center of my organs, at someplace soft, say the liver, and then surging upward, spreading in width as it went. By the time it was flooding all my chest, and the pain was at its fullest, and the rib bones seemed incapable of keeping the flesh above them from exploding, I was lying on my side, clutching myself, I was my own sick child. And that seemed to be the signal for the other coughers. A workhouse is not a company of healthy men. They all, it seemed to me, had been waiting for my initiative; they began. And we coughed all night, retching and groaning, resting a while, then starting in again, heaving our insides at the night. I heard the globs of bloody phlegm spatter on the flags, and some of them must have been mine, but I couldn't tell, for I seemed to sleep between coughs— the desired effect, among others, of the gin—and all in all it was a general chorus of water-dipping and evacuations of the bowel and urine splashes and vomitous coughs and the filthiest songs and, above it, pure despair, the cry of "My son! It's my baby *son* here with me! Can you not under*stand?*"

I tried, first, to not remember what wished to be recalled. In my mind I erected a wall of Heresford sandstone and planted my back against it and told them as reasonably as I could that it was best they not approach. That they nevertheless did come, I could not regard with malice, for they were ghosts and had no home but my mind, and in a way they were entitled to it. They came. And with my back against the wall which I was determined they should not pass over, I gently attempted to turn them away. Barbara, my daughter, would not be deterred. And she floated to me *in situ*, her children in torn grey clothing and no shoes, her tall gaunt red-faced husband, taciturn, working always at the land in Ohio which yielded too little to sell, and hardly enough for them to eat. Her bruised fingers and thin arms, the packed earth floor at her hearth, her feet in a pair of boots which had belonged to a neighbouring farmer, now dead. The long bleak fields about their house, and the dirt track which ran to it, which no one came up. The feeling of the huge nation surrounding them, and not caring. And reptiles crawling closer, and rodents from the field, the starving stone-colored horse too tired to pull at the plow. Barbara looking out the glassless window as her husband dragged the plow himself, while a small child steered, too frightened and weary to speak. I told them

"I am sorry, but no one is permitted to pass here." She came, with no face, but I knew her. And the sky as deep as the sea, purple with sunset, and the burnt-out grass, the grey-brown earth, the hungry children who did not laugh or call, her permanent autumn. All came, and I told them gently "I am sorry." They hung before me, and then within me, and of a sudden I was defending them inside my gates, no longer fending them off. I shook my head and smiled, then rubbed my hands and set about to stuff potatoes with cheese and make them all a meal. The husband looked at me and could not speak; the children were afraid to; my daughter had no face.

But then I was out at the wall again, and telling my wife that No Entry was the rule here. She lay in a dirty bed and could not breathe and did not hear me. I reached to shake her and her bonnet fell off; I saw that much of her hair had fallen out, and what was left was the color of greased paper. I shook her again, so that I might tell her, and her collar fell open, and her arm fell off— there was no blood, simply the hollow *tok* which is made by a rotten squash when it bursts against a wall. I continued to shake her, saying "I am sorry, but no one is permitted in." *Tok,* her other arm fell, and rolled off the bed, leaving a track like a slug's on the flaggings. I dropped her torso before more could fall and cried for aid, but all I heard was a child's sound—the high insistent mindless cry of helpless nightmare.

I woke and looked about me, and quickly closed my eyes. I was covered in perspiration, and shaking. No one paid attention to my quailings, for it was the rule and not the exception here. The odours lay over us like a kind of blanket, and we lay under them like varieties of corpse. We were, actually, not awfully far from a mortuary in distance, and not all that terribly far in fact. Many of us would make the change without noticing it, I thought. In France they call the mortuary *morgue.* I thought of the Chief in Paris, visiting all of those he could. He had said to me once "Dolby, there is a horror in looking at something that cannot return the look. I do not know if I hate it or am drawn to it, but nothing in our lives comes near that singular experience. It *is* a horror. But also, it is not." I thought of my son in Paris, and as I lay on the edge of exhausted sleep, or as I slept, I once more planted my back against the sandstone wall and said No.

I remembered, or dreamed, how once the Chief sent a message to my temporary quarters in London, where he stayed too that week:

MY DEAR DOLBY,

I am thistled and in a species of quicksand, and am in direst need of a strong man to defend me from the winds. Let us walk! I can promise a hot potation of rum at the finish, and perhaps some conversation before that. Can you come at once?

Which meant, to me, that Forster was not available just then for exercise, and the Chief would not be disappointed. I went, of course. He limped. I insisted we return, but he would not listen, so we effected a compromise in that I hailed a hansom, which took us out in the direction of Chalk Farm, where we alighted to walk once more, slowly, and all the while in a storm of his most charming speech. Near the right-hand Canal Bridge stood another carriage, the horse smoking hot in the wintry air, and the driver leaning over the bridge parapet. The Chief said "Ah."

We looked down to see—as he knew we would—a woman lying on the tow path looking up at us with unseeing eyes. She was dead a day or two, the Chief guessed, and was under thirty, and poorly dressed in black. The feet were crossed at the ankles, and her black hair was pushed back from her face and ran onto the ground. All about her was water, and the shattered ice which had dropped from her clothing and face. The policeman and another man who had pulled her out stood above the body, looking down. We all were quiet. And then a barge came floating past, breaking the ice which floated there, and breaking the silence with small cracking sounds.

The Chief tugged at my sleeve. He whispered "Watch!" and I

heard the excitement in his voice. The man on the horse which towed the barge was absorbed in his task, and the woman who steered was looking at the water. The towing rope caught and turned the dead woman's face before our communal cry arrested the rider and he brought the horse up short. His expression did not change for our horror. He simply looked down. The barge floated on, and before the rope could tighten, the horseman rode, making his mount to move the rope daintily over the head and through the hair. The woman who steered looked at us up on the bridge with the deepest contempt, then down at the corpse with a similar face, though less sure, and she drove onward, as the horse stepped up to once more take the lead. The Chief said "*Yes,* Dolby!"

I said "It was awful, sir."

"It was" he said. "And wonderful, in a way. In a *way,* mind you."

I did not answer, I remember. I thought of the rum.

And later, at the Ship and Lobster, as we were sitting at a snowy tablecloth and drinking the promised drinks, watching moisture bubble from a thick log in the great stone fireplace, he said to me "You must not think the worse of me for witnessing that tragedy with relish, Dolby."

"Oh, sir," I said, "you c-cannot imagine that I—"

"Dolby, I can" he said gently. "I have. I forgive you, and you must in turn forgive me. Understand it" he said, settling his small shoulders and straightening a chain across his stomach, and drawing a deep breath; laying his little white hands on the tablecloth the better to gesture. "Understand that I do not rejoice in her death. But of *course* you know that. You know *me.* It is her life I think of when I see her. It is how I can make her life again, and toward an end. That end being to perhaps keep one of her yet unfallen sisters from a similar fate. Now, thinking on it, as you do while you draw at your hot new drink—is it your second already? Stout fellow!—you will see, I am certain, that I am but doing my job, in a certain sense. Am I right? I am *saving* someone, Dolby."

I did not hear the neighbourhood bells chime five or half-five, or even six. It was exhaustion more than the gin, and fear, I suppose, of what else I would hear and see. But I had slept a measure, and I was grateful, even though I'd paid for my rest by dreaming. There was another day ahead, and then a night not unlike the one just past. And, excepting divine intervention, or the accidental making of my fortune in the next twenty-four hours, I had passed that previous day and night through a simulacrum of the remainder of my life.

The workhouse clock sounded, and Sonny came in the door crying for us to waken. Few of us sat up. Most slept on, or lay still, accumulating strength for the long day to come. Some swore, and two began a cursing contest—"cunny" being matched by "chapel of ease," and so back and forth, to high and infantile laughter—and I waited for the justifiably outraged father, stranded here with his child, to protest. But he had learned to keep his silence. When we left, I saw his face; it was whitish-grey, and he clutched himself, and I realized that they'd come to him at night and given punishment. I hoped he was not too sick or broken to earn a few pence for food for his child. Some pauper residents of the house came in to distribute our bundles, and we dressed again in the motley of the streets. It was a charade, of sorts, for most of us would return that night. And if we weren't back at this cold shed, we would be at another. Although some of us might have the luck to die.

One of the men went back through the little door for a wash. I stayed where I was; the thought of the grey-brown broth in the tanks made me gag and start in coughing again. It wasn't too bad yet. Rugs and pallets were stacked, and then the distribution, by the pauper boys, of skilly and bread. I watched a little man steal another little man's round black hat. The thief was caught by his victim. Each recognizing the other from a former street or position of life, they both commenced weeping, and in each other's arms, and I counted them fortunate. When the lad came to me with the skilly bowl and my ragged chunk of bread, I took them and sat down as if I had been struck from behind. I realized I had forgotten to eat my bread the night before. And someone, while I slept, had done it for me. My continued days depended on my wits and physical energies. And I had proved to myself that I fast was forsaking them both. Over the tepid mush, I started in coughing again.

As my Chief would have pointed out, and as in many of his books he did, there are hundreds of ways to react to the same exigency. Another man might have wolfed the new day's bread at once. Another might have stolen a piece from someone else to make up his past night's loss. Still another would have wailed or wept. I coughed, then stopped, then carefully ate the gruel while a hint of warmth remained to it. I licked the wooden spoon. I walked past the spot where I had seen the father and son together and flipped my crust behind me as I passed. I did not look back. I did not listen. And the man had the sense to keep his silence, lest the bully boys decide to commemorate the event. Nothing could be explained. I continued to walk, thinking it wise to get in practice for the exercise to come. And I dreamed of the day approaching. I altered its impending reality so that I spent it in a public house, in the maplewood snuggery, say, before the little stone fireplace, drinking mulled wine and chatting in the light, and smells of sausage, and clatter of glass, about how, once, I had been locked in a workhouse of necessity for a night, and had felt required to give my daily bread to a hungry child. My body glowed with the fictional fire as I circled the shed, dreaming.

In fact, it glowed with the need for a drink. And with my understanding that the drink had taken over, that not only my body but my mind was now affected, since I could not always count on myself to remember that the engine must be stoked—the faecal matter supplied with its rightful content of nitrogen—and that one day therefore I would, and probably soon, fall down weak with want of drink, and lack of food, and die of exposure. Be buried in a mass grave. Be shoveled into the Thames. Be eaten by rats and cats and dogs. Be carted off to the doctors' college for vivisection. Grin and grin with the permanent open mouth at the shabby sky.

The labour for the day, we soon were told (and I had divined it the night before) was crank labour. The cranks which protruded into our shed continued through the wall to the flour mill on the other side. We would earn our night's keep, before Sonny released us to the streets and the long day, by grinding four bushels of corn. The bell up by the ceiling, cunningly connected to the machinery, would sound each time a bushel was ground. So we began. Some of us began. The bully lads strode and swore and laughed with one another, lay upon beds and watched. The little miller came round from time to time, inquiring why we didn't *try* harder. The boys were put in corners picking oakum. And everything went very very slow, the idea being to delay the entrance to the street. The clock had struck eleven before we left. We were all of us hungry again, and all of us again had nowhere to go.

I walked as purposefully as I could, so as to send the blood more vigourously through my body. For although it was only September, I was cold. I was very cold and worried, still, about my having forgotten to eat the preceding night. And worried still worse about the impossibility of further to drink. I had no gold buttons, I had nothing more to offer. My coat was gone, and my hope.

Although few people might sun themselves in the park in September, there still was sun, and there still was the madness in Englishmen which made them hurl themselves upon the ground and grovel whenever the sun shone full. So I went to Hyde Park and walked with my head down, watching for metal glints, for anything useful, not only coins, which might have fallen from the clothes of the recumbent. It is a peculiar place, that park. For you can walk a distance from the road, in among the trees and long groves, and suddenly be unable to hear the Bayswater Road carriage noises. There is nothing but the well-kempt grass as tight as the top of a billiards table, and the sough of wind in the wide old trees all about, and the sense of limitless space in the middle of nothing, just space that goes on, and then the feet. The *shush shush* of patent leather shoes and sturdy walking brogues and boots made for riding and boots made for nothing but being seen. *Shush shush*, the sound of the shoes on the pavings and cobbles that wander from the Long Water to Mount Gate. The spectral dragged sound of feet with no voices above them. No laughter or squeals, nothing of metal or wood. *Shush shush*, the feet of London in early afternoon. The sounds of ease, of there being no hurry, of bulky women in heavy skirts, of men in well-sewn trousers and sturdy coats, walking beside one another, at measured leisure, *shush shush*, saying nothing because nothing needs to be said, because there is nothing that cannot wait.

I went to my hands and knees, I remember, because I was certain that I saw a silver wink in the light of a sun which now seemed horribly distant. I thought of the sun as an egg yolk fried and set down on a table far away and grown cold when no one came to eat it. I laughed, I recall, and then coughed, of course, and stayed, at the foot of a great forked elm, with my head down. Studying. Studying for the silver sign I had seen. I dug into the soil with my fingernails, but could not raise it. I scrabbled further. I noted that the motions of my fingers and arms raised a pain along my chest. I understood, as I dug, that some of the cold which I had perceived in the sun was really present in the air about the park. And that some of it must have leaked into my chest cavity, by a means I could not understand. However, I was not frightened, since the icy feeling was simply an intermediary stage, on the way to the numbness which would comfort me. I heard the cough, and was aware that it made me shake about and spit a certain amount of blood, but I was not frightened. In point of fact, I was, to a degree, given pleasure: for I could not hear their shoes punctuate their silent damned assurance: *shush.*

It came to me, after a bit, that I was on my shoulder and flank. A little girl, as blond and clean and lovely as my own small Barbara once was, looked down at me. I smiled and rolled my head, by way of shaking it in rueful agreement. "Yes—on the ground" I said. She looked, I suppose, at the fluid that lay on my lips and tongue, perhaps my chin, and which I suppose continued to arrive there. For she opened her little mouth and screamed and screamed. I swallowed at the blood so that I could say "I was recently with Boz, you know. Do you understand? We were together much of the time. Nancy-and-Sikes?" But I fear that the swallowing of poisoned substances bothered my stomach, and I embarrassed the two of us by vomiting blood up into the air.

I presume it was her presence, or intervention, or her guardians', and I shall always be grateful. For as I lay in a comfortable, if humiliating, half-slumber, I realized that when I spoke to her I did not stammer. It struck me, in my supineness: I could *speak*. I must say something, therefore. Why else, after all this time, and in the worst of his times, would Dolby find himself capable of saying *capable?* Was the initial consonant of that word any different from the one in *Cambridge,* that rock ahead in his speech? The rock was removed, and if I lived, I would say something. I thought of the Chief as he mimicked my stammer and wished that I could tell him of its disappearance. I wondered what he would think to see me here like this. And I hoped they would not leave me on the grass to die. Nor deposit me at some street corner to perish away from respectable folk. And it must have been the little girl. For I heard horses and wooden wheels and the alarm bell. I was discussed and lifted and hauled, like wood of course, for I was a drunken pauper, but nevertheless I was moved. True, I went from the best of the infirmaries, close by the Park, to the one across the river, Guy's, and then to Fulham. Still, I did not care. For at Fulham I was taken in. It was the child who saved me. And thus, in clean white clothing, and donated slippers, in a bed that is changed when it grows too bloody, in a ward where they do not carp overmuch when I stay up late and write, in a place where I am warm and fed, and where, still, I never stammer, I address myself to the page—mere parody of he who did it best of all since Shakespeare—and I speak.

In the voice of revolutionary Dolby, oppressed and somehow

loving it. In the narratives I have perpetrated, in the guises I have made. In the sly and self-enfranchised voice of Barbara the slut who, had she existed, might have taught that sorry family a thing or two. And in Ellen's voice, her husband's, and Kate's. In the voice his own pen made upon the page. And in the voice his lungs and tongue and heart made true upon the actual air I shared with him. I started out in sullen servitude and learned I loved him as well. I started out emancipating myself and learned that I *was* the tail he wagged. I started out with rage and learned how pleased I was to be wiggled about behind him. And I did learn too how truly he earned a hatred. How much I needed to be free of him to love him. How right had been my pleasures and my sense of pain. Much of the time, I thought of Ellen Ternan Robinson, once mistress, then respectable parish wife, for whom, surely, it must have been as I have described it. How alone she must have felt!

Yet how alone he was as well. And poor Catherine, his wife. Early on, when Maria Beadnell his boyhood love humbled him, then cast him off, he had decided never again to be ruled. Catherine's sin was to be lovely when young, and capable of his domination. Her deeper crime was to be less lovely when old, and too prone to his dominion. He could cast his past away by leaving her behind. And there his own sad drama begins; for he could *not* acquire to himself her youth by capturing Ternan. They all were always alone.

I dream sometimes of his children. And of Ellen Ternan Robinson's—what will they one day think?

I dream of my son and my daughter. Their absence is another pain in me. Especially my boy, George Charles, who carries a bit of both of us in his name. There were those who would have suggested that he carries more than a bit of both of us within his *blood*. To be unsubtle: they would say that my Chief exercised *droit du seigneur* upon my household. To say so even on a private page would be to outrage half of England. It would provoke a question not so much about his character, but mine, and would offend the most dispassionate reader. Of the matter I will say no more. My son is my son. And he is far away.

Perhaps that is the definition of a child.

Bloody right, I say. Moon here. Dolby isn't writing now. I say *Moon is here*, one-eyed nigger baby from Her Majesty's bleeding last Empire. Moon speaking, too right. They call me Moon. Why not? Poor beggar, Dolby, they carted him out last night, after his bit of chat with the Visitor, Matron in attendance, and all the chaps on the ward listening over the roll and rumble of their spit. Moon heard it all, though no one would think so. Tar-baby nigger with the old mounded back and bowed legs and one eye— what can he understand? Dolby thought that too, though he was kinder to me than the rest. Niggers don't understand Her Majesty's palaver. That's the ticket. Old Moon, smuggling spirits in exchange for English lessons, what would *he* understand?

All of it, John Bull. All of it, no less. I served at home on the staff of an unimportant Major of Horse. He wanted us all to sound like dark little Majors of Horse. Even his bloody five-year-old son carried a bloody riding crop and strutted in an officer's uniform and talked like a Major of Horse. I spoke as I was made to speak. When I came here, I saw they wanted ignorance and no conversation. So the wog, for "advancement," keeps shut. Lakshmi wondered if I might care to go into service. Become a bleeding servant in a noble house. Proper swill, that. I'd rather carry dead men's bowels than live like a slave. Now, I can leave after work, I would tell her. If you can leave after work, you aren't a bloody slave. Never could convince her, poor beast. Best chance for us, I'd tell her, is to lie doggo. Creep underground, beneath their notice. Where they wanted us. Become transparent, let their haughty bleeding looks go through us. Live in peace. Cunning and silence in exile's your ticket, I'd tell her. Poor beast. Dead as Dolby's last bottle. Or mine. One more kaffir dead in Her Majesty's green and writhing pauper's boneyard. Lakshmi dead. And my son. And Dolby. Moon lives, and still in secret. Proper fair joke, that. What's the bleeding precious life *for*, now they're gone?

Don't whine, wog.

Right.

Moon here, not whining, in the closet they allot to my time on the service. Dolby's paraffin lamp with me, not yet collected by Matron. And Dolby's precious papers. Filled with his tributes to Moon, and to my cleverness in the provision of drink. Too right. Cost me most of my bloody money, it did. But no complaints. I learned. Saw his bloody England from the inside out. What bent golliwog has such a chance?

And Dolby was my friend.

Now, in 1900, bloody new age all over the land like poison smoke over the bloody Midlands. The Queen fat and ill. International force sent to relieve the legation at Pekin. Siege laid down by Chinese Fist of Harmony—blighters in Parliament call them Boxers. Shrinking the Empire's spheres of influence. Wave of the future, and not a moment too soon. Now they've a Workers' Party here. Member of Lords has risen to point out, fat finger trembling, that the party of labour and the Fist of Harmony seem strangely allied. Proper good joke if it's true. String of Chinese laundries and opium dens uniting the forces of English dissent, what? See it: bloody Fist of Harmony raised in salute by a mob of opium-smoking British workers in front of the Palace of Westminster. Lovely bloody sight.

The English are passing away. John Ruskin dead. Oscar Wilde, famous ponce and bugger, gone too. Henry Sidgwick. Ernest Dowson. Dolby much thrilled, I remember, by mention in *The Daily Express* of a book on dreams by a Jewish chap named Freud. Dolby always troubled by his dreams, poor man. Wanted to sleep without them. Dreaming of the dead is the price you pay for rest, I wanted to tell him. Couldn't. Wouldn't seem within the ken of the shit-hauler and blood-mopper. Wanted also to tell him of the German chap named Zeppelin. Not a Jew. Invented a huge bloody flying balloon with a motor beneath it. Drive through the skies, you see. Raving funny idea, one German up in the air, the other down in our dreams. Of course Dolby was troubled a bit by the

Freud-wallah's being a Jew. Not overmuch, but he noticed it. Wanted to believe it proper for Jews to advance. Didn't concern me a jot. One bloody nigger's like another, I say.

I brought him drink, and he was grateful enough for that. Oh, we'd some grand sprees of laughing, with a bit of coughing from old George. I'd mop the blood and we'd continue. Dolby whispering aloud his notes. Moon, grateful peasant that I was, pretending I didn't read them while he slept. He woke once as I looked through them. Scared me half to bloody death, he did. Opened one eye. Not much white left to it, all veined with the blood of his dying. Surrounded by a soft brown and yellow skin. Eye looked over at me, blinked. Opened wider. Stared. I let the pages whisper back together. Slowly moved my hand to my lap. Sat still. Faithful nigger on watch. Smiled all my teeth. Nodded. Eye closed up. Snores of his sputum in the closing throat. Poor silly sod. He thought much of me, I learned from his book. But not enough.

Matron in later that night to warn me of a Visitor next morning. Wondered if she ever slept. If she didn't go home, she was a slave. Bloody Englishwoman she was, and no question. Told me she wanted the ward to sparkle. Asked me if I could stay late, past my shift, into the daytime. Since she asked, I wouldn't be a slave for staying. Quite nervous, Matron was. Visitor had lost a husband to an inflammation of the lungs. Wanted to give the Infirmary a large bequest in husband's name. Bloody British charity. Wanted to ask her if I should get the dying chaps to cough the worse so as to summon more money up. Told me she wanted everyone on best behaviour. Vision of chaps sitting at attention in bed. Get the Major of Horse to inspect them. He could get them to cough bluer blood. Had to smile. My smile always made her angry. Bloody good fun.

Stayed into the morning. Nothing to go home for, eh? Bilious flare of lamps in dull brown morning light. Sense of the wretched fog at the windowpanes. Great weight on everything, but invisible. Everyone coughing and retching. Smell of dying men's interiors. Dolby's papers neatly at the table with his pen and ink.

213

The silly sodding Chief and his life. And Dolby's own. And Moon's. All turning brown within. As Moon is brown without. Cheap ink. The patients sat in bed, propped with extra pillows. Moon carted them in. Fresh-washed blankets, newly scrubbed sheets. Even their smalls laundered fresh for the visit, though they never wear them. Each of them in clean gowns. Moisture, though, on the dark wood walls. Sense of clamminess of the green ceiling.

As his Chief would have put it in a margin: *In the darkness, pain.*

Sounds of coughing. Everyone trying to spit out what sits inside and eats him. Fifteen beds, fresh white. Slowly, as the Visitor circulates with Matron, the beds turn bright, then rusty, red.

The Visitor a tall angular woman in her late middle years wearing grey Scottish tweeds, walking shoes, heavy bag, a Mac. As if she were traveling in a strange wild land. Dark shadows under her bulging eyes. Pointed jaw, good nose. Face of a flawed actress. Sense of her being accustomed to horses and dogs. Reminded me of the wives of junior officers at home, sick with longing for their England. Wives who knew their husbands never would rise to important command. Widows of husbands killed in minor mutinies by bent brown "natives" like Moon, who speaks on Dolby's crackling paper with his ink.

Matron at her best. Cloak draped over her wide back and bottom. Starched dress crackling. Apron molded against it. Large white shoes. Salt and pepper moustaches neatly trimmed and shaved, powdered. Still visible, of course. Poor thing. Always stern, often angry. Good woman, though, I suppose. Decent to the chaps on the ward. Surrounded by their deaths day and night. Losing them all. Trying to smile, introducing Visitor to each of the coughers. Visitor shrinking in her skin. Nasty place for a well-bred, well-protected woman.

Paused, finally, at the foot of Dolby's bed. Came to it with a sort of motion and expression as to make me think the entire purpose of her bloody visit, well disguised, was to see George

Dolby at his end. Her face under strictest tight control. Moon silently watching. Smiling the old wog-at-your-service smile. Keeping the quiet patrol. Chat among Visitor and Matron and Dolby. His health, his preoccupation with papers at the little table beside his bed. References to his writing, something about where he had come from and how. Eyes of Visitor filling, her neck and head and hands beginning to shake. Admired her control. Wondered why she needed so bloody much of it. Dolby noticed nothing.

She asked him what he wrote. Her voice trembled. Dolby looked past her. Said "Memoirs, notes, recollections." Started in coughing. Everyone waited politely. British always polite. When they torture you with water or gunpowder burns, they are always polite.

Asked him what the recollections referred to. Answered "My former position. My job, ladies."

Asked him what the job was. He told them whom he had worked for.

Terrible bloody silence, then. Disbelief on Matron's face. But *belief* on Visitor's. That was it, you see. She bloody well had known it in advance. Expected it, anyway. Confirmation all over her fine old British complexion. Nodded her head. Closed her eyes.

Then she opened them so wide and helpless. She was just a victim, then. Nothing bloody more. Some cruel hack's minor character. Mucous discharge running from nose, tears from unblinking eyes. The usual bloody victim. Nothing more.

One of us, you see.

Leaned in closer. Asked in choking voice, barely heard it, if he would say it again. He did so.

Visitor came round to bend closer. She flinched as she did, but continued her study. Dolby, poor chap, seemed unaware of the actual terror, then. Thrill of sadness and real fear in every movement she made. Matron sensed it right off, of course. Dolby lay back, sinking into his bones and through them off the mortal bloody whatsit before our eyes. Tears and snot all over Visitor's face. Inquired after more details. Dolby delivered them. Glances between Visitor and Matron.

And then old Dolby smelled it. I knew enough of his heart from his words to tell what he felt. Smelled that he was losing it all. That he was totally lost. Spoke more. Voice thicker, greater passion to it. Described with much precision and detail, though with less breath behind the words, in what capacities he had performed for the bloody Chief. Visitor moved back, then forced herself to hold in place. Hands shook. Clasped them to imitate calm. No luck there, poor bitch. Dolby coughed. Matron wiped at his chin. Held the red towel behind her back. Visitor trembled the more. Like a frightened horse. Dolby described their journeys together. Looked up to see if they believed him.

Their silence. Visitor's injury. Matron's embarrassment.

Poor old Dolby in a proper rage. No helping it, I suppose. Red lips opening, teeth separating, throat all bubbling with the blood and then the words: "And he *did* have Ternan for a mistress, ladies! I mean to say he *had* her!"

Both stepping back. Eyes of the Visitor, then. Dolby rising like a bloody ghost from his sheets to stand on the sodding bed as they retreated. Their holding in place, then. His lips like a feeding bloody animal's. His teeth like parted fangs. His words: "You have heard of his celebrated Readings?"

Matron: "I witnessed one, George."

His smile. Trembling of Visitor. His mouth opening, bloody lips working. Voice coming out. But not Dolby's. Something higher, more from the nose, more commanding. Like watching a fakir in public madness. Stranger's voice coming out on Dolby's own:

"'Ah, yes! Good-bye! —Where is Papa?'"

Their blanched faces. Old Moon fair biting through his lip.

"His father's breath was on his cheek, before the words had parted from his lips. The feeble hand waved in the air, as if it cried 'good-bye!' again.

" 'Now lay me down; and Floy, come close to me and let me see you!'

"Sister and brother wound their arms around each other, and the golden light came streaming in, and fell upon them, locked together."

Then it stopped. As if one of Her Majesty's bleeding pipers with his round ruddy English knees stopped blowing, flattened the air from the sack and snapped to, that voice left off, never had been. Dolby, in his own voice: "Matron, do you recall? Small Dombey? Father and son at the moment of death? Do you remember? Where was it—Cheltenham? Brighton? One of the presentations at the St. James? Eh? Stop blubbering, Moon.

"Or do you prefer—"

Visitor growing older. Shoulders slumping in her coat. Face a wet pitted stone. Eyes not seeing. Vein out on her forehead, throbbing. On Dolby's long face, more rage. His sense of bloody loss, you see. There was, as his Chief would have instructed, *deeper silence.*

His voice taken over again by the other voice. Haunting thunder and snarl: "Once he threw a rug over it; but it was worse to fancy the eyes and imagine them moving towards him, than to see them glaring upward as if watching the reflection of the pool of gore that quivered and danced in the sunlight on the ceiling. He had plucked it off again. And there was the body—mere flesh and blood, no more—but such flesh, and so much *blood!!!*"

Dolby standing on the bed. Bouncing. Voice from another world coming through his own. Shouting down at Matron and Visitor. Blood in a cloudlet hung about him. Chin bright red, his lips as well. Face of darkest delight doing murder.

Then the ceasing of the other voice. And then the bloody puppet strings cut from above. Weak wobbling. Tremor in the knees. Didn't fall, though. Stood and kept his sodding balance. Panted. Blood all over. Everyone perishing motionless.

Deeper silence, still, his Chief might have written.

Then Dolby laughed. Then he laughed and laughed. Howled

like a proper banshee. Chaps on the ward enjoying it all. Relief from the boredom of dying, you know. Laughed louder.

Matron seized hold of Visitor, who was swooning fair to tumble. Cried to her: "*Mrs. Robinson!*"

Now, old Moon, I said to myself. Now you see it, old nigger. Don't you remember *that* one from his book? And still not all that bad, considering her age, the wear and tear.

Old Dolby stopped coughing. Stopped laughing. Made himself breathe deep. Did so again. Sat down slowly on edge of bed. Pawed at blood on his face. Stared with eyes like hers. Said "Who?"

Visitor weeping into leather gloves. Leaning on Matron.

Dolby said "Who?"

His coughing. Her weeping.

Matron: "Moon, fetch Mrs. Robinson a chair!" Nigger padding on foreign feet. Visitor half lying on the chair, but looking at Dolby again.

Visitor panting. Choking on words, saying them out, stopping to rest. Like a patient in the gaspers' ward. "I have sought you" she said. Face smeared like a melted doll's.

"We never met" she said. "We were different aspects of his life." Staring into Dolby's face. Looked like brother and bloody sister, really.

"But you are a final connection. With—him. With him" Visitor said.

"I cannot tell you why" Visitor said.

"Except it is my history" Visitor said.

"*My* history" Visitor said. "*My* history, sir. Not yours."

Dolby at edge of bed. Awe. In a dream. Looking into Visitor's face.

Visitor said "I have been talked of since my girlhood, sir. I have been mulled over and considered. I have been endlessly written about."

Dolby: "Who?"

Visitor's voice rising. Would have been a good bloody officer's wife. Snap the whip, old girl. Said "I have been made to all but dance at the end of a rope of words. Now *you*—you, of all—"

Dolby mumbling. Blinking his eyes. Wiping at the flesh and blood about him with weak fingers on the air. Saying "Is that— you cuh-cuh-c-cannot imagine—"

New strength, his bloody Chief might have said in a margin. "Oh, can't I, Dolby?"

He said "Who?"

Visitor's wicked low laugh: "Haven't I?"

Covering her face with her hands again. Shaking her head.

Dolby asking them "Who?"

Poor sod. Sat on the edge of the bloody bed well after they'd gone. Face leached white. Bald head fair to pulsing. All his final strength gone. I swung his feet back and covered him up to his chin. Sat beside his bed in the Visitor's chair and watched him stare at nothing, close his eyes.

Then another bit of bone-scrape coughing. Much mopping of blood. Then silence, and by the afternoon the usual tired cleric to say the final futile words, and by the night his death. Watched him die. Watched the other gaspers stare every now and again at the long shape wrapped in bloody sheets. Helped the staff carry him off for delivery.

Moon has his job. Not a slave. Vessels of slime to empty and rinse. Vessels who deposit the slime to wrap and trundle away. The long walk home on slippery streets. Daytime sleep in the cold room empty of her except for some clothing, a few sodding combs. Sounds outside of children pelting cats with stones. Hungry endless crying of infants. Sound of slops being emptied down the wall to the streets. And Dolby's papers, of course. Shaggy folded heap of his history.

Heir to Dolby's words. If I keep my health and stay at work and have a bottle when I need it, I will one day start at the bloody beginning. I will bloody well change it all. Rewrite the lives old Dolby set down, his and his Chief's and my own. Why not? It is wrong that a man be imprisoned by language. A man should not be required to lose his bloody flesh and blood. His child. His wife. Everything. That is not correct.

I am Moon, the reader. Such an end to such a book is not bloody fair to the poor bloody reader. One wants something, after all, with a happy bloody ending to it. I will make changes.

AFTERWARDS: AN AFTERWORD

Dickens is alive, as ever. Dear Dorothy Pittman, who helped so much in the birth of this book, is dead. Dear Angus Wilson, who was kind to it and its author, is dead. But I'm still kicking. And Peter Glassgold, who was to edit the novel in 1976, is here to oversee its republication nearly twenty years later. And the book is, as it was meant to be, published for James Laughlin by New Directions Publishing Corporation.

At the suggestion of the Powys scholar Robert Blackmore, my senior colleague at Colgate, I was reading Edgar Johnson's *Charles Dickens: Tragedy and Triumph* in 1974 and I found myself asking of its subject, over and again, "How did anyone live with him?" Since I had often asked this question of myself about myself and other writers of my acquaintance, it was perhaps the analogy of the flea (me) to the lion (Dickens)—this itchiness (my adoration of Dickens' work aside) our only point of contact or similarity—that led me to believe that I would have to answer the question as I tried to answer so many: by writing fiction—in this case, by making up the man to get at his truth.

My first thought was to write a play about him. I had and I have wanted to write a play (and tried, often enough) for years. The effort of 1974 lasted through the writing of these words: *The stage is his mind,* placed at the start of what might have been the first act. Once I reread those stage directions, I understood that I was thinking in a novelist's terms and that I was condemned to the writing of a novel.

I read widely and traveled in Dickens' life. I went to England and toddled in the trail of his long strides. I'd read about and been pleased by his having been, on his second American tour, stranded by spring floods across the railroad tracks in Utica, New York. Colgate University is not far from Utica, and there were times when I, a New Yorker, knew "stranded" in the bone. I found that Moses Baggs' Hotel, on Baggs Square, Utica, where Dickens and his right-hand man, George Dolby, had been forced to stay, had been demolished in the '30s. At the historical society, I asked for the hotel register and was told it wasn't among the society's holdings. Like a minor Dickensian character in a solipsistic trance, I said, "Yes, it is." I remember swiveling my head as I permitted my eyes to widen with no little melodrama. I remember saying, "There is a cupboard upstairs?" And I remember the poor woman's eyes growing larger even than mine must have been. She nodded, I nodded back, and we marched to a kind of attic filled with wooden cupboards and dusty furniture. I pointed to the lower shelf of a cupboard and said, "There." She retrieved a long, black ledger. It was from Moses Baggs' Hotel. We turned the pages and read Dickens' name in his hand.

I wrote the novel in sections, and didn't know what held them together except Dickens' vast personality. My agent of those days, Dorothy Pittman, who died too young in 1992, invited me to visit at her New York apartment. While she read over my pages, I paced Greenwich Village. At a bookstore on Eighth Street, I bought a small volume of Victorian punch recipes: I found that I had found the linkage of my chapters—someone who drank, who loved these recipes perhaps because their sense of orderly procedure was a stay against the chaos of his life. I wrote in the fullness of Moon, who hadn't until then developed as a character. I wrote the final chapter more amply, so that the fiction turned in on itself for the second time. It is Dolby's revision of Dickens and Dickens', especially, of Dolby, in the early pages, that I think of as the first turning.

Dorothy presented the revised manuscript to my original American editor, Peter Glassgold, then a senior editor and now editor in chief at New Directions. James Laughlin accepted *The Mutual Friend*, publication of which Peter had recommended. JL offered me, I remember,

$1500. I whined for more, knowing that only John Hawkes and one or two others on the ND list made princelier sums. JL suggested in the friendliest of ways that I "take the book uptown," see whether one of the larger houses would pay me more, and come back to him for publication if they would not. He has always paid modestly—that is how you stay in business, I suppose—yet he has always been the most generous of publishers, most decent of men. Few of his writers or colleagues have deserved him.

Dorothy Pittman sold the novel to Frances McCullough at Harper & Row, and she asked me to revise a chapter I'd never got right. I had written a cross-examination of Dickens by himself during his writing of *The Mystery of Edwin Drood* (he died after finishing the first half; it was in the second half that he'd planned to show John Jasper, the killer, cross-examining himself). I never made my original chapter work with any intelligence. I wrote a new one, and the novel was published handsomely. It was thereafter published in England by Harvester (now defunct) and then by Penguin; it was republished here by David Godine. And now it comes full circle to the publisher and editor who had meant to publish it first in 1977. I wish Dorothy Pittman were here to know. I do know and am honored to say how much she gave to these pages and to me.

While Johnson, a sense of reluctance weighing down his words, did describe Dickens' affair with Ellen Ternan, he made it clear that, to scholars and gentlemen, overmuch fingering of Dickens' bedclothes was distasteful. I was, when I wrote this book and am now, as I reread it, neither a scholar nor a gentleman. I happily made up the passions of Ternan and Dickens, and Ternan's loathing of Dickens' flesh. Subsequent research—see the biographies by Fred Kaplan and Peter Ackroyd, and especially see Claire Tomalin's life of Ellen Ternan, *The Invisible Woman*—suggest that I did a fair job. Dickens of course did the best job—in *Great Expectations*, in aspects of *A Tale of Two Cities* and *Our Mutual Friend*. He called himself, after all, The Inimitable. He was.

When I gave a reading from this novel in 1977, someone in the audience congratulated me on having pulled off the successful murder of my literary father. Thoughts of the anxiety of influence were freshly aloft, and Oedipus was in the air. I was shocked that this intelligent reader and listener could think that I had anything other than adoration in mind. Dickens is in some fashion the progenitor of much of our fiction, but I had never possessed the hubris to think of myself as any sort of rival to this monumental writer. How does one say this without writhingly sliming about in his 'umbleness like Heep? I smiled uneasily, and we nattered of Harold Bloom. And then, on an airplane, in 1986, I read through a collection of reviews by Anthony Burgess, the exploder of John Bull, iconoclastic citizen of his own literary continent (I thought). I read, without noting at first the author attacked, an onslaught against some American person who had appropriated Burgess's and England's own Charles Dickens for the purpose of tainting him. The American person shrank in his seat; he turned off his reading lamp, but lighted up the aisle with his blushes.

I can't—I won't—operatically declaim my loyalty to even the most quotidian scene of Dickens' least successful novel. Nor will I deny that I loved learning, by trying to invent it, the soul of one of our greatest writers. A novel about Dickens is a novel about storytelling. For all his enormities and pettinesses—some of them so similar to yours and mine—Dickens emerges, as I understand him, a hero of this novel and of storytelling, a hero of story itself.

—F.B.
Sherburne, New York
1993